PRA... ...LLAHAN

## ONCE UPON A WARDROBE

"Heartfelt characters will win over sentimental readers. Callahan's fans will love this."
—*Publishers Weekly*

"*Once Upon a Wardrobe* is a beautiful follow-up to *Becoming Mrs. Lewis*. It's a love letter to books and stories with a meaningful message. Megs and her family learn that fantastical tales are more than mere ways to appease young children. Stories are nourishment for the souls that need joy the most, and sometimes they're the only thing that can help us understand life."
—*The Washington Post*

"Full of magic, nostalgia and a sister's love, [Harlan] Coben calls this novel 'a love letter to those of us obsessed with C. S. Lewis's Narnia series.'"
—*TODAY*

"This is a heartwarming tale about the transformative power of books, with engaging and detailed descriptions. George's earnestness and imaginative nature uplift his family and will charm any reader who enjoys looking at the stories behind our favorite childhood stories."
—Maribeth Fisher, *Booklist*

"This beautiful and soul-touching book is about death and dying, but it also reminds us that new chapters remain for those of us who are left behind."
—Historical Novel Society

"Patti Callahan's powerful and captivating new novel ponders how the events in C. S. Lewis' life, particularly his childhood, inspired him to create the magical and mythical world of Narnia and the cast of characters inhabiting it . . .

Readers will reach for it again and again, eager to be reminded that love will prevail and imagination leads people down fantastical paths. Some books are read and forgotten soon after; others linger forever in one's mind, popping up from time to time when something relevant sparks the memory. *Once Upon a Wardrobe* is certainly the latter and will be cherished by anyone who reads it."

—BookReporter.com

"More than just a clever way to tell the story of Lewis' life, the book explores the power of story and the importance of imagination."

—*The Atlanta Journal-Constitution*

"From Patti Callahan, the bestselling author of *Becoming Mrs. Lewis*, comes another enchanting story that pulls back the curtain on the early life of C. S. Lewis."

—The Nerd Daily

"*Once Upon a Wardrobe* is a tender, enchanting tribute to the power of story and the myriad ways it can both break and heal our hearts. It is the story of a dying boy and a loving sister and the path a treasured story takes from one heart to the other. Perfect and timely and beautiful and poignant, it is everything the world needs right now."

—Ariel Lawhon, *New York Times* bestselling author
of *I Was Anastasia* and *Code Name Hélène*

"Beautiful, tender, and poignant, *Once Upon a Wardrobe* is a rare treasure. Written with elegant prose, warmth, and a clear passion for her subject, Patti Callahan has crafted a love letter to beloved Narnia, and to the power of story to inspire, connect, and heal. Truly magical."

—Hazel Gaynor, *New York Times* bestselling author

"This imaginative and touching book will introduce readers to Narnia or remind them of why they first fell in love with the enchanting land. Among its many layers and the characters' many dimensions, what's revealed to readers is the importance of asking questions that provide more than just one answer. It's a wonderfully immersive book meant for anyone who—well, anyone who loves to read!"

—Laura Tuzzio, *Hope Magazine*

"This fiercely imaginative and endearing novel is Patti Callahan's third in the historical fiction genre ... *Once Upon a Wardrobe* would be a thoughtful gift for fans of C. S. Lewis and for anyone enchanted by stories and the unexplained mysteries in them. Perfect for all ages from young children to adults, this tender tale will make you smile as you turn the last page."

—Glenda Harris, *The Bluffton Sun* and *Hilton Head Sun*

"The stories of C. S. Lewis have long been a comfort and a beacon to me, lighting the way in my darkest hours. Reading Patti Callahan's *Once Upon a Wardrobe*, I felt just as I did upon first discovering the wonders of Narnia: joy, hope, and the sustaining knowledge that grace can be found in the pages of a beloved story. This remarkably moving book deserves to be embraced and cherished as the classic it will undoubtedly become."

—Jennifer Robson, internationally bestselling author of *The Gown*

"Callahan (*Becoming Mrs. Lewis*) once again visits the life and works of C. S. Lewis in this enlightening novel of logic and imagination, faith, and reason ... this enchanting novel of faith and hope is a must-read for fans of C. S. Lewis. Readers will be eager to return to the world of The Chronicles of Narnia with new insights."

—*Library Journal*, starred review

"Enchanting and luminous, filled with the love of family, this is a story for anyone whose life has ever been changed by a book. Megs and George will stretch your heart, perhaps fracture it, then shine light through the cracks and send your spirit soaring. It is impossible not to be swept away by Patti Callahan's exploration of what lies beneath C. S. Lewis's beloved land of Narnia. This is storytelling at its finest, deepest, and most profound. A triumph."

—Lisa Wingate, #1 *New York Times* bestselling author of
    *Before We Were Yours* and *The Book of Lost Friends*

"I so loved this story. Every page is filled with magic and wonder, with insight and wisdom. I am in awe of Patti Callahan's talent."

—Debbie Macomber, *New York Times* bestselling author

"From the very first page of Patti Callahan's new book, *Once Upon a Wardrobe*, I was transported, as if I was finally stepping through C. S. Lewis's famous wardrobe, something I've wanted to do since I first read the

Narnia books. In this powerful, enchanting tale for all ages, readers uncover the inspiration for Lewis's famous books, while at the same time discovering the way in which stories—and myths—weave through our existences, subtly transforming us in immeasurable ways. Stunning."

—Marie Benedict, *New York Times* bestselling
author of *The Mystery of Mrs. Christie*

"Exquisitely heartfelt, *Once Upon a Wardrobe* is a love letter to the magic of stories. I call it the Callahan Effect—from the first page to the last, Patti Callahan's wise and beautiful prose draws you in and doesn't let you go."

—Sarah Addison Allen, *New York Times* bestselling
author of *First Frost* and *Lost Lake*

"*Once Upon a Wardrobe* is a poignant meditation on the lengths we will go to for our loved ones as well as a fascinating glimpse into the early life of C. S. Lewis. Patti Callahan's beautiful, life-affirming novel is a reminder that literature lives inside us, and that when we read someone else's story, we understand so much more about our own. A gorgeous, compelling book."

—Janet Skeslien Charles, *New York Times*
bestselling author of *The Paris Library*

"When it comes to a classic like the great C. S. Lewis's *The Lion, the Witch and the Wardrobe*, we all want to hear the story behind the story, just as Patti Callahan's young, ailing George Devonshire does in the gorgeously wrought *Once Upon a Wardrobe*. And in the book, we get just that: a peek behind the curtain of a story that has enchanted generations. But the masterful Callahan—who has already shown us a more intimate, human side of C. S. Lewis in *Becoming Mrs. Lewis* (2019)—gives us much more, too; she delivers a great gust of enchantment, a draft of emotion, and a zephyr of spiritual insight that will sweep through you the way snowflakes rush through the wintry postwar Oxford countryside. Callahan starts with a simple enough question: where did Narnia come from? But the answer she delivers in *Once Upon a Wardrobe*—a tale full of forests and castles, hope and despair, first love and first loss—will leap from the page straight into your heart. With a touch of fairy tale magic, *Once Upon a Wardrobe* will take you behind the legend and deep into the English and Irish countryside, where you'll encounter not only the inspirations for one of the 20th century's most beloved works but also a tale of heartache, hope, and discovery that will forever change the Narnia you thought you knew. Callahan's poignant, luminous *Once Upon a Wardrobe* honors the legacy of C. S. Lewis's Narnia by giving us a new chapter, one born from the kind of real magic that is only possible when we open our hearts and let the lamplight in."

—Kristin Harmel, *New York Times* bestselling
author of *The Forest of Vanishing Stars*

# BECOMING MRS. LEWIS

"Patti Callahan seems to have found the story she was born to tell in this tale of unlikely friendship turned true love between Joy Davidman and C. S. Lewis that tests the bounds of faith and radically alters both of their lives. Their connection comes to life in Callahan's expert hands, revealing a connection so persuasive and affecting we wonder if there's another like it in history. Luminous and penetrating."

—Paula McLain, *New York Times* bestselling author of
*The Paris Wife* and *When the Stars Go Dark*

"I thought I knew Joy Davidman, the oft mentioned but little examined wife of C. S. Lewis, but in *Becoming Mrs. Lewis*, Patti Callahan breathes life into this fascinating woman whose hunger for knowledge leads her to buck tradition at every turn. In a beautifully crafted account, Patti unveils Joy as a passionate and courageous—yet very human—seeker of answers to the meaning of life and the depths of faith. *Becoming Mrs. Lewis* is an unlikely love story that will touch heart, mind, and soul."

—Diane Chamberlain, *New York Times* bestselling
author of *The Dream Daughter*

"Layered with personal reflection, poignant life events, and the Davidman-Lewis journey toward respect and love, *Becoming Mrs. Lewis* may very well become a literary classic of its own."

—*Hope by the Book*, Gold Star Review

"Spanning more than a decade, this slow-burning love story will be especially satisfying to writers and C. S. Lewis fans, as there are many references to his literary canon and his famous stories of Narnia. Callahan's prose is heartfelt and full of grace."

—*BookPage*

"Callahan crafts a masterpiece that details the friendship and ultimate romance between the real Davidman and Lewis . . . Fans of Karen White and Mary Alice Monroe will enjoy this book. Callahan's writing is riveting and her characters spring to life to create a magical and literary experience that won't be soon forgotten."

—*Library Journal*, starred review

"Readers familiar with the life and work of C. S. Lewis will relish learning about the woman who inspired some of his most famous books. Others will find the slow burn of the romance between the two mesmerizing. All fans of women's fiction, particularly works with religious themes, will appreciate reading about this vibrant and intelligent woman."

—*Booklist*

"Callahan (*The Bookshop at Water's End*) vividly enters the life of a woman searching for both God and romantic love in this pleasing historical novel about writer and poet Joy Davidman . . . Making full use of historical documentation, Callahan has created an incredible portrait of a complex woman."

—*Publishers Weekly*, starred review

"In *Becoming Mrs. Lewis*, Patti Callahan Henry breathes wondrous fresh life into one of the greatest literary love stories of all time: the unlikely romance between English writer C. S. Lewis and the much younger American divorcée, Joy Davidman. Callahan chronicles their complex and unconventional relationship with a sure voice, deep insight into character, and eye for period detail. The result is a deeply moving story about love and loss that is transformative and magical."

—Pam Jenoff, *New York Times* bestselling author of *The Orphan's Tale*

"Patti Callahan's prose reads like poetry as she deftly unearths a lost love story that begs to be remembered and retold. I was swept along, filled with hope, and entirely beguiled, not only by the life lived behind the veil of C. S. Lewis's books but also by the woman who won his heart. A literary treasure from first page to last."

—Lisa Wingate, *New York Times* bestselling author of
*Before We Were Yours* and *The Book of Lost Friends*

"*Becoming Mrs. Lewis* is at once profoundly evocative, revealing an intimate view of a woman whose love and story had never been fully told . . . until now. Patti Callahan brings to life the elusive Joy Davidman and illuminates the achingly touching romance between Joy and C. S. Lewis. This is the book Patti Callahan was born to write. *Becoming Mrs. Lewis* is a tour de force and the must-read of the season!"

—Mary Alice Monroe, *New York Times* bestselling
author of *Beach House Reunion*

"Patti Callahan has written my favorite book of the year. *Becoming Mrs. Lewis* deftly explores the life and work of Joy Davidman, a bold and brilliant woman who is long overdue her time in the spotlight. Carefully researched. Beautifully written. Deeply romantic. Fiercely intelligent. It is both a meditation on marriage and a whopping grand adventure. Touching, tender, and triumphant, this is a love story for the ages."

—Ariel Lawhon, *New York Times* bestselling author of
*I Was Anastasia* and Code Name Hélène

"Patti Callahan took a character on the periphery, one who has historically taken a back seat to her male counterpart, and given her a fierce, passionate voice. For those fans of Lewis curious about the woman who inspired *A Grief Observed*, this book offers a convincing, fascinating glimpse into the private lives of two very remarkable individuals."

—*New York Journal of Books*

"*Becoming Mrs. Lewis* illuminates the raw humanity of seeking faith in a distrustful world. We've heard C. S. Lewis's narrative. Here, Callahan keenly demystifies poet Joy Davidman's story and, in the telling, shows us the power of a greater love. I was wonderstruck by this novel."

—Sarah McCoy, *New York Times* and international bestselling author of *Marilla of Green Gables* and *The Baker's Daughter*

"This finely observed accounting of writer Joy Davidman's life deeply moved me. Patti Callahan somehow inhabits Davidman, taking her readers inside the writer's hungry mind and heart. We keenly feel Davidman's struggle to become her own person at a time (the 1950s) when women had few options. When Davidman breaks free of a crushing marriage and makes the upstream swim to claim her fullest life, we cheer. An astonishing work of biographical fiction."

—Lynn Cullen, bestselling author of *Mrs. Poe*

"With an artist's touch, Patti has woven flesh and bone onto an unlikely love story and given us a glimpse into a beautiful and storied romance. I read this through an increasing sense of awe and admiration. By the final page, I realized Patti had crafted an intimate and daring literary achievement."

—Charles Martin, *USA TODAY* bestselling author of *Long Way Gone* and *The Mountain Between Us*

"This book is a work of art. Intelligent. Witty and charming. *Becoming Mrs. Lewis* is a stunning foray into the wilds of faith—from doubt and discovery to the great adventure of living it out. Patti Callahan's invitation into Joy and Jack's love story is as brilliant as the lives they led. I'm left as spellbound as the first time I met Aslan . . . with these characters now just as dear."

—Kristy Cambron, author of *The Ringmaster's Wife* and the Lost Castle series

"In *Becoming Mrs. Lewis*, Callahan peels back the curtain and allows a glimpse into Joy Davidman's extraordinary life and her love and marriage with C. S. Lewis. With captivating prose, Callahan carries the reader across the ocean from New York to Oxford and into the private heart of this tender love story."

—Katherine Reay, bestselling author of *Dear Mr. Knightley*

"In this unforgettable story of love and passion, piercing intellect and the power of the written word, Joy Davidman has come to claim her own resurrection, and the results are astonishing. Patti Henry has achieved a bold literary magic: *Becoming Mrs. Lewis* heals the cracks in the firmament of our hearts."

—Signe Pike, author of *The Lost Queen* and *The Forgotten Kingdom*

"It's all here: Bill's betrayals. Joy's boundless hope. Davy and Douglas, energetic but vulnerable. The faithful Oxford don used by God. Jack and Joy, arguing over a kiss. In a novel awash with authenticity, we learn their story through the voice of Mrs. C. S. Lewis. I suspect the man himself would say of Patti Callahan, 'She's a corking good writer.'"

—Carolyn Curtis, coeditor of *Women and C. S. Lewis: What His Life and Literature Reveal for Today's Culture* (Lion Hudson, Oxford)

# SURVIVING SAVANNAH

"Fans of Christina Baker Kline and Kate Quinn will love this beautiful, richly detailed novel about a lost bit of American maritime history. In a seamless blending of fact and fiction, Patti Callahan has created an atmospheric, compelling story of survival, tragedy, the enduring power of myth and memory, and the moments that change one's life."

—Kristin Hannah, #1 *New York Times* bestselling author of *The Great Alone* and *The Nightingale*

"In *Surviving Savannah*, Patti Callahan masterfully weaves a little-known historical tragedy, an enigmatic mystery, and a searing family saga into a mesmerizing tale that will captivate readers until the last page and beyond."

—Pam Jenoff, *New York Times* bestselling author of *The Lost Girls of Paris*

"The astonishing story of the 'Titanic of the South' is brought to vivid life . . . This tale of survival, love, and loss, as well as Callahan's epic portrayals of a trio of strong, passionate women, gripped me from the very first page. Simply masterful."

—Fiona Davis, *New York Times* bestselling author of *The Lions of Fifth Avenue*

"Through the interwoven tales of three courageous women, *Surviving Savannah* grips the reader in a spellbinding novel full of mystery, tragedy, sacrifice, and resilience. Layering painstaking research with evocative prose,

Callahan has penned an utterly transportive read while illuminating a heart-wrenching yet largely forgotten slice of American history. Superb."

    —Kristina McMorris, *New York Times* bestselling
      author of *Sold on a Monday*

"Hidden history rises from the watery depths in all its glittering glory but also in its intimate, human detail. Meticulously researched, beautifully written, underpinned by timeless themes of personal trauma and its aftereffects, *Surviving Savannah* is a journey readers and book clubs will treasure."

    —Lisa Wingate, #1 *New York Times* bestselling author of
      *Before We Were Yours* and *The Book of Lost Friends*

"A luminous novel about bravery, connection, and resilience that resurrects a forgotten 19th-century shipwreck and interlaces it with a page-turning contemporary narrative. With lush historical detail and a graceful pen, Callahan raises questions about fate, faith, and human purpose that are timeless. *Surviving Savannah* has the luster of a secret that's been pulled from the depths of the sea."

    —Signe Pike, bestselling author of *The Lost*
      *Queen* and *The Forgotten Kingdom*

"In Patti Callahan's fiercely hopeful *Surviving Savannah*, the past and the present intertwine with ringing authenticity. Disaster and crisis become a powerful testing ground, as Callahan's expertly drawn characters are forced to discover how to live past tragedy, and what matters most in the aftermath. This is exactly the kind of story we need right now."

    —Paula McClain, bestselling author of *The Paris*
      *Wife* and *When the Stars Go Dark*

# ONCE UPON A
# WARDROBE

# OTHER BOOKS BY PATTI CALLAHAN

# ONCE UPON A
# WARDROBE

PATTI CALLAHAN

HARPER MUSE

ISBN 978-1-4002-3347-2 (signed edition)
ISBN 978-1-4002-3297-0 (Canadian international edition)
ISBN 978-1-4002-3283-3 (international edition)
ISBN 978-0-7852-5174-3 (trade paper)

**Library of Congress Cataloging-in-Publication Data**

Names: Henry, Patti Callahan, author.
Title: Once upon a wardrobe / Patti Callahan.
Description: Nashville : Harper Muse, [2021] | Summary: "From the bestselling author of Becoming Mrs. Lewis comes another beautiful story inspired by C. S. Lewis's ability to change the world and captivate hearts-including those of a terminally ill boy and his logic-driven sister"—Provided by publisher.
Identifiers: LCCN 2021007763 (print) | LCCN 2021007764 (ebook) | ISBN 9780785251729 (hardcover) | ISBN 9780785251767 (epub) | ISBN 9780785251781
Subjects: LCSH: Lewis, C. S. (Clive Staples), 1898-1963—Fiction. | GSAFD: Biographical fiction.
Classification: LCC PS3608.E578 O53 2021 (print) | LCC PS3608.E578 (ebook) | DDC 813/.6—dc23
LC record available at https://lccn.loc.gov/2021007763
LC ebook record available at https://lccn.loc.gov/2021007764

*Printed in the United States of America*
24 25 26 27 28 LBC 6 5 4 3 2

*With the greatest love*
*for*
*Bridgette Kea Rock*
*No matter your age, may you never, ever*
*grow too old for fairy tales.*
*Mhamó*

*Sometimes fairy stories may say best what's to be said.*

C. S. LEWIS

# CONTENTS

XIX

# CONTENTS

# CONTENTS

# ONCE UPON A
# WARDROBE

# ONE

# GEORGE MEETS A LION

**DECEMBER 1950**
**WORCESTERSHIRE, ENGLAND**

George Henry Devonshire is only eight years old and he already knows the truth. They don't have to tell him: the heart he was born with isn't strong enough, and they've done all they can. And by *they*, he means the doctors and nurses, his parents, and his older sister, Megs. If they could save him, if they could give their own life for him, they would. He knows that too. But they can't.

The December snow outside his bedroom window piles up like wave upon wave of white. George sits up in bed, propped against the forever-plumped-by-his-mum pillows. Next to him is a dark oak table with pill bottles and a glass of water and a gone-cold cup of tea that his mum left behind. Among all of that clutter is a book, just published, called *The Lion, the Witch and the Wardrobe* by C. S. Lewis.

It has a lion on the cover, and George often looks to this lion as if it might hold the key to all he desires to know.

There is so very much he wants to know.

George once thought that if he lived long enough to be a grown-up, he'd have all the answers. Now he believes adults don't know what's what any more than he does.

But the man who wrote this book—this storybook that transports George out of his bedroom and into Narnia—this man *knows* something. What that *something* might be is a mystery.

"Long ago and far away" often begins the best stories, but this author began his book with just four names—Peter, Susan, Edmund, and Lucy—and a magic wardrobe.

George is waiting for his Megs to come home for the weekend from university so he can tell her about this remarkable book, about this white land where it is always winter but never Christmas, where animals can talk and the back of a wardrobe opens to another world. He loves Megs more than all the words he has to describe the feeling.

Across George's room is his own ordinary wooden wardrobe. He slides from the bedcovers and slips his feet into his fuzzy lamb's-wool slippers. His breath catches as it always does when he jolts the weak muscle that is his heart. He waits as his heartbeat catches up to his plan and then shuffles across the floor. He places both hands on the thick handles and opens the heavy doors.

There isn't a looking glass on the outside of this wardrobe like there is in the book, just carvings of trees and birds.

The doors creak and George spies his few pieces of clothing hanging there. (A boy who lives mostly in bed doesn't need very many shirts and pants.) He sees the family's wool coats and clothes that don't fit into his parents' overstuffed closet. He knows there is no secret back to this wardrobe, and he can't walk through it to find a snowy forest and a lamppost and a faun that will take him on a great adventure.

What he can do, is sit inside this space and close his eyes and take himself to that imaginary world, where he can have his own adventures, where he can escape the very real world, where his body won't get old, and where his mum doesn't cry in the kitchen. She thinks he can't hear her, but he can.

He pushes aside the coats and shirts and dresses, then slips inside. He's a small boy, not as big as an eight-year-old boy should be, but big enough to need to fold his legs up to his chest as he scoots to the very back of the wardrobe, never pulling the door all the way shut, just as Lucy in the book has taught him one should *never* close a wardrobe door while inside.

Darkness envelops him, and it feels quite fine to be surrounded by the aroma of his mum's rose perfume, along with mothballs (just as in the book) and a faint woody scent hinting of a forest. As he leans into it, he feels the solid back of the wardrobe and lets out a long breath. He closes his eyes and conjures the image of a talking beaver inviting him for tea in a dam made of sticks.

George smiles.

He isn't as scared as his family thinks he is. Nothing hurts, and he doesn't expect it to hurt even when his heart stops beating. He's just tired, and sleep isn't so bad.

He's read enough books (for what else is there to do in bed?) to know Narnia isn't real, or not real in the way that grown-ups call real. (But then, what do they know?) The professor who wrote about this magical place, however, *is* real, and he lives only a train ride away in Oxford, where Megs attends school. This man would know the answers to George's questions.

Where did this land of the lion, a white witch, and fauns and beavers and castles come from?

How did Aslan—as true as any living thing the boy has ever known—come to bound onto the pages of a book?

George feels sleep ease up on him as quiet as a lion on the prowl, and he tumbles into it, his hands wrapped around a mane of fur (really a rabbit coat of his mum's). The ice-cold world of a snowy forest surrounds him in a story written behind his eyelids, sketched onto his mind, emblazoned on his dreams.

# TWO ☉

## MEGS FALLS INTO A STORY

There was once, and is even now, a city on the banks of the River Cherwell, a city as abundant with timeless tales as any city in the world. The slow river begins its journey in Hellidon and meets its destiny in the Thames at Oxford, a city of stone towers and gleaming spires where this story and many others begin. Some stories imagined in this ancient place rise above the others; they ascend from the towers, from the quiet libraries and single rooms, from the museums and the cobblestone streets. Some of those stories become legends.

Myths.

Tales that are as much a part of us as our bones.

But I, Margaret Louise Devonshire, called Megs by all who know me, honestly don't care about that. My heart belongs to numbers and equations, my head to thoughts of solving the greatest mysteries of physics.

It is the first Friday in December, and I ride the train

from the Oxford to Foregate station in Worcester, only a mile from my house along the London Road. I've been leaving university on the weekends more often than my fellow students at Somerville College, one of the only colleges at Oxford to have women students, but none of them have a little brother like George, and they seem more than happy to be free of their homes and towns and cities. I call them my fellow students and not my friends, because so far, that's all they are. Maybe because I leave Oxford the minute there is a moment of free time while the others gather in pubs drinking pints, debating politics, playing draughts, and flirting with each other as if that is the easiest thing in the world.

I wouldn't dare tell any of them the truth. I miss everything about my Worcester: the way it straddles the silver snake of the River Severn; the clangs of its Royal Worcester porcelain factory; Worcester Bridge arching over the river, its stone glimmering in the sun; the heath-covered hills; and Worcester Cathedral, sitting proudly in the middle of it all, its spires straight to heaven.

Not that I'm sad to be at university—I'm not! I have worked all my life to get here. All my remembered life, I've aimed my arrow straight at the bull's-eye of Oxford. I'm seventeen, the first woman in my family to go to college, and I'm proud to have received a scholarship for my marks. It seems a bit unfair that I would get such a scholarship and residence rooms fully furnished, with a bedroom and a little sitting room, for something that comes so easily to me, something I love so much.

But of course not as much as I love George.

Home is our Devonshire house, a stone cottage surrounded by the hand-hewn fences of aged alder. Between
the low wooden gate and the front door, a wild garden of
rambling purple fumitory and thick moonwort fern rests
hidden beneath snow. The window boxes Dad once made
Mum for her birthday hang from the two side windows, sad
and empty in the winter barrenness.

Last autumn, as the earth moved toward rest, Mum
worked in the garden with a fervor I hadn't seen in years,
and I believe I know why: she can't keep George alive, but
she can keep the flowers and vegetables growing under
her care.

Today when I arrive at the house, where I'd lived all my
life until I departed for Oxford, the chimney smoke curls
upward from a cap at the far-right end of the cottage. I walk
carefully along the stone pathway that is covered with snow
and glinting with swords of sunlight. I hesitate before placing my hand on the knob of our blue-painted front door.

No matter how I feel, I must appear cheerful for
George.

I open the door, and a rush of heat flows toward me
with a fireplace scent so reminiscent of my early childhood
that my knees almost buckle.

But I can't fold.

I must be strong.

I shut the front door, slip off my jacket and mittens, set
them on the bench, and kick off my wellies. I move slowly

through the house I know as well as anything in my life. I can walk through it quick as lightning with my eyes fast shut and never hit an edge of counter, a kitchen table, or Dad's large leather chair. In a single minute and blindfolded, I could find my bedroom and crawl beneath its worn-thin sheets with a warm water bottle and be ten years old again.

I reach the stone-walled kitchen to find it empty. The kettle sits on the blue countertop next to an empty teacup. On the small dark wooden table, a mystery novel by Dorothy L. Sayers is facedown, the spine of it cracked. Mum is halfway through a Lord Peter Wimsey story. I like thinking about how the author also went to Somerville, how her book connects us through my mum.

I take two rights to George's bedroom. He has the room with the largest windows so he can see outside when the weakness of his heart keeps him from rising. At times he loses his breath so desperately that his lips turn a strange shade of blue. This window is his door to the world.

When I reach his room, I see that his bed holds only squashed pillows and rumpled covers.

My heartbeat thunders inside my ears. Has there been a rush to hospital and no one had time to tell me? It has happened before.

Mum's voice brings her to the doorway. She hugs me as tight as a vise. "You're home!"

"Where's George?"

I point to his empty bed. Mum's gaze leaves mine to scan the room. She startles, calls out his name. I do the same. He doesn't answer. Together we rush through the small house, which takes no more time than it does to call his name thrice more.

Mum flings open the front door and pokes her head out. "I see only your footprints in the snow," she says, and I hear relief in her words.

I rush back to George's room and look under his bed. Then I notice the wardrobe door is slightly ajar.

"Mum, look!" I call out as I yank open the door. There's George, his knees drawn up to his chest, his blue eyes looking straight at us.

"Megs!" He scurries out. I hug him as tightly as I can without fearing I will break the little bones in his chest and shoulders.

"Georgie Porgie."

I lift him and he throws his arms around my neck. He carries the aroma of the rose sachets in the closet and I breathe it in. Slight and frail, he clings to me. And I to him. I place him gently in bed, and he holds to my neck until I laugh and kiss his cheek. I draw the covers to his chin while Mum watches with a look of pure relief.

I sit on the edge of George's bed and it slants toward me. "I received your letter. It was so beautiful the way you told me the story about Dad and the sheep he chased through the garden. When did you learn to write so well?"

George grins, and that hair of his is so blond it appears like cotton. Twilight rests against the windows as if it wants to join us in the bedroom, and I flick on his bedside light.

"George," I say quietly, "why were you hiding in there?"

"I'm not hiding, I'm dreaming," he says, looking out the window as if he can see something we can't. "Imagining."

Mum looks at me and nods her head for me to follow her to the kitchen.

"I'll be right back." I kiss George on his cheek, and he closes his eyes.

Mum sets the kettle to the stove's fire and watches it in silence for a few heartbeats, until she turns to me with tears in her eyes. "It's because of that book that he goes and hides in the wardrobe. He reads that story over and over. He wants to read nothing else. Not even his favorites, *Peter Rabbit* and *Squirrel Nutkin*. Now it's all about Narnia and the lion and the four children who are living apart from their parents during the war. It's about magic and witches and talking animals. It's all he wants to talk about."

"Have you read it?"

"No, I haven't yet. Aunt Dottie dropped it off days ago. It's a new book for children by that author who teaches at your university."

"C. S. Lewis, yes," I say. "One of his other books, *The Screwtape Letters*, was all the chatter. There're more books to come from him, I've heard."

"Well, he best hurry. I doubt your brother will be . . ." Tears gather in her eyes, and she brushes them away with the back of her hand.

"Mum, don't say such things. Please."

"It's true."

"You don't know that."

The teakettle screams, and Mum pours boiling water into the cup over the tea leaves nestled in the silver strainer and watches the steam rise. "Go on now. Take your cuppa and visit with your brother."

She pulls her worn gray sweater tighter around her and buttons it near the neck as if she's holding herself together with the Shetland wool of her father's old farm lambs. I kiss her red cheek and she takes a linen handkerchief and wipes her eyes, then blows her nose into it with a resonating sound. We both laugh.

"Go on now," she says.

His room is warm. During the day it's the sunniest part of the house—intolerable for a few weeks every summer and favored in winter. It's shaped like a perfect square (and I know a perfect square) with plaster walls painted an ivory color. The single bed is handmade by our Grandfather Devonshire, fashioned of oak with four posters squiring up like the tower at Magdalen. The hand-hewn oak floors are covered with a sheep's-wool rug, fluffy in the places not often trod and flattened where our feet walk again and again. The blanket on his bed is striped, alternating blue and green, pulled high over the crisp white linen sheets that Mum irons smooth. The wardrobe across from the bed and between the windows, once belonging to Mum's sister, Dottie, has the trees and birds of a forest glade carved into its wooden doors. I think how each of these things is a part of our family, each made or passed down through a Devonshire or MacAllister line that reaches us now.

George's face is placid, and he rests on his pillow lightly, as if he hasn't enough weight to dent the down feathers inside. His eyes are closed, and I watch him sleep. His easy breaths go in and out.

"George," I whisper.

He opens his eyes, and his grin is wide. "I knew you would come home if I asked. I told Mum so."

"Why wouldn't I?" I take his hand.

"Mum says you are too busy with school. Mathematics exams are very hard, she says."

"They are, but I'm right here."

"I need you to do something for me." He sounds like an old man, or if not old, then just like Dad.

"Anything." I drop into the hard, wooden chair next to his bed.

"Have you ever seen him?" he asks.

"Seen who?"

"The man who wrote about Narnia. The man who wrote the book."

"C. S. Lewis. Yes, I do see him quite often. He walks quickly with his pipe and his walking stick along High Street and Parks Road, as if he's always late for something."

"I need you to ask him a question."

"George, I don't really know him. I've just seen him about. He teaches at Magdalen, and they don't allow women students there. I'm at Somerville. They are a mile and worlds apart."

"It's the same. It's Oxford University."

I can't argue that point. And I'm not one for arguing as it is. "What do you want me to ask him?"

"Where did Narnia come from?"

"I don't understand."

"Have you read it?" He asks as if his question is the answer.

I shake my head. "It's a book for children. I'm consumed with physics and the way numbers hold together the universe. I'm learning about Einstein's theories and . . . I haven't had time to read some children's book."

"You're rarely wrong, sister, but you are now. It's not a children's book. It might look like it on the cover, but it's a book for everyone. Please, Megs. I need to know if Narnia is *real*."

"Of course it's not real. It's a story, like *Squirrel Nutkin* and that book you like about the girl who dropped into a hole in the ground."

"Alice," he says. "This is different. I know you think the whole world is held together by some math formula." His voice has an unaccustomed annoyance in it. "But I've thought about this a lot, and I think the world is held together by stories, not all those equations you stare at." He's rarely angry, and this might not even be anger but something sparks up like a quick flame.

"My, my, I see." I feel my eyebrows lifting. "You've definitely given this some serious thought."

"Please. Just ask Professor Lewis, Megs. This book of his is different. It's as real as Dad's apple tree outside, as real as Mum's flowers, surely as real as this house. I need to know where it came from."

George doesn't have to say any more, because I realize the answer he wants means life and death to him. If my little brother needs to know where Narnia came from, I will find out.

"I will ask him. I promise."

From that moment, the weekend slips through my fingers like I'm trying to hold on to morning fog. I stay with George, and I study until my eyes burn. I flop around the house in an old wool sweater and fuzzy slippers. I think sometimes of the others at university who are having a chat in groups, and I feel so disconnected from them. It's not that I don't want to wear the latest fashion of pleated skirts and cute cardigans and have a smart exchange with a handsome boy in a waistcoat, but I just wasn't made that way. It's all so uncomfortable. I don't understand how girls get their hair in sleek ponytails or wear it in bouffant while my dark curls spring wild in the wind about my round face. Their skin is smooth and porcelain while the freckles on my cheeks and nose will not be covered with powder. They call me cute; I've heard them. But not beautiful, never that.

Mathematics doesn't care what I look like or what I wear, and that's what I've been focused on all weekend. On

Sunday, right before I prepare to leave, I sit down and open the book that has consumed my little brother, that has him hiding in the wardrobe and telling me about fauns and beavers and winters where Christmas never comes.

"I can read to you before I go to the train station," I tell him. "Would you like that?"

He smiles. "Yes."

"'Once there were four children whose names were Peter, Susan, Edmund and Lucy . . .'"

I mean to read for just a few minutes, to show him I'm not such a prig about math, that I can read a fairy tale as well as anyone else. A few minutes, I said.

Just a few.

But when I look up hours later, having missed the train, and the final pages resonant in the room with my tears blurring the last lines, I understand my brother. I understand it all.

We must, absolutely must, find out where Narnia came from.

## THREE

# WELCOME TO THE KILNS

Three days have passed since I promised George I would ask his question of Mr. Lewis. And this is my third time trespassing on his property, which is called the Kilns. December snow reflects sunlight like sequins. The frozen lake behind the house is a silver-gray disc of light and shadow. I sit on a large boulder, which from just a few yards away looks like the head of a giant buried in a mound of winter white. Cold seeps through my trousers, and I don't care. I'm enchanted by the hushed and mystical quality of the woodlands smack in the middle of Oxfordshire. I'm captured by the closest thing to magic—which I don't believe in—that I've ever known.

I've done just as George has asked—well, almost—and I've tracked down C. S. Lewis, the tutor of English literature at Magdalen College. I'd have gone straight to Magdalen, but it doesn't admit women as students. I am more often seen as a girl, not a woman, reminded constantly of my youth and diminutive size. They call me "little lady" and "darling" and "cutie." Let me see them undo an equation as long as their arm; I doubt they can.

So instead of storming Magdalen's gates, I'd decided to attend one of his famous talks. Although the event interfered with my study group, I found myself in the Examination Schools on High Street for a lecture on Edmund Spenser's tales, something I cared little for, but I wanted to hear Mr. Lewis and try to ask him the only question that mattered to me: George's question.

Mr. Lewis entered the dusty, crowded lecture hall in a flurry of black coat and hat and cold air. The room was crowded to its edges with enthusiastic students, some sitting on the windowsills and others standing at the back of the hall. While Mr. Lewis settled in at the lectern, still unwrapping his scarf, and now standing in his black gown, he at once commenced speaking in a bass and booming voice about Mr. Spenser and his book *The Faerie Queen*. "You may hear angels singing—or come upon satyrs romping . . ."

He lectured with such enunciation and clear speech that I heard every word. When he was nearly finished, he reached over and donned his coat and hat, then wound his scarf around his neck, lecturing all the while until he walked out the door.

By the end of his lecture, I did care a bit more about Edmund Spenser and his work and the revival of medieval motifs and how a poet ought to be a moral teacher.

That's how Mr. Lewis is; he captures the mind as quick as a heartbeat.

After the lecture, I followed Mr. Lewis at a long distance as he walked nearly to a run through the town's streets, his walking stick swinging to a secret rhythm. From behind Magdalen he hurried onto a path that ran parallel to the London Road called Cuckoo Lane. I tried to keep up with him on a secluded and walled passageway through gardens, then up the hill toward Headington. I followed at a safe distance, out of breath and carrying my books. It was a charming hidden route, and we passed under an arched stone overhang connecting wall to wall, ivy growing wild and giving me a feeling of the world being made of nothing but stone and vines and hidden crannies. The narrow Cuckoo Lane connected Headington to Old Headington and seemed meant for only a secret few; now I was one of them.

From there I trudged up the long hill to his house. I tried to find my words, to cough out the only question that mattered, but nothing happened. He was oblivious to me, his thoughts wherever an author's thoughts might go. Before I knew it, he had walked through the gate of the Kilns and was gone.

I've been sitting in these woods behind his brick house for three evenings in a row, trying to screw up the courage to speak to him. So far that screw hasn't turned far enough. I've nearly decided to invent a tale and answer for George, tell him that Narnia came from a great box of stories that Mr. Lewis keeps in his study. I will tell George that Mr. Lewis is magical and has his own sources that he refuses to reveal.

But I can't lie to George. I never have, and I'm not about to start now.

This afternoon I rode the bus to the Kilns, and now I stare over the rolling and hilly acreage, thick with fir and alder, lumpy with boulders and tree stumps. The Kilns feels a world away from university. It isn't Narnia—I'm not so deluded to believe I can walk onto the author's property and find a spired castle and a white witch. But there is a lamppost or two along the way, and the trees do indeed appear as if they might house sleeping dryads. The frozen lake might be where Lucy ran across with Mrs. Beaver. That is, if you look at it just right through squinted eyes.

Through the still air, I've heard the voices of the people who live in the author's house and I've come to differentiate them. There are two Lewis brothers and a man named Paxford, whose voice has such a quick-drilling sound I can barely distinguish his jumbled words. Paxford keeps the land, planting and cutting and cleaning. Twice he's walked near me and hasn't seen me hiding. His hands are large, and I was mesmerized by their size as he cut down a branch that blocked the view to the small lake.

C. S. Lewis is called Jack. His brother is called Warnie; I don't know his real name. I suspect these brothers, despite being quite old to me, would understand why I sit on their land and huddle on their rock, because they seem to love each other the way George and I love each other. They would understand my grief and fear. But maybe they will never really know how I feel, because trespassing does not seem the best way to begin a friendship.

I've only seen them once.

The first two times I came, I stayed for hours. Each hour my courage grew only the tiniest bit, as my toes got colder by quite a lot. Soon I would become brave enough to call out their names and blab the question I have come to ask: *Where did Narnia come from? My brother, he needs to know. He must know.*

But I'm a coward, unable to approach them.

The afternoon sun moves behind a bank of clouds flat and low, and the woods start to turn to shadow-shapes. Trees, bushes, and rocks on the white ground appear like cutouts in lace. I think of how the author must've found some of his fantasyland in this place, because I think I can see it too. I can almost imagine Mr. Tumnus ambling from behind a rock or the great Aslan setting his huge lion paws on the ground as it shakes with his majesty. My attention wanders. I let my vigilance flag, and a voice shocks me from my reverie.

"Well, hello there!"

I startle and slip from the rock, landing softly and with a grunt in the deep snow. My legs askew and my arms thrown behind me, I must appear to be quite crazy. A man—I see it is the author's brother, Warnie—is looking down at me.

"I'm so very sorry," I say as I rearrange my limbs to stand.

The man holds out his leather-gloved hand and I take it. He pulls me up. "Are you all right?"

"I am. Please don't be angry. I'm sorry I'm trespassing. I'll leave. I was just . . . sitting here thinking. I wasn't doing anything . . . wrong. I promise." My words tumble out on top of each other.

He bursts into a laugh so wonderful that the trees seem to shake with his shoulders. "I doubt you are here to do harm."

Now that he's up close, I can see him clearer. He's tall with a jowly face and a shaggy moustache. Above his ruddy nose are twinkling brown eyes. A tweed hat sits low, tilted over his forehead, and his body is covered with layers of coats and sweaters. All about him is the aroma of pipe smoke and wood fire. He looks at once both jolly and sad.

"Don't be so sorry. I'm Warren Lewis. And you are?"

"I am Megs Devonshire."

"Is there something you're looking for? Are you lost?"

"No. I know where I am. I'm here on purpose. I was looking for . . . Narnia." It is the stupidest thing to say. A grown woman—well, almost that—claiming such a thing. The heat of embarrassment crawls beneath my woolen coat and up my neck. "I mean—"

"Yes, we've had this happen before." His voice radiates kindness, and he doesn't seem to be chiding or humoring me at all.

I brush the snow from my coat and clap my hands together to remove the snow from my mittens. My hair falls from its clasp; I brush the dark curls away. "I'm not a fool. I know there's no real Narnia. It's for my brother . . . He wants to know how it started. He's sick. He's . . ." Nothing is coming out right. If I had made plans, if I'd thought it all through as I did my math problems, this wouldn't be happening.

"Your brother is ill?" His eyebrows drop and his lips form a straight line.

"Very."

"I'm so sorry. Is there anything I can do?"

"Yes, there is actually." I dig up the brave light hidden deep inside my fathoms of awkwardness and tell him. Because what if there won't be another chance? "He wants to know where Narnia came from. He needs to know. George is eight years old, and he won't see nine, sir. He asked me to find out. I'm his only sister and he asked *me*. I have to find out for him, but I don't quite know how, so I've been sitting here—on this cold boulder on your land— listening and hoping to figure it out."

"Well, I know just the man who can tell you: my brother, Jack."

Laughter bubbles up from under my tamped-down fear. "I know who your brother is, of course. But I hesitate to bother him."

"Then how, Miss Devonshire, will you ever have your question answered?"

"That's just it: the whole of my problem. Do I just make up an answer for my brother? Imagine where such a land as Narnia came from? Or do I become a nuisance and ask the author? That has been my dilemma, sir."

"Will you come with me and we'll ask him together? You don't strike me as the bothersome type."

"Come with you? To the house?" I glance down the hill toward the shingled roof and chimney pot, where smoke coils out and rises to the sky. I've memorized the lines of the house, the windows like eyes and the green side door.

"Yes. You are invited by me—and I, too, live in the house. Let's have a cuppa and warm you up. You are covered in snow."

He doesn't speak another word but tramps toward the house and assumes I will follow. I place my feet into his footprints and make my way past the frozen lake, silver with ice, past the dock covered in snow with tiny footprints of an animal I can't identify, past a tree stump so large it might seat four for dinner, and onto the pathway to the green door behind a low stone wall.

Warnie stops, stamps his feet on the brick entryway, and opens the door. A pale lemony light falls out, and even if I've changed my mind, even if I've second thoughts, there is no turning back now. Golden light beckons me into the home of Jack Lewis and his brother, Warnie.

The hallway is covered in dark wood, making it feel like a cave with a bench that runs along the herringbone wood floor. Coats and hats dangle from metal hooks on the wall.

Dust motes float and sink in the light until Warnie closes the door and turns to face me.

"Welcome to the Kilns, Miss Devonshire. Follow me." He takes a few steps and enters a room to the left, where the first thing I see is the source of the chimney smoke: a crackling fire on the back wall of the hazy room. I blink to clear my eyes and step back.

"Jack," Warnie says, "we have a guest."

"We do?"

That booming voice I heard in the lecture hall is no different here and it fills the room. My sight finds the man with that beautiful sound. He looks up with a beaming smile. C. S. Lewis sits in a large leather chair with a book on his lap and a pipe dangling from his mouth. His eyes are clear and cheerful as he looks right at me.

He stands and places his book on a side table. "Hallo."

He has the same look as Warnie, though perhaps a bit shabbier, if anyone asks me. His brown felt slippers are half on, half off with the backsides turned down; his shirt mussed and wrinkled; his jacket elbows worn almost clear through. "Welcome to the Kilns."

"Jack," Warnie says. "This is Miss Megs Devonshire. She has a most important question for you." Warnie holds out his hand to me. "Do take off your coat and mittens, and while you ask my brother your question, I will go make us some tea."

I unbutton my blue wool coat and remove it, slip off my mittens, and Warnie takes them from me.

Mr. Lewis smiles at me as if we've been friends all our lives. "Well, Miss Devonshire, it's a pleasure to meet you. Do sit down. Now, what kind of question do you have for me?"

Mr. Lewis's voice is so welcoming that again I find myself telling the truth as straight up as if I've practiced.

"My little brother, George, is eight years old, sir. He's very sick, and he asked a favor of me. He asked me to find out if Narnia is real. When I told him that of course it wasn't, he insisted on knowing where it comes from. I'm sorry if I am ruining your lovely evening—Mum does say I can be a pest. But I'm willing to be a pest for this undertaking."

"Dear Miss Devonshire, whoever told you Narnia isn't real?" He taps his pipe onto a tray. He leans closer. "Who?"

"No one, sir. I attend Somerville College reading maths. I'm smart enough to know your story is made up. I just want to be able to explain to George where it comes from. When I suggested your imagination, that wasn't good enough for him. He wanted to know how and . . . sir . . ." My eyes fill with tears threatening to run down my face. "I don't know what to tell him. It feels like both life and death to me, and I don't know what to say."

"Have you read the story, Miss Devonshire?"

"Yes, and I know it's a children's book."

Mr. Lewis laughs with a bellow that startles me. "Our mother had a mathematics degree herself in a time when women didn't do such things. But she was never above a good story, myth, or fairy tale."

Embarrassment floods my mouth with a metallic taste, like I bit my tongue, and I can't find the words to defend myself. He waits. Finally I speak with a stutter. "Sir, I'm not above it. It's just . . . It's a children's book."

"Well, well. It seems you are poorly informed, but sit, sit."

"Poorly informed?"

"As I say in the front of the book, 'maybe someday you'll be old enough to read fairy tales again.'" He points to a chair. I sit, cross my ankles, and prepare to be kicked out of the warm room any minute. "I'm not sure I can answer the question for your brother, but I can tell you a story or two."

The warmth of the room begins to make me dizzy and I just stare at him.

"Did you know there will be more books about Narnia?" he asks.

"I've heard. But right now we only have *The Lion, the Witch and the Wardrobe*."

"The next will be released in autumn of next year."

"George probably won't be able to read that one. He probably . . . Well, Mum says he probably won't . . ." I can't finish, the tears puddling in my eyes.

"Oh, Miss Devonshire." His voice breaks in half with the syllables of my name. "That is tragic in a way words can't contain. He's only eight years old?"

"Yes, sir."

"Let us give your brother some stories to carry with him on his journey."

"Please, sir. Anything at all that I can take home with me."

A rustling noise interrupts, and we both turn to see Warnie holding a black lacquered tray. Atop it is a brown common teapot with three cream pottery cups and saucers. Nothing fancy here, and that brings me comfort.

He pours us a cup of tea, and the three of us sit in a circle as the fire crackles like a man coughing. I wish for sugar but the rationing still prohibits it. Five years after the war, the rationing for flour and chocolate biscuits and syrup has been lifted, but sugar is still a rare treat.

I take a sip of my tea. It scalds my tongue, but I don't flinch. My skin buzzes with nervousness.

The Lewises' common room isn't what I expected at all. I thought that a tutor who is likely the most revered lecturer at Oxford would have a dark-paneled chamber full of books and awards, a musty room with a ladder to the top shelves, and glass cases of rare books. But no! This is a room crowded with well-worn furniture, knitted throws, and books scattered about like toys. Blackout curtains left over from the Second World War are hanging on the windows as if the fighter planes still buzz overhead.

There are masses of books: on the tables, on the floor, on the desk at the far end of the room. The walls must have once been painted a creamy white but are now yellowed from pipe smoke.

Mr. Lewis begins to speak. "Who knows where Narnia came from?" He lowers his voice. "Who knows when exactly a story begins? Probably at the start of time. But maybe Narnia had its first seeds in a land that my brother and I imagined as children in our attic. We called it Boxen. What do you think, Warnie?"

"It's quite possible," replies his brother. "But there was no real magic in those stories. Maybe the magic came later. In Narnia."

"Perhaps I was training myself to be a novelist."

There is a large wooden desk at the far end of the room below the window, almost glowing with twilight, papers piled everywhere. "Is the original on that desk?" I ask. I'm thinking I want to tell George I saw the pages typed up or written in Mr. Lewis's house.

"The original?" he asks.

"The original *The Lion, the Witch and the Wardrobe*."

"Oh, no, no. I don't have that anymore. When I finish a piece of work I flip the pages over and start something else on the other side. After it's all typed up, it's gone."

"Is that where you wrote it?" I ask Mr. Lewis.

"No. That was my mother's desk. Mine is upstairs in my study."

His eyes dim, and he looks at Warnie as if they are the only two people in all the world and their mother's desk holds a secret I can't know.

"I want to understand, Mr. Lewis. I want to understand how you can imagine something like that."

"There is a difference between imagination and reason," he says. "You want to understand with reason; I hear you.

And I once believed they battled each other—imagination and reason—that they stood in sharp contrast one to the other." He takes a draw of his pipe. "But that's not why we are here right now, Miss Devonshire. Maybe that shall come to you later."

I don't understand what he means, but I nod anyway.

"Should we tell her about the little end room at Little Lea?" Mr. Lewis asks, turning to his brother. "Which does, by the by, look like the Kilns, don't you think?"

"Yes, I do." Warnie sips his tea and nods. "And yes, tell her."

Then Mr. Lewis, in his charming accent and thunderous voice, begins a tale of two brothers in an attic in Ireland. He tells me the story as the fire fades and night falls hard against the windows.

# FOUR

## THE LITTLE END ROOM

"I asked him," I tell George as I rush into his room and sit on the wooden chair next to his bed. I drop my book bag and kiss his cheek before I take out the composition notebook with the marble-style cover I'd bought at Blackwell's bookshop on the way home.

"Oh, Megs! You did? What did he say?" George sits up, and the energy in his voice takes away all doubt that I can make him happy with the notebook I hold.

"He's the nicest man in the world. He talks . . . so precisely. I don't know how to explain it. Like every word is exact and he means each one."

George takes my hand. "Where did you talk with him? In a lecture hall?"

"I was hiding in the woods behind his house and his brother found me."

George laughs and his smile fills his face; he throws off his covers to sit straight. "And?"

"The author and his brother live on a property that looks like Narnia slipped out of the book and into their back garden. Or"—I smile—"it slipped out of his land and into Narnia."

"What did you ask him? What did he tell you?"

"Slow down, silly. I'll tell you everything. I promise. He did answer me a bit but not quite like you'd think. He told me a couple stories and invited me back on Monday."

"He didn't answer?" George's face falls and he slumps back to his pillow.

"Oh, he did. Just in his own way. With stories. He wouldn't let me take notes like I do with my tutor, but instead told me to go back to my rooms and write it down as I remembered it. So this"—I hold up my notebook—"is how I remember it."

George takes the notebook from my hands and flips through the pages I'd furiously written on with black ink, my handwriting jammed tightly from side to side and top to bottom. "I can't read this very well. Your writing is . . . scrunchy."

"I know. I wrote it so fast. I'll read it to you."

I take back the notebook and begin. While sleet pelts the windows, I read to George. "Outside Belfast, in County Down, a young—"

"Wait!" George presses his hand to mine. "That's not how you start a story."

"How do I start it?" I ask him, looking up from my words. "Do I say, 'Once upon a time'?"

"If you want." He seems incredulous at this boring start.

"How about . . ." I think for a breath or two. "How about, 'Not long ago . . .'"

"And not far away," he says.

"Or," I say with a grin, "'once upon a . . . wardrobe'!"

He smiles so buoyantly his cheeks rise to his ears. "Yes!" he says, his gaze wandering to the wardrobe across the room.

"Then here we go," I say. "Once upon a wardrobe, not very long ago and not far away, in County Down outside Belfast, a young Jack Lewis, only eight years old, same age as you, lived with his older brother, Warnie, who was eleven years old, his mother, Flora, and his father, Albert. There was a tutor and a nanny, Lizzie and Annie, and his grandfather Lewis also lived there. It was a full house."

George interrupts again. "Who is Jack?"

"The author, Mr. Lewis." I smile. "Clive Staples Lewis. I should have told you that. As a boy, he changed his name. He didn't like Clive Staples. Instead, he named himself Jack. His mother called him Jacksie."

George laughs, and the sound is as glorious as waves on rocks at Brighton Beach. "Jacksie? Like a baby?"

"I think it's just a cute nickname. You know how mums are."

He laughs and glances at the door in case Mum might be listening.

"Now let me tell it," I say.

George nods and presses his lips in a smile.

"They lived in a house called Little Lea. It was a red-brick house on a hill looking over the green land, and on a clear day they could see the wild waters of Belfast Lough and the Antrim Mountains. In this house was an attic full of nooks and crannies and small spaces where Jack and Warnie would play. They could sit at the window and watch the ships in the bay, for their great-grandfather had been a shipbuilder and they were fascinated. During this time, the massive *Titanic* was being built in Belfast, right under their noses, but how could they have known its terrible fate?"

I pause and look to George. I'm not sure this is what he wants, but it is all I have, so I continue.

---

George listens to his sister, her voice telling him the facts, but his imagination breathes new life into the story. George listens and observes his sister's beautiful face. She has more freckles on the left cheek than the right. There is a dimple low by the right side of her lip, and the curls of her hair are alive with her every move. Her smile takes some time but is always worth the wait.

Hours in bed have taught George how to find the soft edges of the facts and drop himself into the worlds he hears about or reads of. He closes his eyes, sets his mind's eye on the words, and floats on them like a raft. Megs's beloved voice continues, and George is transported to an attic with two young boys at a window seat in a place they called the little end room.

The brothers stare out at the emerald land and beyond to the whitecaps of a wild bay and the jagged edges of a mountain that rises into the clouds. Both of the Lewis boys have dark hair; they are quiet while watching the ships sail in and out of the harbor.

"Where do you think that one is going?" The younger boy, wearing brown knickers and a linen shirt, pressed his hands to the window. He pointed to a schooner that moved toward the open sea, where adventure no doubt awaited. The sky spread over the bay with a dome of clouds like sea foam.

"To India," the older boy, Warnie, said.

"You think every ship is going to India," Jack replied with a sly grin. "Or it could be going to Animal-Land."

The brothers glanced at each other with a look of kindness and friendship. Jack did love the view, but it was Warnie who was endlessly enchanted by the ships. The barkadeer and the brigantine, the clipper with three sails, and the galleon with a square rig and two decks. The rally with oars and the schooner with masts.

The exposed beams of a low-slung ceiling loomed over them. All around the attic were doors opening to other spaces. A wooden wardrobe, its handles thick as branches, crouched in one corner. Dust settled in the cracks of its dark etchings. Their mother kept her furs and fancy dresses inside. More than once, and more than twice, the brothers had crawled inside to tell each other a story.

But now the boys sat quietly, watching the ships with sails as big as dragon's wings fly into the bay. Dark blue waves splashed against the sea walls; sails billowed and breathed. Then Jack hit upon something in his thoughts and he turned to his brother.

"Oh, Warnie, in two weeks you will take one of those boats to England, to boarding school, won't you? You will leave me."

"Yes." Warnie tried to be brave when he said this. "But I'll come home often. The days will go by quick as a flash. You have your schoolwork and Lizzie and Annie and Mother and Father . . . and Grandfather."

"I hate my schoolwork. Math is the devil." Jack jumped from the edge of the window seat and walked to a small desk his father had made for him—"Jack's desk"—and sat down: drawings and maps scattered on its surface, piles of papers tilted, and colored pencils stored in boxes.

Warnie stood and joined his brother. "You'll be jolly fine. I won't be gone long, and you have your Animal-Land." Warnie pointed at the drawings and maps and notebooks, some spilling onto the wooden floors. These held Jack's creations: funny creatures that were half human and half animal, others that were all animal but dressed as humans in suits and top hats or in knight's armor, carrying swords. Elaborate maps detailed imaginary places: mountain ranges and loughs and seas and towns.

Jack called it all Animal-Land.

To create this land Jack had used every color in his

pencil box and every piece of paper he could find, filling notebooks, one after the other, with his handwriting—crooked and sideways—revealing story after story about King Bunny and Sir Peter Mouse, Gollywog, and others with strange names. On a sheet of lined paper, in his funny half-capital-letter, half-cursive handwriting, Jack listed all of them under the title *Dramatis Personae*.

Warnie considered the papers for a long while before looking up with a grin. "I have an idea! I have India and you have Animal-Land." Warnie pointed to one of Jack's characters, an owl in coattails named Puddiphat. "We can combine our worlds. Then it will be like we're still together even when we are apart!" Warnie ran his finger along the drawings of Jack's map, the seas crocheted with foam and creatures lurking beneath. The squiggly lines of various kingdoms' territories made puzzle pieces of the land.

Warnie quickly strode across the attic room, ducking beneath a low beam and retrieving his map of India before returning. He held the two maps—Animal-Land and India—near each other, and the edges touched. "Let's combine them into one country! You'll work on them while I'm at Wynyard. Write to me about what happens in our new together-kingdom."

Jack shuffled the papers on his desk and brought out a drawing of King Bunny in full armor. "Yes! We'll make maps and—"

"We'll call it Boxen," Warnie said.

Jack jumped up now. "There will be steamships and

trains. There will be knights like Sir Walter Scott and talking animals like Squirrel Nutkin." Jack's imagination grew far beyond the thing he'd created alone. Now, with his brother, something altogether new was unfolding, yet it took nothing away from his own creation. Outside, the rain ceased, and sunlight streamed through the attic's dusty air.

The brothers went to work on their combined land, and after many hours and an almost-missed dinner, they had established a new kingdom, one that combined their separate lands and brought them together as more than brothers; now they were cocreators.

———————

A week later, an early autumn afternoon spread sunlight as sharp as King Bunny's imaginary sword through Jack's bedroom window and onto the hardwood floors. Jack couldn't go outside. Miserable and tired, he was ill again, as he often was.

His chest ached with heaviness, and his barking cough brought the family doctor running to Little Lea.

"It's his weak constitution," the doctor said in the hallway in a deep voice, believing Jack was out of earshot. But Jack heard him; he always heard things the grown-ups thought he didn't. Now his mother was bustling about and making him stay in bed. The only good thing about being in bed was that he had more time to read the books on his bedside table.

When her footsteps faded down the hallway, Jack flopped back onto his pillow and closed his eyes. He imagined playing with Warnie instead of lying in bed with a cough.

Endless passageways ran through the family's house. Jack would run down hallways and through empty room after empty room. Sometimes when the sunlight fell through the windows, the house was just as jolly as a forest glade. Jack knew that anywhere he looked could be magic if he saw it with his imagination. Peter Rabbit might scurry under the dining room door. Farmer McGregor might be hiding in the vegetable garden, and Celtic faeries could be dancing beneath an oak tree's bough of leaves outside the window.

With his "weak constitution," Jack wasn't allowed outside as much as other boys. That was fine by him, because the house was also full of innumerable books, so many that when they moved from the old house to this one, which his father had built for them, Jack didn't understand where all the books had come from. They seemed to have simply appeared.

Now sick enough to stay in bed but not too sick to read, Jack leaned over to pick up his Squirrel Nutkin book. The bedroom door creaked open and Lizzie, his nanny, with her dark Irish curls springing from beneath her white cap and her blue eyes so vivid they seemed to spark, entered. She spoke in her thick Belfast brogue.

"Jacksie." She pulled up a chair and sat next to his bed,

then set a cuppa on the bedside table and grinned. "I am here to regale you with the one tale worth the telling."

This was his clue that a story was to begin. Jack smiled at her and sat up straight. He put down the book and picked up his tea.

"Across the western sea is an invisible world, a parallel world where one year of time equals seven of ours; where the fairies live in the sidhe, the people of the Goddess Danu."

The familiarity of this beginning soothed Jack and he leaned in, wanting more of the Tuatha Dé Danann and their adventures.

"This," she crooned, "is the story of King Nuada."

"Tell the one where he loses his hand and—" The bedroom door opened, and the loamy aroma of earth and adventure blew in with Warnie.

Warnie reached Jack's bedside in hasty steps, his smile at the ready. "I have something for you!"

The metal lid of a biscuit tin rested in Warnie's hand. He placed it in the nest of Jack's palm. A tiny garden made of twigs and moss rested inside the lid, a miniature world as mightily real as the ones Lizzie had begun to spin from the air. Jack stared at the mossy collection and a feeling passed through him, a warmth and an opening of his heart that he could barely put into words: a yearning, a longing, a wanting . . .

Jack held that tiny world his brother made for him and also held the deep feeling, even as the day of his brother's departure approached like a speeding train.

For the remaining hours and days they had together at Little Lea, the brothers played chess, checkers, and Halma. They read books and created their new land called Boxen.

When Warnie finally departed for boarding school—across the sea to England by ferry and then on a train to Wynyard in Hertfordshire—Jack guarded Boxen and the miniature garden as if his attention to this made-up world would hurry Warnie home to him.

———

One frigid November night, after Warnie had been gone for weeks, the house felt emptier than ever. Mother tucked Jack into bed, holding *The Tale of Squirrel Nutkin*. Jack thought for a moment to protest that he was nine years old now and much too grown-up for such stories, but that would have been a lie. His love for the story was greater than his pride.

Mother sat next to Jack's bed and a light snow began to gather outside the window, a tinkling of sleet and a slip of white building up on the outside windowsill. Jack imagined Warnie in some common residence hall with other boys snoring about him and possibly not enough blankets to warm him. But Mother, with her long black hair piled on top of her head and her warm voice of love, began to read.

Jack's mournful thoughts faded.

He could almost see the impertinent Squirrel Nutkin

slip under the door, running from the owl, Old Brown. Nutkin and Twinkleberry tripped across the story, and Nutkin almost lost his tail when he taunted the owl.

Jack snuggled deeper in the blankets. Safe. Warm.

When the story ended, Mother kissed him good night. As she went to turn off the light, she spied a pile of papers. She lifted them and held them under the puddle of lamplight. "Jacksie, what is this?"

"I wrote it. It's called *My Life*." Jack beamed with pride. "Everyone in the house is in the story."

Mother bent closer to the light as she flipped through the pages. Jack held his breath; he wanted her to love it. Finally a laugh erupted when she read out loud, "'A bad temper, thick lips and generally wearing a jersey.' This is how you describe your father? I am not so sure he'll want to read this."

"But it is true," Jack said indignantly.

"All the same . . ." She read a few more pages, then looked to her son. "You include all the pets: our mouse; the canary, Pete; and our terrier, Tim! You are wonderful, my child, wonderful. You know, I was once a writer."

"You were?" This was astounding. Mother always seemed as if she had only and ever been Mother.

"Yes. Someday I shall tell you about it. But for now, you must sleep." She lifted the pages. "May I take these to read myself?"

"Yes! And, Mother?"

"Yes?"

"Only fourteen days until Warnie returns," Jack said and rolled over to sleep.

The soft sound of his door closing was the last thing he heard.

# FIVE

# INK AS THE GREAT CURE

George's room shimmers with eventide light, pink and buttery yellow, and he sits quietly in his bed with his eyes closed. He is so still; I think maybe he's fallen asleep. I am finished with the first story, telling it as best I know how, and it looks like I've bored him, put him to sleep. Maybe all he'd wanted was a simple answer; maybe I should have just made it up and told him about the fake box of ideas. He'd never know the difference. After I'd left Mr. Lewis, there was just so much to remember, and I'd rushed all the way through this first story.

I press my hand on my brother's and squeeze. "George?"

"I heard every word. I'm here. I saw it all."

My heart constricts with the knowledge that he feels like he has to say he's still in the room, still with me. Tears prick the base of my throat, and I swallow them. His eyes open and he gives me a sad smile. "What happened when Warnie came back from school? Did he still love Boxen or did he grow up and not . . . ?"

"He still loved it; he didn't outgrow it just because he went off to school! They worked on that land for years and years."

"Well, you left out that part of the story."

"I thought you were asleep, silly boy."

"No! How could I possibly sleep in the middle of a story? I was just . . . in the story. Which isn't sleep at all but something brighter and . . ."

"In the story?"

"Yes. Don't you do the same?"

"No, I don't think so."

"When I read a story or you tell me one, I can go into them."

"Oh?" I say.

"So what happened when Warnie came home?"

"Well, close your eyes if you please." I laugh and cover his eyes with my hand.

---

George leans back, and there he is again with nine-year-old Jack waiting for his brother to come home for holiday.

Jack sat in the attic staring past the rolling hills and farther, to Belfast Lough's dark blue water. Flat, low clouds filled the much lighter sky, a faded sea.

On the road that was hidden by high trees, a black carriage carried Jack's father, Albert, down to the docks to retrieve Warnie. In the house, in the rooms and hallways, the grown-ups bustled about. Mother in the kitchen, fussing about the grand meal for Warnie's return. Their nanny, Lizzie, fluffing the sheets high in the air like the sails of a ship as she prepared Warnie's room. Annie sweeping the front hallway of the brown mud Jack had tracked in after running through the garden. And his grandfather Lewis, who lived in an upstairs bedroom all to himself, sitting in a chair in the library, clucking and fussing over the news. Grandfather didn't rush about like the others. He was slow and quiet, a presence of love in the house.

They all waited for Warnie, with Jack the most expectant. While Warnie was away, there'd still been school lessons for Jack—the mathematics he hated, the reading he loved, Latin, Greek, and history. And in between, he'd continued creating the world of Boxen.

Now staring out the window, Jack noticed a ferry had arrived in the lough, squat and low, its broad decks peppered with people. One of those people was surely his brother, but Jack couldn't see that far. He waved from the window as if Warnie could feel his greeting.

Within the hour, Warnie and Jack were in the attic, reunited and standing in the little end room.

"You're here at last!" Jack could not contain his enthusiasm.

Warnie stood tall, still in his school uniform starched and straight as the wall even after all that travel. "I am so happy to be home." He beamed a smile.

"Tell me everything," Jack said. "I want to know everything."

"The headmaster—" Warnie looked keenly at Jack, intense. "His name is Capron, but he's called Oldie. He reads our letters before they are mailed so I can't say everything I want to say. But I don't want to talk about school right now. I want to talk about Boxen. Your letter said that King Bunny has been captured!" Warnie loosened the top button of his uniform and sat down.

"I rescued him!" Solemn words poured out of Jack. "I wrote so many stories for us: 'The King's Ring,' 'Manx Against Manx,' 'The Locked Door,' 'Living Races of Mouseland,' and 'The Relief of Murry.'"

"Oh, that's so wonderful. I want to see them immediately."

"I even wrote a play called *The King's Ring* with Icthus-Oress, who is the son of a dead butcher *and* a singer. And these." Jack pointed to new drawings where mice carried swords and donned top hats. Toads wore three-piece suits.

Warnie reached for the piles of drawings and notebooks and Jack watched him, aware that Warnie was slightly different. Not in any essential way, but something in his eyes had shifted, a hardness that softened with the talk of Boxen.

"Do you not like Wynyard?" Jack asked, wondering if this might be the cause of the change that made Jack feel as if there was something about his brother he didn't know.

Warnie gave a sad type of smile. "I like cricket and being outdoors but—"

"Then I would hate it," Jack said. "You know I can't play those kinds of games." Jack held up his thumbs. "I am too clumsy by far."

"Father says it's only because we're missing a joint in our thumbs, not because we're clumsy." Warnie picked up a drawing of Puddiphat. "And because of that, you are so clever at all of this. Mother would agree that God gives us what we need."

Jack stared at his brother spouting his parents' words and for a moment, a terrifying moment, he believed he had lost his brother to Wynyard and adulthood.

But then Warnie smiled and crouched down. "How shall Pig Land fare in the next battle?"

Before Jack could answer, Annie's voice rose up the stairs. "Dinner is ready, boys!"

The brothers jumped up, leaving Pig Land and Boxen and Puddiphat to await their return.

———

I stop. George opens one eye to verify that I have closed my notebook.

"Oh, Megs! Is that it? Is that all they said? What did the two brothers say or do with you after that? What did the professor say?"

"Well, firstly, George, he isn't a professor—not like the professor in his book. Mr. Lewis is the tutor of English literature but not a professor, so I just call him Mr. Lewis. You could call him a don or tutor or fellow, but . . ."

George looks at me, bored with such facts, so I keep going. "Anyway, after they were done telling me that story,

Warnie bolted from the common room as if his tail were on fire, and he returned with their drawings from that time." I lean forward. "George, they were amazing! I saw a bunny riding a bike and a toad in a three-piece suit. Mr. Lewis had drawn them all as a child. Your age. He said he longed to make things."

"Do you think that was the start of Narnia?" George asks quietly as if afraid to know the truth.

"Neither of them can say." I shrug.

"And Mr. Lewis's unusual thumbs," George says. "Imagine if they hadn't been created that way." He pauses, and I imagine he thinks about his own heart being created differently from others. "What if Mr. Lewis's thumbs had been perfect?"

"I don't know," I tell George. "What if he had been better built with a hardy constitution and had never been done in with colds? Would he have started to draw and make up stories in the sunlit hallways and dusty little end room while he was stuck inside? Maybe not. Maybe he would have been outside with the other boys playing and running, and he'd never have created Animal-Land and then Boxen. I'm not sure if a missing joint in a thumb can be said to have started something that turned into Narnia, but I find it interesting, and so does Mr. Lewis."

"Did you get to read any of it? Of Boxen?"

I shake my head. "Mr. Lewis says he seldom rereads any of his work, but he did say he will sometimes pick up the old notebooks and drawings and glance at them, marvel at the land they created together when they were young. He told me that when their father died, he and Warnie returned to Little Lea and buried their attic toys in the garden. But they saved some of the drawings. Even later, when Jack was twenty-eight years old, he said he wrote an encyclopedia to explain all of Boxen."

George grew solemn. He gazed out the window and asked, "Was that all they told you?"

"I have one more story, but I think we'll save it for after dinner. Remember, they found me lurking like a proper crook on their property. It's incredible they told me anything at all. But they invited me back on Monday. Remember, little brother," I say, ruffling his curls, "it's close to exams. I can't just mooch about with Mr. Lewis all day. I have to study, and he has to teach and lecture and mark exams."

"I know," George says softly. "Out there, the world is a very busy place. But you have one more story?"

I kiss his cheek. "Right before the next story, Mr. Lewis told me this, so I'll tell you: 'And then everything changed.'"

"Well, isn't that a brilliant way to keep you hanging on?" George laughs, and the sound brings Mum into the room with a tray carrying three teacups and one pot with yellow flowers sprinkled about the edges. Her hair is longer this season, graying at the edge by her ear and chestnut everywhere else. Mum is too young, only forty years old, to be showing the signs of age. The skin under her eyes casts a purplish shade, and I wonder when she last truly slept for more than a few hours. But her sweet smile belies all fatigue, and her musical voice fills George's room with cheer. Dad is so very in love with her, and each time she walks into a room, I know why. She possesses a light that everyone can see.

"What is so funny?" she asks as she sets the tray beside the medicine bottles on George's little desk. It should be covered in schoolbooks and notes, but that's not George's life.

"Mr. Lewis. He left Megs hanging on so she would come back to his house. I'm going to get more stories."

Mum looks to me with a stern expression that tells me I best be careful not to lead my little brother down the trail of lies.

"They're true stories," I say as I pour the tea into my cup and think about the very strong tea at the Kilns. "I asked Mr. Lewis and his brother exactly what George told me to ask, and while he didn't quite answer me in the way I want, he told me two stories to bring home and said there are more for us."

Mum shakes her head. "Don't waste the poor man's time. Or yours. Narnia came from his imagination and that just must be that. It is a beautiful story to keep George occupied, but we mustn't hound a busy man."

George leans back and flattens against his pillow. "No, Mum. That is not just that. That is too simple an answer."

"Well, my darling boy, sometimes the simplest answers are the correct answers."

"There's more to it. I know it," he says so forcefully that it brings on a coughing storm. These fits come upon him with such ferocity that Mum and I rush to either side of him and bang on his back until it subsides. He relaxes again, but his fingertips have turned a berry shade of blue and his lips seem to almost disappear without their color.

"Megs," he says insistently, "did Mr. Lewis say if it was hard to make up the lands? If it was difficult to imagine Boxen? Or Narnia? Because . . . don't you see? He was my age when he wrote about King Bunny. He was my age when he created an entirely new world built of the bits and pieces of this world, while he was sick too!"

"He didn't say." I look to Mum, but she is busy watching George for signs of distress. "He just told me all about Boxen and the house where they lived in Ireland, which sounds glorious." I pause and lean closer. "Boxen isn't as famous as Narnia, that's for certain. Hardly anyone knows about it now. But he told me that when a story bubbles up, it's 'like a lion pawing to get out.'"

George nods. "I know. That lion is everywhere."

While I don't know what he means, I try to explain what I mean. "Here is all I can tell you: From the very beginning, Mr. Lewis wrote of other lands from his imagination. Maybe all of these kingdoms came from the same place—wherever that place is—Boxen and Animal-Land and Narnia. I don't know, but I do know that Mr. Lewis said something like this about imagination." I stop and think back; I don't want to misquote him. "'Whenever you are fed up with life, start writing: ink is the great cure for all human ills.'"

"Oh," George says with a short breath. "Wouldn't it be grand if ink could cure me?"

Mum draws a sharp breath. "I don't think that is what he meant, son. I believe—"

"I know what he meant, Mum. He meant the ills of the soul, and he is right." George looks to me. "Megs, when you go back to university, will you get me some paper and colored pencils like Jack's? When you come back, will you bring me notebooks? If Mr. Lewis can write at that same age, surely I can too." He smiles and I nod, because words will bring tears, and that won't help either of us. "Is there anything else to tell me, Megs? Just one more thing before the next story?"

I think hard, going back to that warm common room at the Kilns and what Mr. Lewis told me about making things up. I open my notebook and read a note I'd made. "He did tell me this: 'Reason is how we get to the truth, but imagination is how we find meaning.'" I look to George. "I think he said it better than that, but that is what I was left with. I remember that sentence as clear as if he rang a bell. 'Imagination is the way to find meaning . . .'"

George nods and closes his eyes with a satisfied smile, as if I have told him something he already knew but forgot.

I look to Mum, and she motions for me to walk into the kitchen with her.

Dad is still at work in town, running the local market, most likely busy as can be with the Royal Worcester Porcelain factory just letting out its evening shift, but he'll be home soon. This is the routine; they follow it without fail. My parents have formed the grooves of their life over the seventeen years since I was born, and they are as sturdy as the tracks that carry my train to and from Oxford.

Horrible questions speed through my head: What will Mum and Dad do when George is gone? How will their daily lives and schedules change? Sorrow floods me, and a sound rises from my throat as we reach the brick-floored kitchen and the warm, green AGA stove.

"Darling?" Mum turns to me with a question on her face. "Are you all right?" She sets the tea tray on the thick oak worktable. Something bubbles an iron pot on the stove, a stew, most likely lamb from its rich aroma.

"No, I am *not* all right. There must be something I can do besides tell my brother stories. There must be. What do the doctors say now?"

"The same as they've always said, Megs. There is nothing to be done but what we're doing. The trip to London didn't give us any new information, and the journey and the tests only wore him out further. It's too much to understand, I know. But we must."

"Mum, there is science. It is 1950, and there are huge advances. There must be an answer."

"Yes, you'd think there would be, wouldn't you? The antibiotics have helped us until now, but . . ." Her voice carries the weariness of years. The burden rounds her shoulders and grays her hair. Why am I making it worse by prodding at her?

The crunch of gravel causes us both to look up and out the kitchen window. Dad rides up the walkway on his bike. His dark hair is askew and his cheeks are ruddy with the wind of winter. "Why doesn't he just take the car?" I ask.

"He's afraid we'll need it while he's gone." Mum's voice fades with all she won't say about emergencies and a quick getaway to hospital. "Now put on a smile and greet your dad. No talk of stories and wardrobes and mythical creatures. Do you hear me?"

I nod and yet I know, deeply know, that there will still be talk of such things, because it is the talk George desires most.

# THE RUINED CASTLE

We knew George was sick the day he was born. I was nine years old, and Mum and Dad had been trying to have another baby for many years. Mum went into labor so quickly that cold November day of 1943, while the war raged through Europe and the Vatican was bombed. George was born in Mum and Dad's bed—not nearly enough time to rush to hospital.

And then a boy! A beautiful boy with eyes so blue they radiated like small round oceans from his face.

But he was too soft, too ... floppy. Weren't babies supposed to be squirmy and round-about in your arms? Not George. Yet the sweetest spirit emanated from that body.

His weak lungs and pale complexion, his limp arms and legs, had specialists rolling in and out of our warm cottage, all uttering the same doomed answers. It was George's heart. There was nothing to be done. Blood didn't go to the right place. It was weak. After doctors poked and prodded and tested and x-rayed, the doctors warned Mum and Dad George would most likely not see his fifth birthday.

But he had, and three more after it.

His life was contained by the spaces in and around our house—the kitchen and keeping room, the garden, and once in a while, at his best, a trip to the village for church and picnics. Activities were planned based on how he felt. On a strong day we went on long walks while I pulled him in a wagon. On weak days he stayed in bed and slept and read and was read to. We never knew what kind of day it would be, but winter days were the worst. The frigid cold seized his lungs, so he didn't much go outside. I was grateful for Narnia, for it took him outside in his mind, as did all the stories he loved. Winter was the time for stories of journeys and quests, of adventure and travel. *The Enchanted Wood. Jack and the Beanstalk. Winnie-the-Pooh. Little People of the Woods. The Wind on the Moon.*

Stacks of books.

Stacks of adventure.

I'd read none of them, of course. But I was content that they helped George.

Sometimes in the middle of winter's dark afternoon I would find him in the chair that usually sat next to his bed, but he'd have scooted it to the window. There he stood upon it with his nose pressed to the glass, his breath fogging the pane. It was then that I remembered that his world, although stuck with ours, was his own altogether. Whatever was in his mind—matters of adventure, sorrow, or comfort, I could never fully know. Whatever he saw out the window, or whatever he *wanted* to see out the window, was his alone.

At seventeen years old, I left for Oxford after earning a scholarship for my understanding of the theory of relativity from Albert Einstein, a teacher who had visited Oxford three times. I could grasp his formulas just as clearly as day. Einstein's equations changed the world, and I wanted to be a part of *that* new world, where numbers and equations unraveled mysteries.

But stories? Those were for George. Books kept him occupied, and I do believe alive, during the long convalescence between each worsening bout. Stories and fairy tales allowed him to be another person, another child, another being. He could leave his bed and soar above the stars, or roar like a lion, or fall fast into a river and swim like a fish. Mum allowed him the luxury, but Dad turned away from the fairy tales.

I loved Dad with a fierce love, but I loved George more. Maybe when we know we will lose someone, we love fiercer and wilder. Of course there will always be loss, but with George the end lingered in every room, in every breath, in every holiday.

That December night at our cottage, before I give George Mr. Lewis's second story, darkness falls in a quick way—one minute a golden light resting against the window, then the black of a moonless and cloudy night.

I return to George's room while Mum and Dad talk

about business, the ledgers of the market. George sits awake, reading again, the same book with four children riding on a lion's back under a bough of leaves. *The Lion, the Witch and the Wardrobe.* Instead of sitting in the chair, I scoot him over and slide in next to him on the soft bed.

"Mum is going to come in and make me say my prayers and go to sleep," he says. "So hurry."

"There's no hurrying these stories," I say with a grin and open the notebook. I change my voice, add more sing-song. "Once upon a wardrobe, not very long ago." I pause and look sideways at him.

"And not very far away," he says and we both laugh.

---

George listens as his sister resumes reading the pages in her black notebook. Megs is so beautiful, and he knows the light in her eyes is her love for him. It makes him feel that no matter what happens, he will be okay, and so will she.

"Now," she says, "it is 1908, and we are still in Little Lea in Belfast. Jack is almost ten years old and Warnie is twelve."

His sister loves her facts, but again his mind spins toward the story like he's been transported to Ireland, a place he's never visited except in stories and photographs. He sees a young boy on his knees next to a bed in a room with a wide window framing a murky night.

*Please, God, save my mother. Save her now. Make her well. I cannot live without her.*

Jack was on his knees on the cold hard wood, his knees aching. He squeezed his eyes shut so tight that he felt his eyebrows slide down as he uttered the prayer again and again.

The aroma of ethers—a smell that bit the back of his throat—seeped into his room. Jack was missing his brother more than ever, feeling more alone than ever. He was praying because downstairs, on the beautiful wooden kitchen table where Mother usually kneaded dough or sat with a book or cut a loaf of bread, she lay unconscious, having surgery.

Unimaginable.

Too much to understand.

They called it cancer.

Jack's room was thin with cold, all the firewood burning in the kitchen for Mother, for the nurses who wore their swan-like caps, for the doctors with their serious expressions and terrifying metal tools and scalpels.

Warnie had been away at school when Mother's headaches began. Soon the bustling house had become hushed, and people in white uniforms flew in and out of its doors. Their grandfather was moved to a nursing home because his daughter-in-law couldn't care for him as she had.

If Grandfather had been right, then God would hear Jack's prayers and save his mother.

Jack used all of his mind and heart to imagine her, with the kind smile and moon face he'd inherited from her, healed, taking him on holiday to the beach or Dunluce Castle. Traveling with him to London to see again the great lions in Trafalgar Square. Quizzing him on his Latin or reading him a story.

Alive. It was the only thing that mattered or made sense.

*Sick* was the only word he understood for what was happening. But Jack had been sick, a lot actually, and he was fine and alive. Surely Mother would be also.

The world felt like it was tilting or sinking.

Silence rushed against Jack's ears like a sea crashing on rocks, and he stood from his knees and crawled into bed, sitting up against the oak headboard to wait for good news. He pulled the wool blanket to his chin and stared out the window. His heart hammered in his chest, and he imagined his mother alive and well and holding him.

Perhaps his imagination, combined with his prayers, would keep her alive. If she were alive in his mind, she would be alive in the world. This seemed to be true as far he could tell.

Jack might be able to create a world like Boxen with his brother, but he could not create a world without his mother in it.

His imagination took him to the jagged edges of his trip to Castlerock two years ago, when Mother had taken Warnie and him to Dunluce Castle.

The train had sped, heading north to the tip of Ireland, and rocked them to near sleep as the countryside and its towns flew by: chimneys with rising smoke, church steeples pointing above the roofs, sheep with tangled muddy wool, and farmers who stood behind the wooden fences and raised a greeting of one hand to the train.

Jack and Warnie had sat next to each other in their stiff traveling clothes while Mother sat across from them in a pale blue dress with lace around her collar, a deeper blue bonnet tied beneath her chin with a ribbon. Her dark hair hung in ringlets that nearly touched her shoulders. She tapped the train's tray, where Jack and Warnie's lesson papers on Greek were spread. "Let us finish before we arrive in Castlerock," she said.

Jack looked away from the countryside. "But, Mother, it's summertime. Enough of lessons."

She shook her head with a stern but kind smile. Jack and Warnie each took their worksheet with the vocabulary words and began to translate and fill in the blank spaces. Jack actually enjoyed Latin and Greek, but he loved staring out to the wild Irish countryside and finding more Boxen stories in his imagination.

"Why must we do schoolwork and not you?" Jack asked Mother. It was an absurd question, and he knew it even as the words came from his lips.

"Oh, I had plenty of schooling. When you're old like me you won't have to do lessons unless you're enthralled with a subject." She paused and seemed to be elsewhere for a moment before returning her attention to her sons. "Just as you love to read now, so do I. I never want to stop learning."

This was the first Jack had heard of such a thing. His mother in school?

Warnie lifted his gaze from the words scribbled across his page in tight script. "Where did you go to school?"

"Queens' College," she said with a lift of her chin. "Mathematics and physics."

Warnie let out a sigh of amazement. "Mathematics *and* physics?"

Jack stared at his mother with her sweet smile and her warm brown eyes, with her thin nose and wondered, for the first time, what she must have looked like or acted like when she was his age.

This was astonishing.

Jack never wanted to grow up; his father made it all seem so dreary. But right then, for a moment, he imagined his mother young and in college, and she gave him hope that getting older might be exciting in its own way.

"But you told *me* that you were a writer," Jack said.

"A person doesn't have to be only one thing in the world. You can be more."

"I can't." Jack let out a laugh, and Warnie did too.

"Well, I was," she said.

"Tell me what you wrote," said Jack.

"I liked to write stories. Before your father and I were married, we wrote letters back and forth to each other, and I let him read my work. And this, my boys, is how I fell in love with him, because he took my writing seriously and he took me seriously. He was so kind about my stories."

"Father was kind?" Warnie asked in one breath.

Mother laughed. Jack adored his mother's laughter

and he wished he'd been the cause of it. "Very kind," she said. "Your father would write back to me and tell me how wonderful my stories were. He encouraged me to send them off. And I did. I published a piece in the *Home Journal*. It was called . . ." She leaned forward and used her storytelling voice, the beautiful voice of myths and tales, and said, "It was called 'The Princess Rosetta.'"

Jack set down his pencil and said sternly, "I want to read it."

She laughed freely. "It's gone. I don't know what has happened to it in the flurry of the moves and your arrivals and . . . But your father read it long ago. I know you see him as a harsh father who can't understand you, Jacksie, but he's a kind man whose attention to what mattered allowed me to fall in love with him."

Jack stared at his mother. The idea of falling in love with anything but nature and stories was as foreign a concept as the planets' movements.

They all rode in companionable silence until they reached Castlerock, its beaches, and lazy afternoons.

Finally, on a cloudy and windy summer afternoon, Jack, Warnie, and Mother climbed the hill toward Dunluce Castle. When Jack looked up and spied the castle high on an emerald hill, his breath caught.

Time paused. Everything stood still and quiet, and Jack's heart reached high above him to the ruin of stone and to crumbling towers that once pierced the clouds.

Longing, which he'd only felt in small doses before,

now washed in with the sea's waves, crashing with wild silver spray on the rocks. The castle spread wide with turrets at the corners, its walls without roofs, jagged as if it had grown from the coast. A stone bridge spanned a wide expanse where, if one imagined, both dragons and ogres lived in the furrows of the cliff and would grab for the kingdom at the first chance. Only the bravest of the brave could keep them from conquering. The sea was carved with the troughs and peaks of the waves crashing at the shoreline. Two gulls swooped on the wind. In the rocks below, tidal pools reflected the cloudy sky, and all around the brothers came the pungent and clean smell of salt.

"Warnie," Jack said. "Look."

Warnie did look, and together they imagined what knights and kings battled, what princesses needed saving, and what quests lay ahead for the royal kingdom of this castle.

———————

"Megs!" George calls out to his sister in the middle of her story so that she almost drops her notebook.

"What? Are you okay?" She drops her hand onto his forehead.

Why did adults always touch his forehead as if it told them everything they needed to know?

"Is that . . ." Did George dare hope? "Is that castle in Ireland . . . Is it Cair Paravel? Is it real?"

His sister takes a deep breath and pulls him closer

with one arm. "Dunluce Castle is real. But is it the castle in Mr. Lewis's book? I don't know."

"His mother . . . It's so desperately sad. Did she live?"

"I'm not yet done with the story, George."

"I'm not sure I want to know. I want Jack's mother to live. Does she?"

"Okay, I'll quit now if you want." Megs grins in the way George loves. Her whole face gives away that she will do whatever he wants, but she already knows what he wants.

George sits straight up, his heart beating with the imaginings of a young Jack Lewis and his brother. He needs to know what happened, even if what happened is awful. "Megs . . ." He exhales and snuggles closer. "All stories have the dark and scary part," he says. "Maybe that's where we are now. The dark part before the good part."

"Well," she says, "maybe this is a good place to stop for now. The beach trip to Castlerock and Dunluce Castle is full of beauty and love." She closes her notebook.

George puts his hand on hers. "Keep going. I want to know."

———

Jack's prayers might have worked, or so he thought, because for weeks after that surgery, his mother recovered in her room. Then one March afternoon, when Warnie had come home for a weekend, Jack and Warnie sat by her side in the quiet bedroom.

"Mother," Warnie said, "if we pray hard enough, God will heal you. And we have been praying so hard."

Mother rested on her pillows, her face so pale and her lips so thin that Jack tried not to look too closely; he just wanted to hear her voice. "God doesn't always answer our prayers the way we want," she told her sons. "There are things we can't know about His great plan."

Jack walked to the end of the bed and lifted his chin in defiance and said, "If His plan isn't to heal you, then He isn't real."

"Oh, my sons, I have something for you." She struggled to sit up, then she leaned over and picked up two Bibles from her bedside table. "There is one for each of you to treasure for all of your life."

Jack and Warnie took the thick Bibles from her hand, felt their smooth leather bindings and silky pages.

"Thank you, Mother," Jack and Warnie said at the same time, but Jack all at once felt that they weren't talking to their actual mother, because how could this ill woman in the bed be her? Their mother did not stay in bed; she taught them Latin and Greek. She played outside with them. She took them to beaches and castles and mountains.

She did not lie in bed and give them Bibles as a consolation prize.

Mother gazed at her sons. With tears in her eyes, she took their hands. "Oh, boys, we must ask ourselves . . . We must . . ." She paused and closed her eyes. "What have we done *for* God?" The boys stood stock-still and held her hand until their father shooed them out of the room. Neither of them had an answer.

Only days later, on August 23, his father's birthday, Jack awoke in the night with a gnawing toothache. As usual, he was worried about Mother, but now there was something new to fret about: his own pain, throbbing in his mouth along with a fever that burned behind his eyelids and at the back of his neck.

"Mother!" he cried out.

Jack's bedroom door flew open, but it was Father in the doorway. This was as startling as if a talking beast had appeared. His father, always leaning toward sadness as it was, sat on the edge of Jack's bed. He smelled like sweat and fear. "Jacksie, your mother is very sick."

Jack sat up. "So am I. Send her to me!"

"It's not the same, Jacksie. It's serious. I need you to be a man now. Don't cry out. Don't make this harder on all of us."

The tenor of his father's voice was different, a bit like someone had taken out a vital part of his soul and put it away.

Jack flopped onto his pillow and held back the tears, his fever burning, his tooth throbbing, and he thought about his mother and how she could not be too sick, because the world and everything in it depended on her.

But she was leaving them even as Jack was wishing for her to come help him, her soul rising from her ravaged body.

The Lewis family's world unraveled with the words

of their father in the morning. "Your mother has gone to heaven to be with God." Warnie and Jack huddled close together as their father uttered this impossible statement. "She is gone. Now come see her and say good-bye."

See her? Jack recoiled. "No. Do not make me." His lips quivered as he tried to control the grief. If he started crying, he might not stop.

Father bent down, his hands on his knees as he directed his youngest son. "You must see her and say good-bye."

Warnie squared his shoulders as if to protect his little brother, as if to protect himself. "No!"

"Now." Albert pointed at the door, and the brothers had no choice but to obey.

Later, hours later, when friends and family had gathered at Little Lea and the drawing room was overflowing with people who spoke in whispers, as if death warranted secrets, Jack escaped to the kitchen to find the comfort of Lizzie. As he scanned the room for her, his gaze fell on the calendar hanging on the plaster wall, a calendar that had been the outline of their days, now full of weeks and years without their mother. Jack read the quote for August 23, 1908: a line from King Lear: "Men must endure their going hence."

Jack stared at that line, one he knew from his Shakespeare lessons, a phrase that was as true as anything he'd ever read.

He wept for his lost mother.

———

Megs closes her notebook and George shakes his head, wipes at the tears in his eyes. "Poor, poor Jack! Can you imagine, Megs? Can you even imagine?"

"No, George, I can't. When Mr. Lewis told me this part, I cried right there in front of him in his common room, snotty tears on his cotton handkerchief."

He reaches for his sister's hand. "It's okay, Megs. It's part of the story. There's lots of parts to a story."

Even as he feels Megs watching him, George closes his own eyes. He's so tired, and he wants to see all that she showed him, to think about Mr. Lewis losing something so beloved and then later creating something so marvelous.

George wants to consider it all.

He longs to climb inside the wardrobe and watch the story come together just as it happened. He doesn't want to change the author's life; he wants to watch it turn into something new, something with snow, a white witch, and a lion that calls to George even in his sleep, its roar far off and deep, both comforting and terrifying.

# SEVEN

# TO SEE WITH OTHER EYES

Oxford in the dead of winter has its own beauty. The pinnacles and stone towers glitter, and the wind blows wild and without warning. I've decided to walk to the Kilns this afternoon. It's a gorgeous path of sidewalks winding only two and a half miles through Oxfordshire. If an old man with a walking stick can do it, so can I.

When I reach the Magdalen Bridge over the Cherwell, where the river splits into two and where the Thames is then called Isis, I gaze down to the flowing water. There are no punters on this cold afternoon, and the banks of the river sparkle with ice. Birch and alder trees are bare and thin and seem taller without their leaves to fluff them up. To my left, standing staunch and proud, is the stone edifice of Magdalen College. The tawny-colored wooden gates with ironworks are shut. The architecture of this college on High Street makes me almost believe the building was built during the medieval times and a dragon once turned the corner flapping its wings and roaring fire.

This is how George has influenced me. I am starting to see stories where I hadn't seen them before. I've obviously been thinking too much of Mr. Lewis's lion book.

Something in me wants to burst through the Magdalen gates and run to the tip-top of its tower, just as the boys' choir does every first of May, and gaze out over all of Oxford while shouting my indignation at death, at sickness, and at the sheer indecency that women students aren't admitted into Magdalen College.

Instead, I walk slowly past the gates and over the bridge so I can climb the hilly terrain toward the Kilns. I think of George while I walk, my hands warm in my red mittens and shoved deep into the pockets of my wool coat, my head bowed to the wind as it threatens to rip off my blue knit cap that Mum knit for me last winter.

I imagine George warm in bed and what he'd give to trade with me for a red nose and runny eyes as he trudges toward the author's house.

If I could gift George one thing in his life, other than a new heart that pumped blood to all the right places, it would be this: to give him answers to his questions about his beloved Narnia. Mr. Lewis and Warnie—whom I discovered they also call "the Major" because of all his time in the army—will tell me another story today over tea. I will listen, but I also promise myself that I will ask for one fact beyond the story, one solid thing I can take home to George, like the biscuit tin with moss that Warnie gave Jack.

But meanwhile, my exams barrel down on me; I feel like I'm carrying my heavy and unshakable books between my shoulder blades.

"Megs!" A voice stops me in my thoughts, and I skid a bit on the icy sidewalk over the bridge and grab the stone railing. I turn to see a figure running toward me. It's a boy I know from the one time I went to the pub with Delia, a girl from down the hall. He attends Magdalen, his name is Padraig, and he studies literature. That's all I remember, although we'd chatted for about five awkward minutes while sipping our Guinnesses. He has a girlfriend; I'd met her and quickly forgotten her name. She looked like all the other slick-ponytail, red-lipstick stylish girls I would never be.

Padraig rushes from the side gate and runs toward me, buttoning his coat and slipping his wool cap over his wild red curls. His presence makes me a bit jittery, and I know enough to know the feeling isn't fear but attraction. Stupid, unnecessary attraction.

"Megs!"

"Hello, Padraig." I nod at him as if I don't care. I have somewhere I need to be.

"You remembered my name!" He grins as if I have given him a gift. "Where you headed?" He stops short next to me. "Want to be getting a pint with me?" His brogue gives away his Northern Irish origins, and his grin dares the world to be anything but what he wants it to be.

"Thank you, but I can't. I'm going to see a tutor."

Padraig looks over his shoulder, then to me. "You're going the wrong way."

I laugh easily, which is lovely. "I'm meeting him at his home."

"That sounds a bit untoward." He draws his chin back in mock disapproval.

I shake my head. His inference, even if joking, makes heat rise in my cheeks. "No, it most definitely is not. It's Mr. C. S. Lewis and his brother, Warnie, at their place. They've invited me to tea. He's not *my* tutor; he's telling me stories. It's hard to explain." I wipe my runny nose with the back of my mitten, thinking Padraig surely must see me as a mousy math student.

"If I walk with you, will you try to explain? If it's so complicated, I want to hear it."

"I'd love the company," I tell him honestly. We start to amble across the Magdalen Bridge and then from High Street to Plain. Padraig keeps stride next to me, so close that if he reached out his hand he could take mine. But of course that is not what he is going to do.

"You see," he says, his breath coming in large puffs. "He's my tutor for English literature."

"He's your tutor? What's that like?" I pause, and two little boys running full pell-mell up the street bang into us. We stand fast and Padraig holds out his hand to steady me. I am struck mute by his touch. But I want to know—is Mr. Lewis different with Padraig than he is with me?

Something like jealousy flares in my heart, but curiosity quickly smothers it.

We are on a corner where we need to cross to St. Clements. Padraig holds out his arm for me as he looks left and right and then nods for us both to cross. I am warmed by this, by his simple courtesy. We hurry and he cheerfully keeps talking as if we've done this a thousand times.

"He's a right genius, he is. And so serious until his wit comes through like a firecracker. Some students say he's a bully but most love him. He pushes us hard. He suffers no fools and some can't abide that. But if you really want to learn to read, he's the right tutor."

"Well, he's the grandest kind of storyteller," I say. "I went to his house to ask him a question and then . . ." I pause but it is quick, because Padraig's open smile allows me to launch into the story of my brother and his request—a story I haven't yet told anyone.

It takes a few blocks, but when I finish and we reach Headington Road, Padraig exhales as if he's done all the talking. "Wow." His voice is so quiet I only *think* that's what he says.

I tell him, "It's silly, maybe, gathering stories of someone else's life. But it's the best I know to do for my brother."

"Have you read Mr. Lewis's other works?" he asks. Our words come in puffs of air into the cold afternoon.

"I haven't."

"They're really good. There's *The Screwtape Letters* and *The Great Divorce*. A scientifiction trilogy, and of course the one that everyone is talking about since he was once an atheist, the lion book."

I stop in my tracks. "Mr. Lewis was an atheist?"

"Indeed." Padraig takes off his wool cap and runs his hands through those unruly curls. He grins with satisfaction at telling me something I don't know.

"Well, I don't know much about him. I study physics, not stories." I feel defensive. "I'd only heard his name about university until my brother asked me to do this. I didn't know his work or his life."

"Maybe that's good. Maybe all you need to know about Mr. Lewis is what he tells you."

I shrug, my shoulders and neck aching from the hours bent over books when I studied in the hush of the Bodleian Library.

Padraig smiles warmly and seems to bounce with anticipation. "Will you tell me what he says? Will you tell me the stories?"

"They aren't what you think," I say, meeting his green eyes, which had been the first thing I noticed about him when I met him at the pub. Delia had insisted I go out that night with her, for it was her birthday. I'd ended up taking her home as she leaned on my arm, stumbling and stopping at least twice as she was too worse for drink.

"What do you mean?" he asks. "Not what I think?"

"They aren't Narnia stories. No matter how many times I ask where Narnia came from, he and his brother tell me stories about their lives and childhood. Did you know his mother died when he was only nine years old? Isn't that dreadful?"

"Maybe he's answering your question and you just don't realize it."

"I'm sure that's true. He's not one to waste time—for goodness' sake, he barely puts his slippers all the way on his feet."

"Well, in Narnia, aren't the children without parents?"

"Separated from them, yes."

Padraig smiles. "Stories have their own truth."

I nod, not fully understanding his point, but wanting him to keep his attention on me; it feels nice, even if he does have a girl with long blonde hair and a giggle that sends all the boys running to the bar to get her an extra cider.

"I need to be getting on," I say. "It was jolly to see you. Thank you for keeping me company."

Padraig nods and spins around, departing as quickly as he'd appeared. I watch him go. A few steps down the sidewalk, he turns around, catches me watching him. He waves and smiles. I'm blessedly glad he can't see my blush as I hurry on.

Only half a mile remains, and I reach Kilns Lane just in time. I walk quickly, dodging the icy bits until I approach the green door of the Lewis house again.

I knock and Warnie opens it. A blast of warm air hits my cold cheeks, making them tingle.

"Come in. Come in!" His voice echoes in the house and I step inside, shed my coat and mittens, and place them on the settle bench at the side of the hallway where other coats and hats and mittens are jumbled together in a party.

"Hello, Miss Devonshire. My brother is running a bit late, but let's sit in the common room and warm you right up."

From where I stand, coats and hats seeming to be the ghosts of their inhabitants hanging straight on the hooks, I can smell the woodfire and tobacco, and I smile at its comforting aura. I follow Warnie into the common room. "Tea is waiting for us," he says.

I sit in the shabby but comfortable armchair I occupied on the last visit and cross my legs at the ankles, trying to be a most proper girl in the home of scholarly men. A tray with all the fixings for tea, minus the rationed sugar, sits on a wooden table at the far end of the room. A stout woman stands there, and she turns to me and smiles, her wild white hair pointing in all directions and her left front tooth askew.

"Hello, Miss Devonshire. It is a pleasure to make your acquaintance. I am Mrs. Rounder."

I nearly burst into laughter at how her name matches her body, but I don't. How very rude that would be.

"It's a pleasure to meet you," I say. "Thank you for making the tea, ma'am."

She smiles and looks at Warnie. "A right proper one she is. Enjoy your afternoon."

And with that, she disappears through the doorway. Pots and pans clang a room or two away and then suddenly, without the sound of a door opening and footsteps, Mr. Lewis appears.

He wears the same clothes I saw him in last time: a tweed jersey that has worn patches on the elbows and a thick sweater beneath. A pipe hangs from his mouth with a little plume of smoke rising in front of his warm brown eyes.

"I am so sorry for the delay," he said. "I was visiting Minto at the nursing home."

"Minto?" I ask, thinking I had forgotten a story I was supposed to know.

"Mrs. Moore. Oh, you shall learn about her soon enough," he says and sits down. "But not today."

I smile because this means there are more stories to come.

When we're all settled with our tea, which I have to say is very strong, Mr. Lewis looks to me with a grin. "Now where were we?"

My words rush like a river. "You don't have to tell me so many stories. I know this is Michaelmas term's end and you must be quite buried in papers and maybe if you gave me just one clue, one factual thing I can take home to George. He was so enchanted with Boxen he asked me to bring him a notebook and a box of colored pencils."

"Well, isn't that marvelous!" Warnie says.

Mr. Lewis sets his pipe on a tray. "One clue? One fact that tells George where Narnia came from . . ." The tutor's voice trails off. "What did you tell us you were studying?"

"Mathematics and physics, sir."

Mr. Lewis and Warnie reply at the same time.

"Ah!"

"Ah!"

Mr. Lewis leans forward. "With stories, I can see with other eyes, imagine with other imaginations, feel with other hearts, as well as with my own. Stories aren't equations."

"I realize that. I just thought . . . Well, I don't want my brother to escape into fantasy, that is to say, to believe something is true that isn't."

The brothers look at each other as if deciding who will tell me how very wrong I am. I can feel it. But the world, it is so hard—don't they know that? There is false hope everywhere, and I want to give George the kind of hope that is good and true, not a disappointing sham.

But I sit still.

"Miss Devonshire," Mr. Lewis says and looks out the window as if what he wants to say dances in that dormant winter garden. "The fantastic and the imaginative aren't escapism."

"How so?" This seems important.

"Good stories introduce the marvelous. The whole story, paradoxically, strengthens our relish for real life. This excursion sends us back with renewed pleasure to the actual world. It provides meaning."

"Yes," Warnie says. "It takes us out of ourselves and lets us view reality from new angles. It expands our awareness of the world."

The significance of these statements creates tingles on

my arms and neck. I realize fantasy and imagination aren't just for escape. And to dismiss them is absurd. But I say nothing. I sit and wait.

Mr. Lewis nods to Warnie. "I also wrote and read because I was so terrible at maths." He looks to me again. "Horrid, as matter of fact. When we reached the horrible school, it was one of the things that earned me cruel discipline from Oldie."

I have the irresistible urge to hug Mr. Lewis, but he doesn't seem the hugging sort. I want to press my hand to his heart and ask him if it is okay, but instead I ask, "How did you live through so many awful things?"

Mr. Lewis looks at me as if deciding how to answer.

"So dreadful," I say.

"Yes." He smiles. "There was a fourteenth-century mystic named St. Julian of Norwich. Have you heard of her?"

"Yes, sir."

"She has written many beautiful lines, but the one that echoes through the world is 'All shall be well, and all shall be well, and all manner of things shall be well.'"

"I don't always believe that, sir," I tell him. "So many bad things happen."

"Yes, they do and always will, and yet, all will be well."

I can feel inside that it is true even as doubt whispers the opposite. I listen, afraid that if I do or say anything else, he will stop talking.

When the brothers tell me this part of their story, they look back and forth to each other as if to check that the other is doing just fine.

## EiGHT

## EXILE

Studying for my own exams while also thinking about George and the tales of Mr. Lewis set my brain fizzing with distraction. The usual focus I have for my figures and sums becomes muddled with stories and, oddly, with thoughts of Padraig's kindness to me.

Since that afternoon four days ago, Padraig has twice sent a note to my dormitory to meet him for a pint, and twice I've refused him. Not because I don't want to see him or gad about in the pubs with his friends, but because I can't get my mind in the right place to enjoy myself. As it is, I'm also not one for gadding about. I never know what to say in a crowd, what to talk about, and I worry I'm not wearing the right thing or that my jersey is the wrong color or that my hair is out of style. I feel old-fashioned in 1950, as if I were meant to be young in the 1930s and 1940s like Mum.

Now I sit on the train as it rocks its way to Worcester, and I carry a bag from Blackwell's bookshop loaded with papers and colored pencils for George. I used my weekly allowance to get them, and I can't think of a better use.

By the time I get to the house, shed my coat, and warm myself in the kitchen with Mum, it is late afternoon. I sneak into George's room to surprise him, holding out the bag of art notebooks and pencils to make him holler with glee.

His bed is empty. I glance about the small room to find it the same. Maybe he's gone to sit in Mum's study at the far end of the house, where her stash of mystery books topples over each other. Sometimes George goes there to curl into her chair and read.

But then I notice the wardrobe door ajar. I slip my hand behind the carved wooden door. It creaks open and there is George, sitting cross-legged and staring right at me as if he expected me to find him just as he is.

"Georgie Porgie." I bend down. "You're in here again?"

"It's nice in here." His hair is all adrift as if he's been in a forest, as if the wind has taken its hand and tousled his curls. "It's quiet and dark, and nothing bothers me so much."

I show him the bag. "Look what I brought you!"

He holds out his hand. I give the bag to him. He is *not* coming out of that wardrobe. He opens my gift, peeks inside.

"Thank you." He looks up and his eyes fill with happiness. "I am going to fill up that whole notebook. Just you wait and see."

"I can't wait." I grab a pillow off the bed and drop it to the floor in front of him. I sit on it cross-legged. "Guess what else I have?"

"What?

"Three more stories."

"Three!" He claps his hands together. "Did Mr. Lewis tell you where Narnia came from? Where it is? Where Aslan lives?"

"No. He just won't answer me that way."

George nods. "I understand."

"I think he wants us to figure it out ourselves. Like a puzzle," I say. "That's the best I can guess."

"I don't know." George stares past me, over my shoulder to the window. "I think he's trying to show us that there *is* no figuring it out."

"Huh?" I open my notebook of facts and stories.

"Just tell me the next one . . . ," George says, his words trailing off to quiet. He shoves the wardrobe door wider, so we are face-to-face and the light from the lamp across the room shines in his eyes.

---

George looks at his sister and smiles at her. It's sweet how she wants it all to make sense, but all he wants is for her to begin the next tale.

"It's about school," she says. "He told me about going away, and it wasn't a very nice school."

"Go on," he says to her. "Tell me."

"Once upon a wardrobe, not very long ago," she says with a sly smile.

"And not very far away," he says.

Then it happens: George leaves the small room where he sits in a wardrobe and enters the kind of library he's always wished for, full of books and woodsmoke and soft leather chairs.

The whole library was overflowing with books. They rested on tables, shelves, the floor, and even a chair. Leather-bound and clothbound, old and new. In that library in Little Lea, nine-year-old Jack sat at a desk, one too large for such a young boy, and his head was bent over a huge and old atlas of the world. It was bound in soft cloth, and the edges were smooth from use. Jack was flipping the pages and smiling as if painted sea and earth rose from the book itself.

On a middle page he stopped: Italy.

Jack traced his finger along the squiggly edges of the borders of a town called Narni. He spoke the word out loud in the empty library: "Narni." He paused and then tried the word on his tongue again, liking the feel of it. "Narni."

He flipped the page again. "Jacksie." His father's voice startled him.

Jack twisted in the chair to see his tall father, grief fading the man's countenance in a way that made him seem smaller, less vital, even less frightening. In a room that had often given Jack comfort, Mr. Albert Lewis spoke to his son in a stern tone.

"It is time for you to join your brother at the Wynyard School."

Jack had known this was coming, but panic ran

through him. "No," he said, sitting as straight as his father and matching his tone, holding up his chin as if the library were a courtroom.

"Yes, you will. It's what's best for you."

Jack's resolve faded and his lower lip shook. "I have Annie and Lizzie. I can learn here. I don't need to leave. I do not want to leave."

"It was already decided. Even before we lost your mother, it was decided." Jack's father walked out swiftly, leaving Jack in the soft leather chair. Jack closed his eyes as his life barreled along without him, taking him quickly to a place he did *not* want to go.

With both his mother and the fight gone from him, Jack packed his trunk and valise and set off on a journey to a new life. He had no idea what awaited him besides his brother.

That must be enough.

For the journey to England, Jack wore a suit that itched him enough to be nearly unbearable, an armor of a completely different kind than the ones he wore dashing about the house and garden. In the back of a coach with his white Eton collar nearly choking him, Jack sat next to Father as they bumped over the roads to Belfast Wharf, where they boarded a broad and fast ferry.

The boat sped across the waves of the Irish Sea to Lancashire, rising and falling while Jack thought of the many times he'd sat at the attic window and watched this harbor, imagining boarding one of the great-masted ships himself and leaving on a grand adventure. Now he imagined that boy still sitting in the window watching this boy leave on a ferry. The English accents, the clipped sounds without the Irish lilt, formed a hollow loneliness inside him; the strange voices were alienating already.

From Lancashire, Jack boarded a train with his father, then stared out the grimy window until they transferred at Seven Sisters station in London, and then there was yet another train to the town of Watford. Barreling along the tracks, Jack sat quietly, his heart a stone. The countryside changed from rolling hills to industrial and back again as his world that once held his mother's comfort faded quickly. With each train transfer, with each town they passed, Jack left his childhood behind.

Only motherless days lay ahead of him. This journey to school felt like an exile.

———

Jack held his valise in his hand, glowering at the Wynyard School, which squatted on rolling fields in the town of Watford. It was a boring and drab brick building with nine windows unevenly placed on either side of the front door and two chimneys that weren't puffing one bit. Right off he knew he'd find no comfort here. Jack reached the front gates with his heart in this throat. Even the gray clouds seemed ominous, pressing down.

Soon, with his father gone, Jack unpacked his bag in

the frigid residence hall, where everything reeked of a toilet, rank and old. He shuddered and then donned his uniform, which had been starched to the stiffness of slate. Within the hour he found himself in the headmaster's office. Reverend Capron, an Anglican priest—nicknamed Oldie behind his back—sat behind a wooden desk in a sparse and cold room. His white hair was combed back from a high forehead and his thin lips were nearly colorless. His broad and thick hands rested on the desk like slabs of meat.

"You are Warren Lewis's brother, am I right?" His voice was uneven, climbing up and down the steps of each word.

"Yes, sir." Jack held his hands behind his back to hide their shaking. Where *was* Warnie?

Oldie stood and his doughy face jiggled. "Another Lewis boy." He shook his head. "Understand that I will have none of your Irish wit, do you hear me?"

"Yes, sir."

And that was how it all started.

Days later, after Jack had finally figured out the routine, and how to dodge Oldie in the hallways, he ran on the muddy fields with Warnie for a cricket game. Wynyard students wore their sporting clothes of black shorts, tall dark socks, white collared shirts, and soft leather shoes, tossing about the ball with a quick-footed assurance Jack would never have.

Thrilled to be outside, to be with his brother and the boys who weren't bowed over books in the only classroom, Jack ran with Warnie. But Jack's prowess for writing and

learning, for quick wit and quicker understanding, did him
no good on the athletic field.

An older boy tossed the ball to Jack. Instead of catching it, Jack stumbled and fell. Trying to rise in the mud, he
looked up to see a crowd of their wolfish faces hovering over
him, blending into one taunting scowl. They laughed. They
laughed at *him*, and Jack's heart slammed shut. He would
never be the boy with physical prowess.

Ever.

He didn't even want to be that boy.

He slipped and slid and finally stood.

When the game was finished and the other boys had
hustled off, Warnie dawdled as he talked to Jack in the
game house. The place smelled of sweat and mud and over-
flowed with balls and bats and uniforms. They were to be
getting ready for dinner, but the brothers sat on a bench
together in their misery for a few moments. Suddenly, a
boy came from behind, a boy whose face looked as if it
had been ironed flat, his blue eyes dull and mean. The boy
thwacked Warnie over the head with the edge of a board, a
sickening sound of wood on skull.

Jack cried out and Warnie groaned and put his palm to
his head, then looked at his hand to see blood. Jack jumped
up and lunged at the boy, but Warnie grabbed Jack by the
arm, stopping him.

The boy laughed and darted from the room. Jack pried
loose from his brother's grip. "Why'd you stop me?"

"That boy, that demon, is named Wyn. He is Oldie's son, and if you go after him there will be more hell to pay."

Jack gazed at his brother. "How many days until holiday?"

"Exactly ninety-two," Warnie told him as he sat on the hard bench of the game house with blood dripping down his cheek.

"Why'd he do that to you?" Jack asked.

"I didn't change quick enough. That's his job: to make sure we're all at dinner on time."

Rage poured through Jack, and he didn't like the feeling. He thought of Lizzie and Annie, of the Irish fairy tales and of Boxen, of the little end room in Little Lea, and of his view over the emerald hills to Belfast Lough.

Why had Mother left them in this situation?

Warnie dropped his hand on Jack's shoulder. "Let's hurry to dinner."

Together the brothers cleaned up. Warnie wiped the proof of Wyn's cruelty from his face, and the brothers quickly changed into their constricting and itchy uniforms and made it to the dining hall with the long wood tables and benches on time. Warnie and Jack slid into their seats just as the food arrived, gray lumps of indistinguishable piles. Potatoes, meat, and vegetables all seemed the same color.

Jack wanted to cry. He could feel sobs begin in his belly and rise to the back of his throat, but there was no better way to be abused and taunted than to weep in front of the very boys who had just beaten him on the field. It wasn't the beating; he could abide such things. It was the cruelty that felt evil and inescapable.

Jack nudged Warnie. "Look up there. Wyn is eating the same food as his father while his sisters and his mother are eating the poor stuff we get."

Indeed, at the headmaster's table on a riser above the rest of the boys, Wyn sat near his father. Wyn's and Oldie's plates held lamb chops with sprigs of thyme, potatoes whipped white with melting butter, and a pile of green lettuce. Mrs. Oldie, with mousy and messy hair, her head bowed to the food, sat next to a string of three quiet sisters in pale yellow bonnets whose plates all were piled with the same gray food as the students'.

Evan, from Northern England and with a smooth accent that belonged in a lord's castle, sat next to Jack on the other side. He leaned close. "Do not ever get in Oldie's way. Just two years ago he beat a boy so badly he was sent to hospital and some say he died. Oldie was almost arrested for it, but he was let off. He will, I promise, kill you if given a chance. So just eat your mush and be quiet."

"He's evil," Jack said simply.

"What did you say?" The voice bellowed behind Jack, and he turned to see a tutor he hadn't yet met.

Jack thought of the two things he could do—lie or be quiet, and he chose the latter. Jack stared at the tutor, who had spittle on the edges of his lips and eyes so narrow Jack thought they might be closed. His ears poked out so far from the sides of his head that it was difficult not to laugh.

"What did you say?" the tutor asked again, louder this time so that the row of boys and Oldie and his son looked up. The brown-haired sisters and disheveled wife kept their heads down.

"Nothing, sir," Jack said.

"Then nothing is what you shall have." The man picked up Jack's plate and walked off with it. Jack's stomach rose with nausea and then settled again in a rock of fear and shame.

That night, in his room, he pulled out a crisp white piece of linen paper, good stationery his father had given to him, and began to write a letter.

Dear Father,
This is not a school. This is a house of horrors. You must come get us and bring us home. We must find a new school. The food is intolerable; the teachers cruel; the flat-faced son of Oldie a monster.

Surely Father would retrieve them, arrive in a coach as fast as a bullet, and take them home so Annie and Lizzie could continue their education in Little Lea.

"Jack. No." Warnie's voice came from behind. Jack's chair squealed on the wood floor as he turned to his brother. Hard evening light spilled from the window onto the stationery.

"Do not write home to Father about this. Oldie will read it and make us pay."

"Father needs to know, Warnie. He needs to bring us home."

"He won't come get us. And you can't tell him. He's never believed me, and Oldie will tell him stories about us that aren't true. Father will believe the headmaster. He always has. We must do our best to survive and count the days to holiday."

Jack crumpled the lovely paper and tossed it into the trash, biting back the tears that were entirely different from the ones he'd shed for his mother. These tasted like hatred and anger, and he loathed the flavor.

What could he do here to sustain himself? What would mean the most?

"We shall start a reading club," Jack said.

"A reading club?" Warnie pulled up another chair to face his brother.

"Yes. A reading club for magazine stories." Jack couldn't buy all the magazines he wished to have—*Captain* and *The Strand* and so many more. "It will be our own kind of club, different from the banging about on the fields."

"Yes!" Warnie said.

It was Warnie who invited the first boy, Evan, the one who had sat next to them at dinner and warned them of beatings, to be the first member. After that, Jack and Warnie drew a crowd, gathering in the library or the residence rooms. Each boy subscribed to a different magazine, and they would pass them about, gab about them.

"Do you think this or that man was worthy of his station?"

"How could another find his way out of the cave?"

Again, Jack found solace in the imaginary world that existed alongside the one he must endure. In the real world, where Oldie beat, taunted, and terrorized the children, Jack read stories, did his lessons, kept his head down, and counted off the hours and days until holiday and the return to Ireland.

At times light fell through, as on Sundays, when they walked into the sleepy town with cobblestone streets to attend the parish church, then afterward ambled about to whittle away their time. They watched trains appear and disappear from the mouth of the tunnel, bought candies and sweets, pottered about on the canal bank, and learned how to be part of a group of young men finding their way in life.

Also, Jack found a new fascination: entomology. "Do you know," he said to Warnie one night at the dinner table, "everyone here treats animals as if they are dumb beasts. Even insects: they kill them and place them on slides."

"You're the very one who can't stand the idea of a spider anywhere near." Warnie grinned with their secret knowing, and Jack shuddered. A spider in his hair was one of his worst fears.

"But these aren't spiders, and even if they were I wouldn't be cruel to them," Jack said.

"Well, not everyone feels as you do about animals . . . as if they are like us."

"Well, they are." Jack imagined King Bunny and Mr. Toad, and he thought about the insects that were torn apart for study. He would never see them as anything but what they were: beautiful, valuable creations.

Then there was math—the subject that brought Jack even more misery than the games on the field. Oldie seemed obsessed with geometry.

One bleak winter afternoon Jack sat with equations he could barely answer. Figures and the $x$ and the $y$ axes and what seemed to be hieroglyphics blurred together in a terrible headache. Jack stared at numbers with his pencil poised above the paper, waiting for it all to make sense. Yet he could *not* find the answer; he could *not* set his pencil down.

Oldie, his spectacles low on his nose, walked by a younger student, a cowering boy with greasy hair, and lifted his paper.

"You have nothing here," he said in a voice that made the other boys scribble on their papers even if they had no idea of the answers.

The boy looked up. "I need help with that problem. I don't—"

Oldie grabbed the boy by the ear, pulled him to the front of the class, and made him stand there and face the other boys. None of them would meet his gaze; he was as scared as Peter Rabbit being chased through Mr. McGregor's garden.

Jack glanced about the room to see if anyone would help, but all the boys looked down.

"Turn your palms up. Now." Oldie took a step toward

a cane behind his desk, a thin rattan stick the tawny color of a cat, the end rounded like a shepherd's hook.

The boy held up his palms. Jack was not entirely sure of what might come next, but knew it would be fierce and entirely unfair. This was a new terror.

Oldie lifted the cane from the green iron hook and brought it down with a *thwack* across the boy's palms. He cried out and snatched his hands behind his back.

"Now sit down and do your work." Oldie's voice echoed about the room.

The boy hurried back to his seat and lifted his pencil.

That night Jack imagined a welt forming across the boy's skin. Icicles formed on the windows like cage bars, and Jack told himself a story about a young boy who escaped a dungeon guarded by dragons.

The next day, as they filed in for breakfast, Jack's eyes on the wood floor where dust gathered in the cracks, Warnie stepped up next to him. "Did you hand in your sums?"

Jack nodded. No one received breakfast without handing in their sums.

"Let me tell you a secret," Warnie said. "If you do the first ones right they never check the rest. So get them right, then you don't have to worry about it. You'll have breakfast every morning."

Jack nodded and hated math all the more for being the very requisite that decided whether he could have breakfast. He looked to his brother with unspoken gratitude and sat on the cold seat waiting for his porridge.

The term passed, and together they avoided Oldie in the hallways when they could, running from him if they saw him come near, moving quickly if he caught their eye. Jack and Warnie huddled with their reading club and did their work. They rose before 7:00 a.m. in a corner of the residence hall and washed with freezing cold water. They ate their parsnips and gray potatoes. They did the best they could until they returned to Little Lea and to altered lives.

# NINE

# THE DARK AND THE LIGHT

I finish the story and George stares at me with wide eyes. We sit facing each other in the fading light of his bedroom. George is still in the wardrobe, and I'm sitting on the pillow on the hard floor.

"Why does he tell you these sad things about his life?" George asks, climbing out of the wardrobe and into my lap.

"I don't know," I tell him. "I just write them down as I remember them best I can."

"It must be because it has something to do with Narnia. But I don't know exactly what," George says.

"Perhaps, but I'm not sure, really, if even he knows. I think he just wants to give me something to bring home to you."

"It's more than that. You know, sister, the children in Narnia are away from their parents too, just as poor Jack was in boarding school. Maybe . . ."

"Padraig said the same thing and—"

"Padraig?"

I brush my hand through the air. "No one. But I don't think Mr. Lewis wants us to do that, to assign the things of his life to the things of his story. I think, if I'm guessing right, he wants us to see that stories are all tangled together. Like physics theories that are true and contradictory at the same time."

"Does that happen?"

"Yes, it does."

"Like I can be brave and scared at the same time." George stands up and stretches, and I rise also.

"Yes, like that."

"What else did he tell you before you left?"

"When he finished I asked him what happened to Oldie and he told me . . ." I pause, because maybe this isn't something George needs to know, but then I decide that truth is always the best. "Oldie ended up in an insane asylum. And I told Mr. Lewis it sounded like he right well should have been there all along. Then Mr. Lewis grinned and those eyes of his sparkled, and he said he jolly well should have been. I told him I hoped that wasn't what all of his schooling had been like, because I love Oxford, and how horrible it would be if school was always awful for him. And he told me, George, he told me with his chin lifted in the air that it wasn't all bad, because his next stories are about the Knock and Norse mythology."

"What's the Knock?"

"We'll find out," I say and brush his hair off his pale forehead. "But not now."

With that, George climbs into bed with the bag that holds the sketchpad and pencils. He spills the colored pencils onto the bright quilt and lets out a sound of glee.

I watch him. The thing is, I want a miracle for George. I want something or someone like Aslan to prowl through the door and save us, save us from the sorrow and the pain and the absolute loneliness of it all.

But no one had saved young Jack.

When George starts drawing, I slip from the room, taking my notebook of Mr. Lewis's stories with me, tucking it into my school bag. I make my way into the kitchen to find Mum sitting at the table, staring straight out the window. Concern has deepened the lines of her forehead.

When I touch her shoulder, she jumps before she lifts her gaze to me.

"Darling."

"Mum." I sit down next to her and she blows her nose into a handkerchief, crumples it into the palm of her hand. "Where's Dad?" I ask.

"He comes home so late now. It's hard for him to be here because he can't fix things, and he's a man who fixes things. He loves us so much, but he doesn't know how . . ." She pauses with her hands knotted so tightly that I reach over to undo them, to loosen her grip on herself.

"Are you okay?" I ask, although it is most likely the stupidest question I can utter. Of course she isn't.

"I don't think you should read your brother any more

of those stories." She says this without inflection, in a cold way that makes me shiver.

"Why?"

"I heard you today. That was a scary story. There's no reason George needs to know about a young boy losing his mother or going to a dreadful boarding school. That is just awful, and I want George to be happy, to hear good stories."

"But it *is* a good story, because that same boy grows up to be the man who wrote *The Lion, the Witch and the Wardrobe*. It's a good story I am telling George because Jack was brave, and he became the man who . . ." I don't know how to articulate what I mean so I sit quietly for a minute.

We both do.

"Mum, all fairy tales have a bad part. They all have a scary part. George knows that. It helps him to know that."

Mum listens and I forge ahead even though I don't really know where I'm going, but the words are rising, nevertheless. "Mr. Lewis has been telling me stories to write down for my brother, but maybe, now that I look at it, they're also stories for me. He doesn't say what he means by them. He just tells little tales of his life, and when I leave, somehow I know more about the world and my own life. I don't know quite how to explain it. He once said to me that he'd never wanted to grow up because his father made it look so dreary. Adulthood frightened him, but then there it was—thrust upon him."

"I haven't read his book yet," Mum says. "I will. What is it really about, Megs?"

"It's about four children who have to go to the country-side during the war—"

She interrupts me with a sound that is halfway between an *uh* and an *oh*. "I remember all of that. Operation Pied Piper they called it. I remember so clearly. You were about seven years old, and I kept imagining what it would be like if we lived in London and I had to send you away." She shudders.

"Well, that's how the book starts—four children are sent away to live in the house of a professor. They find a wardrobe that leads to a land called Narnia. They are to be kings and queens but they don't yet know that, and there they have all kinds of adventures with talking animals and a witch and a faun and a lion named Aslan."

"That's what he talks about the most," Mum says. "Aslan."

"Yes, I think he's God . . . or maybe supposed to be God. But Mr. Lewis doesn't actually say. Anyway, the children become kings and queens and it's beautiful, really. I don't want to give too much away because I want you to read it."

Mum nods and then stands. She walks to the counter where I notice, just then, that a pot of stock is boiling. She drops bite-size pieces of potatoes into it, then turns to me. "Megs, forgive me for saying you shouldn't tell your brother stories. You tell him anything Mr. Lewis tells you. I don't know the right answer to anything these days."

"Neither do I, Mum. I don't know if anyone does. Only math problems seem to have right and wrong answers, far as I can tell lately."

She almost laughs, then she holds out her hand for me to take. I stand and go to her and hold her hand in my own. She squeezes my fingers before she lets go to chop the carrots.

Because even with the dark parts and the light parts and the good parts and the bad parts, dinner must still be served.

## TEN

# THE MAP OF IMAGINATION

George joins us for Saturday morning breakfast in the kitchen. Mum, Dad, and I are talking over each other while George sits quietly at the scarred wooden table where generations of the Devonshire family have sat. He draws in the large black sketchbook I'd given him yesterday. The pencil is moving fast on the paper making scratching noises; he pauses every few moments to stare at it and choose another color from the box.

Mum is asking me about exams.

"I'm ready, I promise," I tell her.

Dad sets down the *London Times* and shakes his head. "America and Australia are asking us to intervene with the prisoners of war in Russia." Then he looks to me. "And it appears a mathematics man, an author, Bertrand Russell, has won the Nobel Prize in Literature, of all things." He leans forward. "Math and literature combined." He shakes his head. "Megs, we love having you here, but maybe you shouldn't come home so much. Perhaps instead you should be studying with your friends at school? Preparing for your exams?"

"Dad!" George says, but he doesn't even look up from his coloring. "Don't say that."

Mum laughs and sets one poached egg on Dad's plate, kisses the top of his dark hair. "She is fine. Our smart girl knows the right thing to do."

"And anyway, my resident mates don't help," I tell Dad. "They're only at university to find a husband."

He smiles at me and I feel warm. Dad's smile is like the sun when it finally comes out after long days of rain. I scoot closer to George and peek at his drawing. I take in a quick breath. "George!"

It is beautiful.

No.

That's not a big enough word.

It's stunning.

George is drawing a sketch of a young boy in an attic. The boy, obviously Jack Lewis, is bent over a desk and he's writing. Behind him, unfinished but obvious, is a lion lurking in the corner. His mane is wild as a forest, his eyes amber and clear, his nose a dark leather, and his countenance kind. That lion—he's no less wild than one in a jungle, but he's also gentle and watching over the young boy.

"You're an artist," I exclaim. "A true-blue artist."

Dad looks side-eye at George's drawings, not moving his *Times* one inch, as if he doesn't want us to know he's peeking. Then he smiles; I see it even as he flips the page of the newspaper.

"Look at these," I say. "I had no idea you knew how to draw so beautifully."

"I did," George says and takes another bite of his toast with orange marmalade. "I had an idea." The jam sticks to his lips and he wipes with the heel of his palm.

Mum looks over my shoulder. "You sketched that?" She sets down her kitchen towel and sits down on the other side of George, puts one arm around him.

"You didn't know he can draw so well either?" I ask, and I wonder why we haven't noticed. Have there not been colored pencils and art notebooks in our house? No, there haven't been.

"Sometimes he draws little doodles on things," Mum said. "But this . . ." She looks to her son. "These are so beautiful. Did you copy this from somewhere?"

"From my head," he says with a shrug. "When Megs is telling me the stories, I see pictures in my head. I can see it all and then I just draw it."

"Your imagination," I say. "It's extraordinary."

"It is?"

Mum touches the notebook. "Yes, it is. It's exactly what Megs said."

We are all silent as we realize that even though we've hovered over George for all these years, we haven't noticed this talent of his. Not because he hid it from us but because perhaps we paid mind to the wrong things.

I realize George's imagination is taking him places while I ramble on about stories and facts about Mr. Lewis. George takes something of this world and travels to another, as if the story world and the real world run right alongside each other. Or maybe they are inside each other. I warm with this new knowledge, with the idea of these worlds all running next to each other. Einstein found one, Mr. Lewis another, and my brother yet another.

For a breath or two, I wonder about this magical world we live in. It's a mystery we can never understand. For a moment, a small and breath-holding moment, I know it to be true: there is more, something more I can't see, a vivid truth that can't be described by logic or words alone, a truth that delights the heart.

And then my feeling—or was it a knowing?—is gone. I am back in the winter light, and I realize that maybe this was what Mr. Lewis was talking about with his biscuit tin and with Squirrel Nutkin and with nature. I suspect he understands that joy, that sudden longing or knowing that comes and is gone so quickly.

I want it back.

I want it back as badly as Edmund wanted more Turkish delight.

————

Later that morning, after I've worked through a few equations and after George takes his morning nap, Mum and Dad go for a long walk in the crisp snow-covered town, leaving us alone. We sit on big fat pillows in the living room facing a fire that snaps and sparks like stars rising up the chimney.

"What do you want for Christmas?" I ask George. "Tell me."

George wiggles his toes near the fire and lies back, stares up to the ceiling. "I want to go to Ireland."

"No, silly. I meant, what do you want me to get you? To bring you?"

George sits up. "You already bring me everything I want. I have the art book, pencils, and stories from Mr. Lewis. There's nothing else I need. I want to *go* somewhere. I want to have my own adventure. Everyone in the books has adventures, and I want my own." He is so matter-of-fact that I know this isn't the first time he's thought of it.

"Well, that's why they're in a book, because we don't have a magic wardrobe."

"That's nonsense." He crosses his legs and his cheeks flush red with energy. "I want my own adventure. I want to go to Ireland. I want to see it."

I play along. "Okay, what do you want to see in Ireland?"

"I want to see Dunluce Castle, where Jack's mum took him on holiday before she died. I want to see the wild sea and the ruins. I want to . . . feel it." George lifts his face as if the bursts of Irish air swell and rise around our tiny cottage in the middle of the English countryside.

"How shall we do that?" I am beginning to feel like this is a terrible and wonderful idea, to take my brother somewhere other than his imagination, to take him from the bed and the cottage and Worcester.

To take him from safety.

He shakes his head as if I have no idea about anything at all. "How are we to do that? Most likely the same way other people go to Ireland."

"I don't think it's safe for you," I say. "Not now."

"In Mr. Lewis's books, would Peter or Susan say it's not safe?"

I stare at my brother. He's arguing with me about children in a book. "George," I say, "Peter and Susan are made-up people."

"They're more than that, and you know it."

George stands and walks to a large oak hutch that stands against the far wall. On its shelves are piles of plates and rows of teacups and glasses, linen napkins and bowls and serving platters. George opens one of its drawers and pulls out a paper map. He brings it back and unfolds it on the floor in front of us both.

"I wish we had an atlas," he says.

"Now *that* I can try to find you," I tell him as he spreads the ragged map flat.

A spark flies from the fireplace and hits the edge of the paper, sizzles. "Here we are." On the map, he points to Worcester in the West Midlands, our borders wiggly with lines that separate us from Birmingham and Hereford. "And there you are when you're not with me." He points at Oxford, just south and east of our town. He runs his finger down the map lines, and I realize he's done this while I'm away from him; he maps my way from home to university and back.

"And here is how to get to Dunluce Castle." He traces his finger west across England, over the Irish Sea to Dublin, then up the coast of Ireland to the top above Belfast, above Londonderry on the edge of the sea.

"That's so far," I say. "A full day's journey, and where would we stay?"

George shrugs and smiles. "I don't know. You're the grown-up."

I laugh and pull him close. "We can't do that."

"You asked what I wanted," he says. "You asked."

"Dunluce is just a bunch of ruins. A long-gone castle without real rooms or—"

"It's Cair Paravel."

"It's not. It's definitely not."

"It's not and it is. And I want to see it."

"I wouldn't even know how to get there. It's—"

He interrupts me with a laugh. "You might be a genius at math, but you're not so smart about real things in the world."

I laugh at him; I take no offense.

He ticks two things off on his fingers. "You drive a car and then you take a ferry."

"But I don't drive, and I don't have a car."

He shrugs. "So find someone who does."

"Mum and Dad would never, ever allow it. You know that."

"I bet you'll find a way," he says. "Now please tell me the next story."

"Now that, George Henry Devonshire, is something I can do." I open the notebook to the next pages. I have labeled them *Norse Mythology.*

"Once upon a wardrobe, not very long ago . . ."

"And not very far away," he says.

"Jack is thirteen years old and has left the horror of Wynyard, spent a bit of time at a school outside Belfast called Campbell College, and is now at a place called Cherbourg House."

"That's a lot of schools before a boy turns thirteen," George says.

"It is, but I have to tell you about all his schools to get to the day he found out about Norse mythology. You need to hear all about his reading life."

"His reading life?"

"Yes. Mr. Lewis wants us to understand his love of Norse mythology, and he wants us to know about the books that influenced him because he says that in many ways they have formed his life."

"Like me, he reads a *lot.*"

"He does." I pause. "So here it is. It is the year of 1911, and Jack is thirteen years old. He is attending Cherbourg Preparatory School at Malvern while Warnie is at Malvern College. Their school buildings are close to each other, both in Malvern, but they aren't together in any classrooms."

"Wait!" George sets his hand on mine. "That's here

in Worcestershire, right? They both went to school right down the road from us?"

"They did indeed."

George pauses. "So they aren't so very different from us, are they?"

"In some ways, no, they are not."

"Go on, then. Go on."

# ELEVEN

# FINDING NORTH

George listens closely. His sister is getting better at telling Mr. Lewis's stories. As she begins to talk, George can hear the slap of waves against the hull of an iron ferry, seagulls crying over two brothers at the railing of a ship that just arrived at England's Lancashire wharf.

In their brown travel suits and stiff Eton collars that Jack abhorred, Jack and Warnie stood on deck, waiting for the ship to dock. Warnie was wan and looking like he wanted to be off that vessel more than anything else. Huge ropes as thick as tree trunks were tossed and tied before the brothers climbed down the gangplank, the first passengers to disembark. The wharf smelled of seagull droppings and coal, of oil and sweat. The waves crested silver and dark against the walls of the wharf, smashing and falling away.

A September wind blew like a hidden storm was behind it, and the brothers, Warnie and Jack Lewis, fifteen and thirteen years old, walked toward the train station, carrying their cases while a scowling porter rolled their trunks on a cart. Warnie wobbled with leftover sea legs as they stepped onto the high metal stairs of the train. They walked through the short tunnel between train cars to locate seats at the back.

Jack couldn't help but ponder how he almost avoided attending another new school this autumn when his father couldn't find the key to his trunk. For two full days, Jack believed something or someone had intervened to keep him in Little Lea, but then the key was discovered in the top drawer of the hallway table.

Hours later, settled in and headed toward Malvern, Jack unwrapped the sandwiches they'd bought when they'd transferred at Paddington station, but Warnie turned away, waiting until his travel stomach settled. The train rattled through the countryside while they talked about books, about visiting their aunt in the countryside during the summer, and about what this new school might be like. Jack read a *Captain* magazine and Warnie flipped through a *London Times*, always caring a bit more than his brother about current affairs.

Finally they reached Malvern, where they had to part, Jack to the preparatory school and Warnie to the college, each on a separate path. Jack headed into what was now his third school.

Jack settled into Cherbourg quickly, now accustomed to finding his way amid taunting boys and strict head-masters. As usual, he counted the days until winter holiday.

One afternoon halfway through the semester, Jack walked into an empty, dusty schoolroom lit only by the sunshine bursting through the dirty windows and onto a desk. There Jack spied a magazine called *The Bookman*.

Resting under a spotlight of sun, the magazine pages lay open as an invitation.

Another story!

Jack approached it with the kind of anticipation he always had for new adventures, with a casual glance as he pulled at his collar. He glanced down and everything stopped: his fidgeting, his thoughts, and his preoccupation and boredom, because there, for the first time, he read the lyrics to a Wagner opera about Norse mythology.

> *At the world-ash-tree once I wove*
> *when far and wide from the stem outbranched*
> *a wondrous verdant wood.*

A quickening ran from Jack's head to his heart—it was that feeling again, the one he'd once felt when his brother had brought him the biscuit tin, the irrepressible emotion he'd felt when reading about Squirrel Nutkin and the experience of autumn, the emotion he feared had died with his mother and again in the desert of Wynyard School.

Jack called it joy.

He picked up the magazine and did more than read the operatic words of Richard Wagner's *Siegfried and the Twilight of the Gods*—he experienced them; he sensed them; he was immersed in them. Though he already loved Celtic and Greek myths, Norse mythology was new and astounding. This was Asgard and a Valkyrie. This was a grand story about gods of the north, and young Jack found himself enchanted, waking from a kind of life-oblivion that had lately surrounded him, a spell of sleep.

———

When the dinner bell clanged through the hallways of the schoolhouse, Jack looked up from Wagner's mythic tale with astonishment. He was still in Cherbourg, still a boy reading a book, still in the so-called real world. The desire that had been so intense while reading the story of the Norse gods was gone.

What would Jack do to get it back?

Almost anything at all.

He stared out the window and wondered how to feel it again—that remote, that severe, that thrilling desire that Wagner's opera had brought to him. The feeling was bigger than desire and still without a word to explain it, and it flooded his heart.

And was fleeting, gone so very fast.

He'd not yet heard the music of the opera, merely read its story.

And yet as he wandered the stark hallways of Cherbourg, moving from class to class, avoiding sports games, avoiding the flagging and taunts of the Bloods—the cruel, self-appointed rulers of the school who were like the bloodthirsty dark elves of the opera—his mind brimmed with images of the Norse myths: fauns and dryads, river gods and talking beasts, dwarfs and gnomes and elves.

Jack took himself to the library and browsed until he found every book on Norse mythology he could find. He dusted them off, found hidden corners of Cherbourg where he could read, immersed himself in what he called "the Northernness." He found the *Mythos of the Norsemen*, *Myths and Legends of the Teutonic Race*, and *Northern Antiquities*.

Autumn approached the edges of winter, and Jack found a book of poetry by the Irish poet W. B. Yeats, the pages drenched in Irish folklore. Jack took the book to his room and read until he fell asleep, the lines soothing his homesick heart as a cough began deep in his chest and a fever raged beneath his skin and behind his eyes. The coming sickness was a cruel reminder of the dreadful night when Jack burned with illness and his mother hadn't come to him; instead, Father had arrived with the terrible news.

This time, though, Jack lay in his residence hall cot, unable to move, desiring nothing more than sleep and solitude. Yet school beckoned, the headmaster raged, and boys taunted. Finally the stern headmaster with unsmiling lips and greasy hair stood over Jack's bed.

"Clive, I believe it best that you return home, that you recuperate where you can't infect the other boys."

Jack looked up from his pillow, his head so heavy and his fever raging. He barely understood the headmaster. A nurse arrived and put pills on Jack's tongue, then packed him up, bundled him in his scratchy coat and traveling clothes, and scurried him to the train station.

Feverish delirium blurred the journey to Ireland, usually full of camaraderie with his brother and a sense of anticipation for the holidays.

Finally at home in Little Lea, Jack tumbled into his own bed. His recuperation was long and punctuated by quiet afternoons reading with his father, but also with large swaths of time alone. Jack slowly recovered. The noise and chaos of Cherbourg faded, and the world outside his bedroom window felt full of possibility.

But mostly Jack read Norse mythology to his heart's content.

When Jack again sensed the world's edges without the soft padding of fever, when his chest no longer ached, he began taking long walks in the garden. Winter came early and dark, and the pathways that led through the hedges wove under the bare branches of the maple and alder trees and the brown leaves of the hornbeam. He'd always enjoyed the view from the top of Little Lea's lawn with sweeping views to the bay, but now it was different. Now, since reading the Norse stories, everything of the land felt . . . mystical.

He wandered the garden, imagining scenes from Wagner's story. There behind the hedge, Mime might meet Sieglinde. There around the bend, Siegfried might be listening to a bird or an elf. Jack became so immersed in the story world that he glimpsed it out of the corner of his eye in the real world.

One late afternoon, the sickness having ebbed and nearly gone, and Christmas holiday and Warnie's return approaching, Jack found he had come to love nature for itself and not just as a stage for Wagner's astonishing story. The gardens of Little Lea were no longer just a place for Siegfried and a dwarf to rise from the mists. Now nature itself, as itself, enchanted Jack. And just as Jack had this momentous thought, a figure darted from behind the hornbeam hedge.

A dwarf?

A gnome or elf?

Or Balder or Thor?

Jack stopped flat in his tracks, the sun weak through winter's low clouds, and his eyes scanned the familiar garden. He shook his head.

It hadn't been real.

Or had it?

That feeling of joy arrived again, and it felt like a desire even greater than the very thing he desired. He felt as if pure Northernness washed over him, took him over completely. He imagined open spaces, twilight, solitude . . . a place far away; a place he could not yet find.

---

The days passed as they do. Months later summer arrived, and with it, freedom. The trees opened sleepy branches with green and greener foliage, the sun warmed the waving heather grasses and the tops of the brothers' shoulders, the waves of Belfast Lough sparkled like they were lit from within.

Father had sent Jack and Warnie, now fourteen and sixteen years old, off with their bags to visit their aunt, Helen, who lived in the countryside of Dundrum. Near the Wicklow Mountains in Ireland, her home was nestled on acres of land as wild as the stories they loved. She wasn't strict; Helen allowed the boys to wander without supervision, to read to their hearts' content, and to be free of the constraints of school. With family enough to satisfy and freedom enough for the imagination, Jack and Warnie loved Helen and loved Dundrum.

One fuzzy afternoon the rain crashed against the windows of Aunt Helen's library. Jack stared through the glass, bemoaning the lack of an afternoon spent in the countryside. He turned his attention back to the room—and there it was! Again!

Right there on the wooden table *Siegfried and the Twilight of the Gods* waited for him. And this time it wasn't just words in a magazine. No! This was a book with illustrations by an artist named Arthur Rackham, who had brought the Norse story to life in a way Jack's brilliant imagination hadn't even done.

"Warnie!" Jack called for his brother, who came running.

"Look," Jack said as Warnie entered the library. "I thought I'd never see it again. And this time with illustrations so glorious . . . they . . ." He lost his words.

Warnie stared at his brother. In this, they had nothing in common. What did Warnie care for the printed version of an opera about Norse mythology? And yet Warnie loved his brother.

"I must have one of my own," Jack said. "I must own this book."

"You've never even heard the music of it," Warnie said. "Only seen the words." He glanced down. "And the pictures."

"You must help me. We'll save our money and . . ."

Warnie sank into a chair and picked up the book, flipped through its pages. It was quite magnificent with its drawings of nymphs and dryads, of fierce gods, the sketches both wild and energized as if the creatures might burst from the pages. But Warnie had loads of other ideas about how to spend his shillings.

It took months, but Jack saved up his money, and Warnie, out of love, chipped in. Jack bought the book for fifteen shillings.

Now possessing the art of the very story that awoke the Northernness within him, Jack sat alone for hours with that illustrated book, a pure pleasure. He slowly flipped through the pages, the story of Siegfried rushing over him like a waterfall, drenching him in the beauty.

In *Twilight of the Gods*, Ragnarök was a thrilling non-stop series of events that finished with the death of each god, and yet there were those gods who died and rose again. Jack met the wolf Fenrir, the son of a god, who devoured the sun. There were journeys to the end of the world with creatures who dwelled in marshes and forests, in caves and on mountains. And somehow Jack felt as if he already knew the stories, as if they'd been buried deeply in his soul.

Finally, inspired to try his own hand at something so beautiful, Jack set ink to paper and began composing his first long poem. Writing the first three stanzas, he felt the poetry come alive beneath his pen, words so real and true that he ached. But by the time he reached the final lines, he felt his words and ideas falter. He sensed the dread of trying to write exactly what he meant and raise his work to a higher realm, a Wagnerian realm.

Jack wanted to do as Wagner had done, and yet . . .

He abandoned the poem, ripping it to shreds and feeling, for the first time, he knew what writing actually meant. It wasn't just words, one after the other. Composing a poem required more than lining up sentences one right after the other. And yet he knew he'd write again. One day he would try again.

In the meantime, dwarfs and dryads, wolves and witches, mountains and gods, and endless winters, all found their way into Jack Lewis's life.

———

George and I sit by the dwindling fire. Mum and Dad are taking longer in the village than I'd expected, and I wonder if they've gone to visit Uncle Brian. I pull George close and wind the well-worn knitted blanket around us, tucking the edges around his legs.

"Where were you when he told you about the Norse stories?" George asked.

"Outside," I tell him, "walking around that lake behind his house, our feet mashing the snow, winding among the trees that look like they are trying to grab the clouds. I walked behind him and put my boots into his footprints when"—I try to sound mysterious and bend closer to George—"all of a sudden, Mr. Lewis stopped at a tree that looked as if it could bend over and whisper to us, an old man's face almost whirling in the bark. I could see, I did see, how he would have looked for that Wagner opera in nature. I was doing the same just at that moment, wondering if his woods were full of fauns and a white witch and talking beavers."

"Oh, Megs, you are so lucky," George says. "And look at you, telling a very good story about a walk in the woods."

I feel surprise catch me. George is right. I described it differently, with more detail, I'd say, than I had before. "I know I'm lucky, George. I wish it could be you walking with the brothers. You're the one who should be there, not me."

A log in the fire pops, and we both startle and laugh. "Go on. What else did you talk about?" George asks.

"I told him I looked for Narnia in his woods the way he looked for Wagner's story in the nature of Little Lea. I've already figured he isn't too keen on me trying to get something factual from his stories. So I tried to get 'round him. I asked if he wrote a fairy tale because he liked fairy tales."

"And?" George asks.

"He told me his friend Mr. Tolkien says, 'Myth-making is the art of the sub-creator.' And then Mr. Lewis stomped his foot against a tree trunk, banging snow from his boot." I smile, hoping it tells my brother how much I love him, how I wish he could stomp through the snow with Mr. Lewis and that I am doing it for him. But I do believe the smile also tells him that this adventure, the one he sent me on, is one I am beginning to enjoy.

"Then he told me something else."

"What?" He nudges me.

"He told me that when he was young, his secret and imaginative life were quite separate from his real life. He said his imaginative life was as important as breathing—or I think that's what he said. He told me he never confuses the two, the real and the imaginary. Even Boxen wasn't something they put themselves into but something they created. And Wagner's world—it wasn't something to believe *in*. It was something that brought him that feeling of joy."

"Joy," George repeats the word. "It even tastes good saying it, doesn't it?"

I laugh and pull him closer.

"I wonder," George says. "What was it about *that story*—of all the stories he'd read? Why the Norse one that took him over? He had the Greek ones and the Celtic ones and—"

"I asked him the same question. He said he had a poet friend named Charles Williams who once wrote a line that

says, 'the sky turned round,' and that's how it felt for him when
he found Wagner's opera, as if the sky had turned round."

"Have you felt it, sister? Have you felt that joy?"

I want to answer him. I close my eyes. "I think so. When
I solve a problem or equation that seems impossible, it's like
there's some kind of light breaking through, or the knowing
leads to some kind of satisfaction . . . and maybe joy. Or when
I walk outside on a spring afternoon and the first crocus is
born from the snow and the sunlight runs across the spider
webs like messengers from tree to tree, that's when I remember something, something I've forgotten and is waiting for
me, something larger than me. And then it's gone. And I
want it back. I think that's what Mr. Lewis is talking about."

"Like when you finish a story and you wish you could
read it like you'd never read it before. Like you want to read
it for the first time again," George says.

"I think so," I say. I pause while our breaths synchro-
nize. I ponder whether I want to tell George the next
question I asked Mr. Lewis.

I decide I will.

"I also asked him what his favorite parts of the Norse
myths were."

"And?"

"He said 'Northernness,' and then he said 'tragedy.'"

"Yes," George said as if Mr. Lewis's wisdom had reached
out and beyond the countryside, past the trees and then
over the train tracks, and landed smack in the middle of
the common room at the Kilns. "Tragedy."

TWELVE

# THE OTHER PROFESSOR

George pulls at the blanket around his legs and looks to his sister. He wants to hear another story. He wants the stories to last forever.

Nothing does, of course.

Not even winter in Narnia. Even it was finally broken.

"Tell me the next one you brought home?" he says to her and she nods.

His sister can't see what he sees, and she can't hear what he hears, and that's okay. Because she's doing her best to turn facts into story, and he knows how to take it the rest of the way.

"Once upon a wardrobe," Megs says. He grins and she continues, "Not very long ago."

"And not very far away," he says.

"Sixteen-year-old Jack Lewis arrived at a train station . . ."

The fire burns low in their cozy living room. George closes his eyes, then the *pop* of the fire turns into the *click*

125

*clack* of a train arriving fast, smoke pouring from its stack, its brakes squealing into the Surrey station at the town of Great Bookham.

In the crisp September air, a crowd pushed and shoved to disembark the black train before the men in suits and the women in tight-waisted dresses waiting on the platform climbed the stairs into the car. A young man stepped off the train.

Jack was taller now and he carried a valise. His brown hair caught the wind of the train as it departed, leaving him looking around for a man he didn't know and hadn't ever met.

William Thompson Kirkpatrick would recognize Jack Lewis, or so Jack had been told, because he had been Jack's father's headmaster once a long time ago and, more recently, Warnie's tutor before Warnie had set off for Sandhurst to train in the British army. Jack thought of his brother training for war. Over and over he dreamed of Warnie caught in a battle or stranded in a field. Jack worried for his brother and tried to imagine him slaying every dragon, defeating every giant, conquering every Fenrir-type wolf of Germany that he might cross.

Jack glanced around the station for the man Warnie called the Knock. He was weary and nervous, a combination that made his stomach queasy and gave him a deep ache for his mother, the pain like a savage wound that would never heal.

The platform was bustling with families and couples

and children rushing along holding a parent's hand. Across the way stood a tall man with white hair and a pocket watch that he kept checking as if he were the rabbit in *Alice in Wonderland*. Was this Kirkpatrick?

The man spotted Jack, then took long strides across the platform. As he drew closer, his features became clear. His face was thin and muscular, his nose sharp and his eyes alert as an eagle. To Jack, Mr. Kirkpatrick looked as old as Father Time. A mythological creature.

Jack was tired to death of cruel schoolmasters, and he hoped what his father had told him was true: that this man, Mr. Kirkpatrick, was sentimental.

"Mr. Clive Staples Lewis, I assume?" he said, holding out his hand.

"Yes, sir."

After gathering Jack's bags and trunks and books, they loaded into Mr. Kirkpatrick's car and drove toward his home in the Surrey countryside, where Jack would live for the next few years. The landscape was a deep and emerald green, its rolling chalk downs, the heath grasses, the woodlands dotted with autumn golds and reds that made Jack think of home and Squirrel Nutkin and a biscuit tin with twigs and moss.

The silence in the car seemed to beg for words, and Jack blurted, "I didn't expect it to look so wild."

"Wild?"

"Yes." Jack stared out the window at the thick clusters of alder and oak, mossy rocks and bushy slopes. "Yes, that's what I do mean. It has a certain wildness about it that I didn't expect."

Mr. Kirkpatrick stared forward, his hands on the steering wheel, gripping it so tightly it seemed it might break off in his hand. His brow dropped as if Jack had said something insulting.

A sinking feeling, a nearly debilitating premonition formed by the present and also left over from the past, rolled over Jack. Had he said something wrong once again? Maybe tutors were always cruel and, until that faraway day when Jack finally finished school, this misery was the way it would be.

His new tutor spoke low and firm. "And what does that word mean, Jack? Wildness? And how did you come to use it?"

Jack thought for a moment, watching as the geography passed by, a landscape suggesting something more than just a place but also an emotion. "I don't know, sir. It was just an opinion."

"We don't speak our opinions unless logic backs them up. What did you know of the Surrey countryside before you arrived, and what did you expect? Have you been educated in the flora and geography of Surrey to base your opinion on something other than what you expected?"

Jack's head buzzed with responses, but not one of them sharp enough for this man's flinty questions. Jack slumped in the seat. He would have to live with this man? With his pointed questions and inability to make small talk in a quiet car? The Knock, who now stared out the windshield, brought Jack to silence.

Jack's hopes fell quiet too. There was no use talking about what he saw out the window or what *wild* meant to him, because he wasn't sure himself. And above all, miles into the trip, Jack knew the old man was right. Nothing had turned out as Jack had expected, even the man himself whom Jack thought would be sappy and sentimental. So maybe Mr. Kirkpatrick was right when he told Jack, "You have no right to that opinion."

Soon the car arrived at a cottage in the middle of the wildness that Jack had no right to have an opinion on. A short woman with brown hair pulled into a bun, her face round with bright red cheeks, as cheery as she was short, bustled out of the front door, waving and greeting Jack as if he were her long-lost son. She welcomed him into the warm home, fed him mutton stew with vegetables from the garden, then showed Jack to his room.

A room all to himself. His room. With a desk and a comfortable bed that had a view of the countryside and gardens. A room with soft blankets and a little wardrobe for his belongings. Maybe, just maybe, it wouldn't be all bad.

The house was cozy with a fireplace that dominated the living area. The wood piled outside would last a long autumn and winter. There was hot water and a bathroom to share, food and countryside, and most important, books were everywhere.

As he fell asleep that first night, he told himself this

was not Wynyard nor Cherbourg nor Malvern. There were no sporting games or Bloods or cruel boys. And with that knowing, and the comforting thought of a vast library to explore, Jack fell asleep.

The next morning Jack began to keep a schedule that never changed in all the years he resided there. The strict schedule—their paces, as it were—set an example for Jack of what a perfect day might be like. The ideal day was set in his heart there in the house of Mr. Kirkpatrick, "a Bookham pattern," as he came to call it.

They were up by 8:00 a.m. for breakfast with toast and jam and a poached egg. By 9:00 a.m. Jack was at the desk in the library to read, study, or write until 11:00 a.m.

The first day at the desk with Mr. Kirkpatrick, there was no gabbing about what might or might not be going on in the world, nor any idle talk of the weather or health. Instead, the Knock set a large leather-bound book in front of Jack—*The Iliad* by Homer.

In Greek!

"Sir," Jack said, "my mother taught me some Greek, but I don't yet read it fluently. If we are to study *The Iliad*, I believe we must do it in English."

"Just *some* Greek? Well then, we do have work to do, don't we?"

The studying began, and continued just like this every day until 11:00 a.m., when they were interrupted by the kerfuffling of Mrs. Kirkpatrick bringing them cups of tea. Sometimes after tea Jack might step outside into the countryside, which grew increasingly familiar. He was back at the desk until lunch, then took another walk or reading at 2:00 p.m. Jack resumed work from 5:00 until 7:00 p.m., then came time for a real meal and conversation. He was in bed by 11:00 p.m., the covers tight about him, exhausted while his mind was swimming with stories and languages and logic and numbers.

But Sundays? As at school, Jack had the day to himself. But here there was no church to attend. Mr. Kirkpatrick was an atheist. On Sundays, Jack's tutor tended to his garden more than to spiritual matters. Those were the days Jack wandered the countryside and town, down the narrow lanes and through the landscape dotted with villas and farmhouses to a countryside of rolling hills, solemn alleys of trees and hedges, waving heath, and wild blooms that changed with every season. During those long afternoon walks in nature he came to believe that one must shut the mouth and open the eyes and ears, for nature only asked of him to look, listen, and attend.

After the walks: more reading.

Jack ordered books from Messrs. Denny in London, and after days of great anticipation they would arrive in the post wrapped in gray paper. Usually it was an Everyman book, which cost only a few shillings. Those plain packages hid entire worlds and foretold of afternoons whiled away.

The years flew by in a routine that felt as comfortable as it did familiar.

One March afternoon he went for a haircut in

Leatherhead. He stood in the station waiting for his train back to Bookham, a quick five-minute ride, and from a speaker overhead, the announcement of the train stops echoed across the high-domed ceiling. Early for the train, he wandered the station's bookstall and discovered there, on a shelf of other Everyman books, ragged and slightly used, an edition of *Phantastes* by George MacDonald. With a free weekend of reading and tea (his favorites) waiting for Jack, he bought the book for a mere five shillings and tucked it into his bag.

Once back at the Kirkpatricks' cottage and settled in the library, Jack opened *Phantastes* to discover a world filled with his favorite things—not that he had even known them before this moment, but here they were! Quests, a medieval romance, and fairies. The outside world faded away while he turned the pages. When he lifted his head from the book, the light had changed, and the room filled with the dusk of winter. Jack needed—no, he desired—to share the experience with someone he loved.

He jumped from the chair and grabbed stationery from the desk to write to his new friend, Arthur Greeves.

Arthur was Jack's age of sixteen and lived down the street from Little Lea. A heart condition kept him from doing as much as Jack. During a visit to Belfast, in the fresh stillness of an early morning when Jack had visited Arthur, Jack had spied *Siegfried and the Twilight of the Gods* on Arthur's bedside table. Before he could verbalize the truth, Jack knew, deep in the hidden places where truth sometimes hides, that Arthur and he would be lifelong friends. Now he wanted to share this new story with him.

> Dear Arthur,
> Have you read *Phantastes?* Surely you have not, or you would have told me . . .

From that moment, Jack's reading life unfolded in a new way. He began to read any book he thought might be like MacDonald's. These included *Tristan and Isolde* in French and Edmund Spenser's *The Faerie Queen*. On the front flap of *Phantastes*, he wrote a long list of George MacDonald's books, making it his goal to read each and every one.

Two and a half years passed in Great Bookham, and Jack Lewis sharpened his mind, his language, his reading, and his writing. He came to understand that judgment should be based on logic. He studied Greek, French, German, Italian, and read great classical literature. He learned to read for more than pleasure, and to translate, to debate, and to study. During his long discussions with the Knock, Jack became more skilled at defending his thoughts.

What he most longed to hear from his tutor were the words, "I hear you." This meant Jack had hit the live wire of debate, and the conversation could go on. What he didn't like to hear was "Stop!" or "Excuse me."

When at long last it was time to leave Surrey, the Knock and Jack stood silent at the train station. The train pulled in front of them—again the smoke and the squealing brakes—but this time they were saying good-bye.

"Mr. Clive Staples Lewis," said Mr. Kirkpatrick.

Jack almost laughed at the echo of their first meeting, and he held out his hand and shook his tutor's. "Thank you for everything, sir. You have taught me so very much. My gratitude to you and Mrs. Kirkpatrick is great. You have taught me that talking and writing aren't merely for chatter. They are, above all, a means to discovering the truth."

"I hear you," the Knock said. "I hear you."

Jack climbed onto the train without a backward glance, for there had been nothing else he wanted to hear but those three words.

———————

I watch George sit silently. The flames in the fireplace lick the edges of the bricks, the logs falling into chunks of glowing ember onto the grate.

"Megs, did you hear that?"

"Hear what?" I ask.

"His best friend . . . Arthur, right?"

"Yes?"

"He had a heart condition. He spent a lot of time in bed." George's voice rises and falls with the absolute wonder of the one thing I hadn't registered.

We sit in the silence of that truth, the connection that reaches through time.

"Do you think . . . ," George asks. "Do you think it's why he's being so nice to us?"

"No," I say. "I think it's because he's a nice man who . . . Oh, I don't know."

And I don't. I realize that for all I do know, for all I want to pretend I know about life and death and the universe, I don't know what matters most to George right now.

"Is he still alive? His best friend with the weak heart . . . is he still . . ."

"Yes!" I tell George. That much I do know. "Yes he is, and he's in Belfast, and Mr. Lewis visits him every summer."

I set my notebook on the floor.

"I bet," George says, "I bet Mr. Kirkpatrick is the professor in the book." George grins as if he's discovered treasure in my telling.

I stand and toss another log on the fire. A spray of sparks flies upward, and I turn to George. "I asked him the same thing and all he said was, 'The professor is the professor.'"

George shakes his head. "Mr. Kirkpatrick is the professor. He is. I know he is." George grins the great smile of a child whose confidence far outweighs his knowledge.

"I don't know, George. It's possible, but Mr. Kirkpatrick was married, lived in a town, and wasn't much for flights of fancy. To me, the professor in the book reminds me more of Mr. Lewis than anyone else."

George perks up. "Maybe." He stares off and then back at me. "Sometimes you leave things out of your story," he says. "What else did Mr. Lewis say about his tutor?"

"He told me he wrote a poem about him. He told me that he was indebted to him and would be for all of his life because that man taught him about logic."

"Is that why his tutor was an atheist—because of logic?"

"He never really said. I think maybe that's part of it."

"But Mr. Lewis isn't an atheist. Not one bit."

"He was once. I don't think we've gotten to the part of the story where he isn't."

"And all those books he reads . . ."

"He's read so many books, George. There's certainly no way I can list all of them. But he told me that *Phantastes* is the one that baptized his imagination."

"If I grew to be old," George said, "I would read as many books as Mr. Lewis. I know I would."

Despite the roaring fire, I almost shiver. It isn't that I always think about how George will not grow old, but at a time like this, I have no decent reply but a hug.

# THiRTEEN

# SURPRISED BY ENCHANTMENT

After returning to Oxford, I walk through the trodden snow, thinking of how many stories Mr. Lewis has read and how few novels I've actually read. Even the ones I have read are because I've been told to read them or because they helped me understand mathematics. What if I read a book that made me fall in love so hard and so fast that I would search for more of its kind?

It seems implausible.

Honestly, those kinds of books, the fairy tales and Mr. Lewis's book about the lion, stir me up inside and make me feel things that bring tears. And I do not want to cry. I want to be strong and good for George. The last thing I need is to get sentimental and squishy. Something—I'm not sure what—in Mr. Lewis's Narnia story makes me weepy.

In many ways, Mr. Lewis and I are opposites. He abhors algebra. I adore it. To me, the world makes much more sense as a sum or a string of numbers. I can feel them. I understand their language.

George feels the same as Mr. Lewis. The truly heart-breaking thing is that he won't live nearly long enough to read all the books Mr. Lewis has read. Life is unfair; it's not the story I would write for myself or for my family or the world.

I mope along High Street, then head toward my rooms at Somerville when I stop mid-step. A chill of something other than the weather runs along my arms and heart as I pause in front of the Bodleian Library. It radiates. Warm light spills from its windows onto the icy sidewalks. Christmas lights have been strung unevenly along the pathways and seem to lead me toward the door. Bicycles are parked on bike racks and a few have tumbled into each other. The Bodleian's dome glows. I think this majestic building must hold more books than even Mr. Lewis could ever read.

People come from around the world to visit this library, and here it is on my walking path every single day, a reliably quiet place to study when the residence halls are too loud. It holds manuscripts as old as can be found and a copy of every book that matters, or so they say. I've heard that within are secret tunnels and leather-bound treasures.

This whole town emerged unscathed from the war because the evil man Adolf Hitler wanted to preserve it for himself. What if a bomb had hit this beautiful library?

I stand outside, gazing up at the Bodleian, taking note of its charms in a way I haven't before so I can catalog a full description for George; I want to tell him about this place he can't visit.

The midafternoon sun sits like an egg yolk in a sea of clear blue, faded in winter hues. Students rush into and out of the building, little clouds coming from their mouths or cigarettes or both. They climb onto bikes and rush past me as if I don't stand there at all.

Everything seems to be moving quickly: the world, the days, Mr. Lewis's stories. I step toward the library door. I walk inside and look about more carefully than I usually do. I want to paint this scene with words George will appreciate. Dark wood surrounds me. In the alcoves, sunlight falls like yellow dust. Stacks of books smell of aged paper and hushed voices sound as if they might know secrets. The furniture is so old and so solid I wonder if it has been there for all time.

I wander until I find myself at a wooden circulation desk, asking a woman in tortoiseshell glasses and bright red lipstick for a copy of George MacDonald's *Phantastes*.

"Mr. MacDonald has an entire section on the second floor." She smiles at me as if she's waited all day for just this question. "Do you love fairy tales?" she asks.

"I'm not sure yet."

"You haven't read his work?" Her smile lifts higher and her round cheeks rise with it, and I realize that for some reason the thought of me reading MacDonald for the first time thrills her. What were these stories?

"No, ma'am. I haven't read anything of his. Or any fairy tales at all, to be honest."

She walks around from behind the desk and turns to another woman with black hair pulled into a tight bun. "Sylvia, I will be right back." She turns to me. "I'm Miss Collins. Come with me."

"I can find it, I'm sure."

She looks over her shoulder, ignores my comment, and motions for me to follow.

"It's for my brother," I say. "I think he'll like it. He loves *The Lion, the Witch and the Wardrobe* so I thought . . ."

"I do believe you should read it first," she says.

I don't understand why I can't tell her the book is for me. Ashamed of fairy tales?

I follow her up the winding staircase and through the labyrinth of books until we stand in front of a section far, far away from the physics, math, and sciences area. She pulls *Phantastes* from the shelf and hands it to me, then walks away with a smile of satisfaction, as if her job for the day is done.

I look at the cover, a thick maroon leather binding with gilt design: *Phantastes: A Faerie Romance.*

What, if anything, could possibly be inside these pages that would inspire a man to nearly, or actually, change the course of his life? I sit at a desk scarred with scratches where a gooseneck lamp drops a circle of light. I open the book and begin to read.

That's when it happens, as it has never happened to me before when reading a story: time falls away as if it doesn't exist at all, as if the cosmos holds still while I read. As if it waits for me to read this story.

And maybe it does.

I look up hours later, and only one other person sits at a desk a few feet over. I've read half of *Phantastes* and within its pages met the Maid of the Alder, who was cold and white and had invited Anodos to her cave, where she gave him tea and lulled him to sleep. Familiar, of course, as Mr. Lewis's Tumnus and Lucy and another cave, but with a different outcome. Here, there is no wardrobe to walk through, but an oak desk is a portal to another world.

Maybe that's why Mr. Lewis writes stories—to find a different way to tell a tale than has been told before.

Or maybe that wasn't why at all.

I might be looking for answers where there are none. Maybe I'm digging for something to give George when there is nothing to give. But that thought is too dreadful to ponder. If I can do nothing, then I am as powerless as a loose feather in a windstorm. All these Jack Lewis stories that I scribble in my notebook, and all these fairy stories that exist in the world—can they do a bit of good?

I don't need to be reading these tales or even thinking about them. I need to be studying for my exams. If I fail those tests, I fail my family in a way that is far worse than not bringing some stories home to George. Thinking hard about this, I sit straight as a board, my hands clenched into fists and eyes screwed tightly shut.

"Megs?"

I startle and look at the boy who calls my name.

"Padraig." Ah, so he is the other person at the desk in the dim corner. He's been here all this time.

He stands and walks toward me, grabs a chair to sit next to me, and drags his chair so closely I can see the freckles at the edge of his ears. "What are *you* doing here?"

"Most likely the same thing you are." My voice feels unsteady, and I wonder if he feels it too. If he does, he doesn't give any hint. He just keeps up with that goofy smile and talking away as if we're in a pub or on Magdalen Bridge.

"I'm studying," he said.

"Well, so am I. I always study here . . . just usually not in this part of the library."

"Not many math students study George MacDonald." He taps the book. "Jolly good one right there."

"Yes, I think it is. I have half of it to go but . . . I need to get back to my own studies and stop with these silly stories." Moving quickly now, I begin to gather my things: my notebook, my mittens and hat, my coat.

"Don't rush off. Those aren't silly stories, Megs. They're something else altogether. You should feel that by now."

I stare at him for a moment, and a once-hidden door to a beautiful conversation seems wide open, waiting for me to walk through. For reasons that escape me, I try to slam that door shut. "They aren't important when it comes to my scores. I need to go."

"It's like you don't want to love the stories, but you just can't help it." He grins again and I stand, frustrated and annoyed without real reason.

"You think only stories can move you?" I ask. "You think only stories can take you somewhere you had no idea you were going? That's not true."

He sits back and that red hair seems to flame from his head, but his smile tells me he is enjoying this. He is giddy, like I've told him he is the most enchanting boy I'd ever heard or seen.

"Don't dismiss my work because it's not as magical as yours," I say. "It's most likely more magical."

"I don't think that at all. I suspect you are the one who thinks that only your discipline holds the true answers."

"It does. The mathematical equations have to come to a conclusion. And there aren't numerous answers. There's only one."

"Oh, is there?" Padraig's eyes hold stars in them. His smile is mischievous, but I will not be charmed.

"What does that mean?"

"Well, from what I understand, both Einstein and Newton are correct, and yet their theories contradict each other. I'm no math genius, just a medieval literature student, but that's how I understand it."

"They can both be right. There's a theory that will explain it all. And I bet Einstein finds it."

"Someone will. But that's not what I meant." The left side of Padraig's grin lifts. "You know what Einstein says about imagination, don't you, Megs?"

"No."

"I went with Dad to one of his lectures, and Einstein

said that the true sign of intelligence was not knowledge but imagination."

I sit back down, softening. "So what did you mean?"

"It's all a mystery, Megs. The stories and where they come from. Physics and how the universe works. We're privileged to try to figure it out, whether it's a story or a math equation."

"Surely you know physics is more important than fiction?" This is an absurd discussion. I can rightly enjoy a good story, but thinking novels are the same as Einstein's and Newton's theories is absurd.

"I think they are neither more important nor less important," he says to my surprise. "No. Not one bit."

"But we cannot understand our world without the genius of the mathematicians. It's a language of the universe," I say.

Padraig causally drapes his arm over the back of a chair. His worn gray sweater and vibrant green eyes make it appear as if he is as comfortable here as at home. "You are ignoring imagination; you need it for your work too. But I can't really understand my life without stories. They offer me . . . they offer all of us the truth in their myths, mysteries, and archetypes."

I stare at him and shake my head and stand up to in another meager attempt to leave.

"Just like my father," Padraig says in mild exasperation. He leans back in his chair and for the first time in his cheerful demeanor I see something like melancholy. Not so much anger as sadness.

"Your father?"

"He's a professor. And he'd agree with you." Padraig stands also. He is at least five inches taller than me, and I have to look up to see his eyes. "Sorry I bothered you, Megs. Go back to your plus and minus signs. Go back to your equations that might add up but can't soothe a heart."

I let out a puff of resignation and sit again. "I'm sorry. I'm being a dolt. I just can't figure out how to help George, and this whole thing is frustrating me. At least with a math problem I can work on it until the right answer shows up."

"Shows up?" Padraig sits again also, then scoots even closer so our knees are touching. "Like a character."

"How so?"

"When I'm writing—"

"You write stories too?"

"I do. But that's not the point."

"Must we have a point?" I try to make light, to lift some of the darkness I've painted onto the quiet room.

He chuckles. "No. But I think what I was trying to say is that when my fictional characters show up, or the ones you're reading about in that book, they have a place they're going. A journey. A math problem does too. I've seen Father spend years on one equation until it shows him the way it is meant to go. That's what a story does with me. I'm not trying to convince you, Megs with the flashing blue eyes, that my work is more important than yours, but maybe it's *just as* important."

I nod and feel the ugly blobby lump in my throat that hints I might cry.

"I bet your brother doesn't want you to read him a math problem." Padraig sets his hand on my shoulder and my stomach does a little flip.

"No, he doesn't." I push my fingers into the corners of my eyes. "But he also wants something I can't give him. He wants answers I cannot find. And I'm trying so hard. I'm listening to Mr. Lewis's stories and writing them down, and I'm trying . . ."

"Oh, Megs." Padraig slides his fingers down my arm and takes one of my hands in his and holds it gently. "I wish I could find the answers for you. We aren't always in control of these things, are we?"

"I want to be."

"So do I."

"Maybe it's not so much about finding the answers as it is asking the questions," he says. "And using your imagination."

"That makes no sense, Padraig." I search in my mind for a smart rebuttal, one that will convince him. "One of my Somerville fellows, her name is Elizabeth Anscombe, likes to quote Wittgenstein, who says, 'The world is determined by the facts, and by their being all the facts.'" I pause. "The facts. That does not include imagination."

"If you really think about it, you'll see that it does. All my life I've watched Father trying to find the one big answer that will explain the beauty of the world with science— all that measuring and adding and subtracting." Padraig rolls his eyes in such a childlike way I almost laugh. "It's important," he says. "Trust me, I know. Advances in science will happen because of people like my father and you, but it's not *everything*, you know? You can't measure everything. And there is more than one way of understanding our lives."

"Your father. He sounds very smart."

"He is."

"Is he in Ireland?"

"Not any longer. He's a professor. Here."

"What?" I lean forward. "What is your last name?"

"Cavender."

I exhale. "I've been to his lectures!"

"I thought so."

"And you didn't say anything?"

"What does it matter? Mathematics snobbery isn't a family trait, and I didn't want you to think I was—"

My laugh erupts, and I shush myself quickly, although we are the only two in the darkening library with our books scattered about. "Mathematics snobbery? I do believe there is some snobbery in literature, *non?*"

"Of course there is. But you won't find it here." Padraig taps at his chest with an open palm.

I glance at the large wall clock. "They close in five minutes," I say before I lean closer to him, lowering my voice. "So do you think stories have a beginning? A place they come from? Like the universe? Like the Big Bang with a single primordial atom?" I take a breath. "I'm asking for George."

Padraig ponders in silence, and when I look closer at him I think to myself that I'm looking at a friend. I've not really had many, not in the way others speak of their friends. I had one girlfriend in Worcester, but she moved across the ocean to take a job in America. I've never had a boyfriend to kiss me under the willow tree like some of the town girls do. I've always had my family and George and the village and my numbers and a few acquaintances. But Padraig, he is beginning to take the shape of a friend. I can feel it and see it, and it makes me nervous.

"The beginning?" He looks off as if I've asked him something he has never thought of before: where *does* a story start?

"Yes, the beginning. I think that's what George wants to know: Where does it come from? But Mr. Lewis just keeps giving me *more* stories."

"Every mythology in the world has a beginning story," says Padraig. "They call it an origin story. Every culture has a legend about where *we* began. But no one—not in science or story or myth—can really say where stories start."

"That doesn't help me."

"I didn't think it would. You know, Megs, you and me, we're trying to answer the same questions, just in different ways. You don't have to be so against one kind to be working with another kind."

"I'm not *against* anything."

"You seem to be. You seem embarrassed that I caught you reading MacDonald. You should feel proud. Your life just expanded."

The floor behind us creaks, and we turn together to

see Miss Collins, the librarian who brought me up hours before. "Closing time." She wraps her pale green cardigan closer and nods to my book. "Have you enjoyed it so far?"

"Very much so," I tell her the truth, and she smiles and walks off.

Padraig and I gather our things, then emerge from the library to find ourselves in a snowfall. The only light comes from flickering gas lampposts, the moon hiding far beneath the layers and layers of snow clouds.

"May I walk you home?" he asks.

"I'd like that."

We amble along so our arms bump each other, and the warmth of him waves toward me. We don't talk of myths or Einstein or school but instead about our favorite hike on Shotover Hill, and the way Longwall Street curves like a snake and how anyone could ever truly enjoy punting when there is always a lurking possibility of falling into the river.

We reach my residence hall and stand on the steps, snow falling like white dust in his red hair, the ends curling in the moisture. "Thank you," I say.

"I'm glad I ran into you, Megs," he says before sauntering off and leaving me with a flipped inside-out feeling.

# FOURTEEN

# THE SECRETS INSIDE A STORY

I stayed up most of the night reading *Phantastes* instead of working on my equations and preparing for exams. The snowfall persisted through the following day and only stopped an hour ago. Oxford is hushed and secretive, hidden beneath inches of new fallen snow. It is evening now and I'm standing at the bus stop in front of the Bodleian Library.

The bus trails down the street's untracked snow to where I wait on the corner in coat, mittens, and hat. I am as bundled as a package ready to be mailed. The bus's tire marks dent the soft blanket of white as it comes to a stop, and I climb aboard.

I'm the only passenger. The bus driver with his black hat and broad shoulders smiles at me. "Out on an evening like this? Most are at the pubs, if I'm a betting man." He winks. "Which I am."

"I have an appointment, so no waggling about for me."

I smile in return and feel it holds some pride. I *am* proud of my appointment. How many people get invitations to the Kilns?

I climb into my seat and stare out the dusty window as he drives. The world is covered in white, hushed and looking brand-new. The mounds of snow change the trees' shape, and the pavement and road blur so I can't tell where one starts and another begins. The driver is careful on the icy roads.

I can tell myself that I keep visiting Mr. Lewis out of obligation to my brother, or I can also admit I'm enjoying the time and his stories. He seems to have answers he isn't revealing, and there I am, slowly realizing I have questions of my own. Those questions had been lurking below, hidden beneath the snow of my own certainty, and now I find myself wanting some answers. There has been born in me a hope that one day Mr. Lewis will say something that will have me understanding all the pain and death and joy that seem to bump into each other in my life.

Mr. Lewis doesn't talk about love, not yet at least, but I also want to understand the peculiar grip that Padraig has on me. The way I feel when I see him is both fuzzy and clear, as is the way I think about him when he's not around. Padraig is obviously a fantasy; my wondering about and longing for him is powerful and false. It does not add to my life—I have no doubt about that.

I stare out the window of the bus as it climbs the hill, skidding a bit and then regaining ground. I run my fingers along the frosty condensation my breath leaves on the glass and think about yesterday evening in the library, how Padraig's eyes have a blue rim around the green.

I push aside these images and think through what I want to ask Mr. Lewis. The questions run through my brain like locomotives, one after the other, coupled together, until we arrive at Mr. Lewis's street. After a wave for the friendly driver, I exit the bus, trodding toward the Kilns and leaving footprints in the pristine snow.

The routine is unaltered: the hedges glistening with ice, a slippery walk over the bricks, the green door, the friendly greetings, the strong tea in the common room, Mr. Lewis asking after my studies, my family, and my brother. Then there is a pause, and Mr. Lewis stands and walks toward the house's entryway.

Is he leaving? Will I get no story today?

"Come outside with Warnie and me," he says in his jolly voice. "This story might best be told while walking about."

"It's freezing," I say with a hopeful smile that might convince him to stay by the roaring fire.

"All the better." His grin spreads to his eyes, and I follow him into the hallway with Warnie, watching as he dons hat, coat, gloves, and scarf. "This is a tale worth telling in nature."

Warnie nods. "I agree, brother, even as this fire beckons me to stay. But let us go."

I had just removed my coat and hat, and here I am again putting them on. I pull my scarf tightly, and we exit the green door and take a left. Neither of the men speak as their smokey exhalations puff out. They know where they're going, and the brothers' silent language leaves me outside their realm.

I realize we are headed to the lake and the wood behind the house, where Warnie had found me the first time only two weeks ago. Has it truly only been two weeks? I feel I know them so well that I almost reach out my hand to hold Mr. Lewis's in mine. But I don't.

Silently, we reach the edge of the icy pathway and they stop to wait for me. Warnie stares off into the hushed forest. "What are your favorite books, Megs? Tell me what you love to read."

"I'm not sure I can say, sir. I've not been a big . . . reader. I know that seems opposite to everything you've both based your lives upon. But this whole expedition isn't about me. It's about Narnia. And where it came from. And your brother doesn't seem to want to tell me." I smile to let them know I'm aiming for levity.

"Oh, but I am now and have been." Jack pauses and stomps his feet before walking again. He seems to carefully consider his next words. "After a book is written, it is hard to know where it came from. Can anyone—can you—say exactly how things are made up? How one of your physicists comes up with a new theory? How imagination rises up to make meaning? When you have an idea, can you tell George or your friend exactly how you thought of it? Its genesis is very mysterious."

"I can't, no. Sometimes I think things and I don't even know why I'm thinking them. Like the thoughts are thinking themselves."

"Exactly." Mr. Lewis lifts a hand for emphasis.

"Is that why reading is so important to you?" I ask.

"Have you not been listening?"

"Oh so carefully. I have. I promise."

Warnie walks ahead as if he has somewhere to be, while Jack continues chatting. "Every life should be guided and enriched by one book or another, don't you agree? Certainly, every formative moment in my life has been enriched or informed by a book. You must be very careful about what you choose to read—unless you want to stay stuck in your opinions and hard-boiled thoughts, you must be very careful." His light voice lets me know a story is coming.

For half of a breath, I think of telling him that I've read most of *Phantastes*, that I spent the night wondering about it, that I am ready to return to it as soon as possible, but I don't speak. Not yet. I want to finish the book first and think more about it before daring to speak to him of it.

Instead I ask, "This may sound silly, but do you think you choose these life-changing books, or do they choose you?" I am muddling my words, mixing up what I mean. "Maybe you choose what is already interesting to you or . . ."

His laugh echoes through the forest. A flock of black birds fly overhead, cawing disapproval at being disturbed. Warnie turns and smiles, waits for us now. "A good question!" he says, and somehow I know he won't answer. Indeed, he moves on. "Now where we were last?" he asks.

"You told me all about Norse mythology and George MacDonald and stories; you were still living with the Knock and—"

Warnie's laugh interrupts. "Ah, then shall she know about your exams?"

Mr. Lewis playfully ignores his brother. "Ah, yes, then university is next." Mr. Lewis keeps talking, his walking stick making small holes in the snow. "I took the exams and the lion of mathematics came for me. I failed algebra— devil take it."

I take in a sharp breath. He failed? He didn't attend Oxford as a student? Where had he gone? I had assumed . . .

"Isn't it odd?" he says and stops in his tracks. "If it wasn't for the war, I might not have been admitted at all. Yet here in Oxfordshire, my entire life has unfolded. And you, you are here for math." He shakes his head with a chuckle. "So differently we are created. Isn't that wonderful?"

Warnie laughs, meeting my backward gaze with a lifted eyebrow. "And don't you know—they almost didn't admit Jack for his poor math score, and then he went and graduated with a rare Triple First." Warnie paused with a bragging grin. "The highest honors in three areas of study: in Greek and Latin literature, in philosophy, and in English."

"Oh," I say. "So many . . ." I acknowledge this fact with a smile, but my thoughts have already taken off toward

Mr. Lewis's mention of the war. "And you were in the war?" I ask. "How . . . awful."

Mr. Lewis nods and looks at Warnie. Something passes between them, something I guess will never be in a story or possibly even be formed into words.

I persist. "Where did they send you in the war, Mr. Lewis?"

He takes a few breaths and regards me. "France."

# FIFTEEN

# BEING BRAVE

Exams are finished, and my brain feels as if it is made of soft pudding. My pack is heavier than usual as I'm carrying my things home for holiday. So this time I will take the shorter way home instead of the path I prefer on the Severn Way running alongside the river. From the railway station I trudge along the Foregate Road and see Worcester Cathedral's tower grasping for the low clouds. I hoist my pack and head toward the London Road and home. It does not escape me that the London Road in Oxford is the one that leads toward Mr. Lewis's house, and this one to mine.

Beneath the fatigue, I'm slightly annoyed. Mother said she would pick me up with the car and she didn't show, perhaps mistaking my arrival time. But the air is light and cold, and the walk isn't so bad; the sky is deep blue, without a cloud to be seen. Neighbors along the mile wave at me as I pass: Mrs. McReady, standing with her broom on the front stoop pretending to sweep but in truth watching for any impropriety she can report at teatime to her friends. And Mr. Litton, coming home from a trip to market and opening his front door.

On this holiday break, I plan to sleep to my heart's content and read stories to George. I've brought with me *The Light Princess* because it was written by the same author as *Phantastes*. If Mr. Lewis loved George MacDonald, perhaps there is something deeper in these tales that George will also love.

We will figure it out—George and I. We will piece these stories together and deduce where Narnia was born.

I turn the corner to home and see that the gate to our cottage is flung wide open.

Something's wrong!

No smoke rises from the chimney, smoke that usually signaled comfort and family. Paying no mind to the icy walkway, I run into the cottage, drop my pack, and rush through the kitchen and then to George's empty room.

Fear like barbed wire snags my breath. I know better than to guess why the rooms are empty—there can be as many reasons as there are wild dreams. I fling open the wardrobe: empty. On his bed are scattered pencils and the open notebook. I glance quickly—pages and pages of drawings of lions and castles, scenes of the stories I have told him. In each one, George has added a lion: sometimes roaring, sometimes resting or just watching.

I drag in a few breaths and rush back to the kitchen.

Mum knew I was coming. Before leaving, I'd rung her from the residence hall.

I see it: a note on the kitchen table, the place where most of my life has unfolded.

*At hospital.*

I flip the torn paper over but there is nothing to console me, nothing to tell me why or when. I'd phoned three hours ago, so this is no planned doctor visit. The left-open gate already told me that.

I grab my satchel and run out the front door, slam it shut, then bolt down the icy streets, my bag flapping against my hip for the two miles to hospital. I race down the London Road past the houses and neighbors, skirting the empty Port Royal Park. I'm accustomed to walking that far but not running, and running seems to be all I can do.

I cannot stop the thoughts. George not breathing. George crying out for help.

I remember the time Mr. Lewis asked me, "Can you explain how ideas come into *your* head?" I hadn't fully understood his question, but now I do—for how am I to explain all the ideas now flooding my thoughts? I don't want these thoughts. I don't want these ideas, but here they are: thinking themselves, as it were, like a dream making itself in the night.

I finally reach Charles Hasting Way and burst through the scrolled iron gate of the brick Worcester Royal Hospital. I take the marble stairs two at a time and bolt through the doors of hospital where warm air surrounds me. The door slams shut behind me.

In front of me is a faded yellow linoleum stretch of counter covered in papers and pens and clipboards. Behind this barrier stand nurses in white and doctors with the snakes of stethoscopes.

"George Devonshire," I say, catching my breath. "Where is he?"

A nurse with tangled auburn hair wears a white cap with a single streak of something dark at its edge. Red lipstick has smeared on her front tooth. My senses are hyperaware, waiting for something to calm me. "Dear girl, who are you? Are you family?"

"I'm his sister, Megs. Where is my brother?"

"He's in a room on the second floor."

I start to take off when her voice stops me. "Wait!" Her white shoes squeak as she moves toward me in a rush.

I halt abruptly, almost tripping over my own feet; I don't even know how to get to the second floor. Where did I think I was going?

"Wait here," she says and walks from around the counter.

"Is he . . . ?" I don't even know what my question is. Or I'm afraid to know.

The nurse—now I can see her name badge: Eleanor—is at my side. "He's okay. He's getting some oxygen. You just wait here. I will retrieve your mother."

A thousand years or more pass, then Mum walks out of an elevator and comes to me, throws her arms around me. She's wearing a pair of brown tweed pants and a white buttoned shirt that might be Dad's, not an outfit she would ever be caught wearing outside. Always a tight cinched dress and pearls for Mum.

"He's fine. He's fine. He's fine." Three times, as if that's truth's magic number.

I pull back to stare at her, tears rising as surely as the Cherwell after a storm. "What happened?"

"He couldn't breathe. He just would suck in air and nothing would happen. His lips were blue, and I threw him in the car. They gave him oxygen. He's fine now. Sleeping with pink lips . . . He's okay." She trembles with the memory. "He's okay."

"Did he try to do something? Go somewhere?"

"He was in that wardrobe again, Megs. He can think or talk of nothing else."

"Going from his bed to his wardrobe would not tire him that way. That's not it. He's getting worse, isn't he?"

"Yes." Mum obviously has no energy for anything but the truth. She would not and could not put two squares of sugar on this for me or for anyone else. George is getting sicker. Mum turns to me. "How is my darling girl? Are you studying hard for exams?"

"I'm finished with them, Mum. I thought you knew."

"You look tired."

"Take me to George."

"Don't be frightened by all the equipment around him. It's all okay . . ."

I nod.

For all the times my brother has been to hospital, I have never been with him here. Now the odors come to me—slowly, like all my other senses are returning now that I know George is breathing. Alcohol, bleach, vomit, and something tangy I don't recognize. I'm frightened it might be blood. Shoes squeak on tile floors, and there's the soft hum of voices and high buzz of bells and disorienting overhead beeping. I feel dizzy and place my hands on either side of my head as we enter the elevator.

With a ding, it lets us out. I follow Mum down a narrow hallway with closed doors on either side, names in chalk on the doors. The halls are decorated with children's drawings, paintings of a circus and balloons and bright colors splashed everywhere. This is the children's ward. Christmas lights are strung along the nurse's desk, and a picture of baby Jesus in a manger hangs on the wall.

Mum reaches room 236 and pushes open the door with her hip. I rush past Dad, who stands at the end of the bed, his hands clenched around its metal rail. I mean to go straight to George, but there are poles and tubes in the way. Some tubes go into his nose and others into his arm. I stop fast and look down at him. His eyes are closed.

"George."

He opens his eyes. "Megs."

Just that is enough to bring my heart to its knees.

"Did you bring me another story?" he asks with a smile. The tubes in his nose push up, pop out. He fixes them himself as I lean down to whisper.

"Yes, I did."

George's cloudy eyes grow brighter, and he moves over in his bed like he expects me to crawl in. His curls splay over his forehead, and his arm with the needle and the tube is placed carefully on his chest.

Mum notices his movement and steps forward. "You cannot crawl into that bed, Margaret Louise."

"I wasn't planning on it, Mum." I grab a plastic chair and draw it forward and next to his bed. It screeches, and we all jump. "I'll sit here with him. You and Dad go take a break. Get a cuppa."

They look at each other, and for the first time I catch Dad's gaze. His warm brown eyes are wet with tears. He nods at me as if speaking will spill those tears. Together they walk out hand in hand. I reach into my canvas satchel and slip out my black notebook.

In this entry, my handwriting is frenetic and sideways. The details were numerous, and I'd wanted to get it all down before forgetting. The war. What happened to Mr. Lewis.

George speaks in a whisper. "Has Mr. Lewis said anything about the faun or the Witch or the lion? Where did—"

"Not a single word, my dearest."

His face falls and lips tremble. I become furious at Mr. Lewis. Why couldn't he just give me a straight-up answer? Again I think to make one up, to lie to George and tell him where each of these characters comes from. The Witch is Mr. Lewis's aunt. The lion is from his favorite

PATTI CALLAHAN

zoo. The faun is from Norse mythology. But George never abides by lies, even well-intentioned ones. Besides, I love him more than that.

"I will ask him again," I tell George. "I promise. But for now, another story. Maybe you'll see something of Narnia in it."

"I like the stories," he says. "Even the scary ones. I like to know that even Mr. Lewis, the man who wrote about the biggest bravery in the world, was once scared."

"Yes, he was."

Opening the notebook, I begin to read. The beeping of the hospital room's machines become the background of the war, and the *rat-a-tat-tat* sounds of a ravaged French countryside.

164

# SIXTEEN

# THE DREAMING SPIRES

Everyone seems more frightened than George of the hospital. He doesn't mind it much. They put tiny tubes in his nose, and he can breathe so easily it's like swimming in oxygen. But the visitors to George's hospital room are distressed. As Megs sits next to him, her hands are shaking. Her cheeks too. George wants to tell her that it's going to be okay because it *is*—even if everything turns out differently than she wants.

She opens her black notebook and wipes a tear off her cheek with the back of her hand. "This story," she says with a false smile, "is about the Great War." She looks up nervously. "Maybe we should wait on this one. I could reread my story on Norse mythology or the one about the Knock."

"No, go on please," he tells her. "It's okay to tell me about the war. It's probably what gave Mr. Lewis the idea for the battle in Narnia. Or perhaps it wasn't the idea, but the"—he searches for the word—"the experience."

Megs nods. "Mr. Lewis was about to turn nineteen."

"So right after he left Surrey," George says.

Megs smiles, her hands now steadier on the notebook. "Yes, but first he attends university."

"Start right, Megs!" George orders. He wants to slide into the story with their shared words.

"Oh, yes!" She sits up straighter. "You ready?"

"Yes."

"Once upon a wardrobe, not very long ago . . ."

George pauses so she'll smile, then says, "And not very far away . . ."

"Jack Lewis sat at a desk in Surrey, preparing for exams."

Megs continues with her story, and George finds himself inside Professor Kirkpatrick's Surrey home while Jack Lewis suffers over algebra equations.

———

Jack was determined to gain admission into Oxford. He'd studied under Professor Kirkpatrick's scrutinizing discipline, and his eyelids burned as he'd studied day and night for admittance exams. As algebra was sure to be in the tests, he buckled down, practicing equations, pushing himself harder than he'd ever done before. Memories of Wynard School and cruel Oldie flooded Jack's mind each time he'd sit down to do an equation. Yet he persevered in his studies. His education would not be dashed on the shores of his loathing for mathematics.

The day Jack headed from Surrey to Oxford to take the admittance exams, he thought of what Mr. Kirkpatrick had once told his father. "You might make a writer or a scholar out of him, but that's about it." This was all fine and well by Jack, but to be a scholar or a writer, he still had to pass the mathematics portion of the exam.

On the train ride to Oxford, Jack again read *Phantastes*, because by now he understood that all books worth loving were worth rereading over and over. Finally he arrived at Oxford station, the train exhaling black coal smoke as Jack stepped off. Of course he'd imagined Oxford in his mind. The fabled city a thousand years old; the medieval city of thirty-two colleges under one Oxford name.

Jack exited the station and ambled a few blocks, confused by the dullness of the city he entered. He'd heard so much about this regal place, about its beauty and ancient feel, and he was flooded with disappointment. Oxford was merely a row of shops, one after the other, stretching along a ribbon of asphalt, without much to write home about.

Jack had expected and desired to be awed. With confusion and an itching annoyance, he turned around to find his way to the college and there—behind him, not in front of him—was the city of Oxford.

He'd stepped out of the wrong side of the train station and walked into the town of Botley.

There is only one first view of Oxford, and it paused Jack's heart. The city was a glorious cluster of dreaming spires and jagged towers, a skyline of medieval romance.

It felt like an echo of a song he'd heard but forgotten. This first impression of its beauty was forever engraved on his mind and in his heart.

He hoisted his pack with a lighter spirit and set his feet quickly to Oxford. He found the cobblestone streets and domed library, the brick and stone colleges, the fair greens of the parks, the book-stuffed bookshops and warm pubs. Jack found the twin rivers meeting the Thames, and where he imagined his new life was to begin. He ambled along Holywell Street to the corner of Mansfield Road to locate the Tudor single house where he would spend the night.

The next morning he muddled through the tests, his head bowed over the desk in the dusty exam rooms, his attention on the questions, not on dreams of a new life.

He finished the exams and boarded another train, then a ferry back to Ireland. Jack arrived home to Little Lea and walked through the door of his family home. He stood before his father and the truth burst out of him in an anxious confession. He was sure he'd failed the math portion of the exams. There was no doubt in his mind, and he didn't want to waste any time on false hope of admittance.

With Warnie in Sandhurst with the British army, he didn't even have his brother to complain to, or for companionship. He would run to his friend Arthur, tell him of the injustice of mathematics and his ruined life.

He would make new plans. His inability to figure and do equations had cost him the chance to attend the prestigious university. But there were other universities, to be sure.

Jack sulked through the holiday, his father's disappointment like smoke clouding the house. He berated himself, even as he read Spenser and MacDonald. He walked the garden paths of his childhood, stared over the lough, despair following him. Why hadn't he spent more time on equations? Why couldn't his mind understand numbers when it could easily learn languages and higher concepts?

It was said that math was another language, and Jack had mastered many: Greek, Latin, German, and French. But how was Jack to be a writer or a scholar if he couldn't gain admittance to university?

Christmas Eve arrived and with it a knock on the front door of Little Lea. In the post was an envelope with the name Clive Staples Lewis typed on its front. On the back was Oxford University's logo, stamped deep into a yellow wax seal.

Right there in the entry foyer, with ancestors' portraits watching over them, Jack's father ripped open the letter that would seal Jack's doomed fate. Jack would be brave; he would stand and accept the verdict.

Albert Lewis read aloud the words.

Dear Mr. Clive Staples Lewis,
    Congratulations on your admittance to Oxford's University College . . .

Jack's tight fists of dread unfolded. He was stunned, but he also knew these were odd times. The war raged, and there were fewer men to attend university. Most British boys of his age were already in France. Oxford must need students; the result was that Jack Lewis was admitted.

In the summer—Trinity Term—of 1916, Jack moved to the spired city of Oxford. After he ambled from the train and through the gates of University College with the azure arms of a cross between five martlets, he was escorted by a tall and thin porter to his rooms. It was a gabled college with an emerald green quad surrounded by a tawny stone cloister, iron lanterns, and gargoyles. Jack reveled in the deep medieval feel of it all.

Jack followed the skinny porter, who looked as if he might break if he touched his toes. They walked along stone hallways, up a narrow winding staircase to a dimly lit residence hallway. The porter opened a door and stepped in. Jack followed and was about to drop his pack when he stopped mid-step to stare. This was a plush two-room residence with warm wood paneling. Covering the walls were oil paintings of old men in professors' cloaks. Bookshelves heavy with books crowded every corner, leaving no room for more. There was a study and a separate bedroom Jack could see behind an open door. He dropped his duffel bag, unsure if he should tell the porter that this fancy room could not possibly be his.

To boot, in the center of the room, proud and large, stood a piano.

This young man had quite obviously taken Jack to the wrong room.

Jack looked to the porter already halfway out the door. "This can't be right. It's brilliant, but it can't be mine. This must be for a . . . wealthier student. I think you might have me confused with someone else."

The porter stopped and looked at Jack, his eyes narrowing like a crow eyeing a shiny object he may or may not dive to retrieve. "Yes. It was another student's room, but he's been sent to the front lines. It's yours for now."

The porter shut the door. Jack sat on the large wooden desk chair with the plush cushioned seat and stared out the iron mullioned window to the green quad where students hurried this way and that, carrying books and smoking cigarettes on a summer afternoon. The war raged far away while he sat in the two-room suite with a piano and shelves extravagant with books.

Until then, Jack had considered the war a nuisance, something that kept everyone from getting on with their lives, a bother that kept Warnie from him. But this room—it had belonged to a boy who now most likely sat in a trench somewhere in France. A boy who might not return to university or to his family.

Jack's mind coiled around the opposing worlds of horrifying war and this warm, book-rich room. He decided right then he would not shelter in luxury, evading what his brother and other students were enduring, and he'd enlist in the British army.

An Irishman, Jack could have avoided serving in the military, but he joined the Officer's Training Corps. During the rigors of marching and artillery training, he had to move his rooms to Keble College. There he was assigned a roommate named Paddy Moore, and they became good mates. Together they promised each other that if anything happened to either one of them, they would take care of the other's family.

Meanwhile, Jack's studies at Oxford took precedence. The military training was an added duty. It never felt truly likely that he would be sent.

War was merely an idea, an event far off. That is until Jack's nineteenth birthday, when he found himself in France's Somme Valley on the front lines, a member of the Third Battalion, Somerset Light Infantry.

When the shelling began, war was no longer an idea or a scene in a book or something Jack acted out with his chivalrous mice in a Belfast attic.

———

Fear trembled through the earth as well as his heart as Jack hunkered down in a muddy trench near his mate Laurence. Jack's wool uniform was tight, his hat tilted to cover his forehead and keep him warm along with his lit cigarette. The dissonant explosions, screams, buzzing, and pounding echoes resonated through the air. Jack bent lower, awaiting orders from his lieutenant, when something whizzed so near his ear, he froze up. More accurately, it whistled past him. It was a sound like nothing he'd ever heard.

A bullet. It had missed his head by an inch at most, and after it had passed, a thought flew through Jack's mind. *This is war, just as Homer wrote about.*

The cold, the wet mud, the marching; it was what Jack had prepared for during his training, yet he was completely unprepared for the reality.

Now that he was on the front lines, his body could do nothing more than go along for the ride. He had never been out of Ireland or England, yet there he was, crouched in a trench with Laurence, the mud thick and dense beneath their feet, the frost biting and frigid. They were hunkered down so low that all he could see were the muddy wood slats of the trench walls, while above them the war raged with sounds like nothing he'd heard before.

The trench was as real as cold, thick mud, as real as hand-grenade blasts nearby, as real as marching to another miserable battlefield until he was marching while asleep, waking to his feet and worn boots still moving, as real as the sleepless fear that crawled through the trenches like smoke. The green grass of England was replaced by a scorched and barren landscape. He wriggled along the ground to inspect barbed wire, slept sitting straight up against a cold muddy wall. This landscape was far away from his university rooms of dark paneled walls, innumerable books, and a piano waiting to let loose its music. But just as he did at university, Jack carried a notebook inside his pocket. He scribbled in it whenever he could, often lines of poetry.

A few months after his birthday, Jack woke in his

barracks with a fever and hallucinations: vivid images of a frozen wasteland inhabited by wolves and dryads; the stars trembling in the firmaments and the earth opening in jagged chasms. Faces, distorted and half animal, emerged and faded. His body trembled as if someone was lifting him like a child and shaking him. Jack didn't know what was real or what was imagined. Eventually they sent him to a hospital and called it trench fever, a disgusting disease caused by lice. Kind nurses tended to his every need, wiping his fevered forehead, bathing him, feeding and caring for him. How he missed his mother those months of illness and all his life.

Lying in the hospital bed one afternoon, a nurse with whom he had interesting discussions about literature brought Jack a different book by George MacDonald: *The Princess and the Goblin.*

Jack consumed the story as if it were his last meal. One George MacDonald book after another followed: *Lilith, At the Back of the North Wind, The Golden Key.* He returned to what had sustained him in past times of fear and sorrow—reading and writing, poetry and myth—until finally he took pen to paper and wrote more poetry.

It took five months for nineteen-year-old Jack to get better in that hospital. When the fever weakened and his strength returned, Jack was back at the front lines for the battle that would change his life. On April 15, 1918, Jack Lewis and his regiment were part of the British offensive attacking German defenses near Arras. Bullets whizzed past. Bravery mixed with cowardice as idealistic and frightened young men fought for freedom, defining courage not by being free of fear but by fighting in spite of the fear.

Seven days of that battle were shaped by blood and shattered bones, collapsed buildings, and smoking piles of rubble. It was a nightmarish world. By the end of the battle, the Somerset Infantry had taken the village of Riez du Vinage and captured sixty German soldiers. On that cold April morning, a British shell was shot toward the Germans, but it fell short, scattering its lethal power at Clive Staples Lewis, his mate Laurence Johnson, and Sergeant Harry Ayres, a man who had become very much like a father to Jack. Sergeant Ayres took the brunt of the explosion and Laurence also fell. Pieces of shrapnel bit into Jack's body.

Jack crawled through mud and dirt, through debris and bodies, to find his way to a stretcher bearer for his sergeant and mate. He wasn't a hero; he was another soldier trying not to die by bullet or bomb. Jack was whisked away to a hospital in Étaples. Those jagged scraps of a British shell made to wound the enemy were lodged in Jack's body: his left arm, his leg, and most dangerously, his chest.

Laurence and the sergeant were dead. Jack survived, but even as he was taken to Liverpool to heal, he could not reckon with the fact that had any of them switched places, if he had been two steps to the left or right, or if Harry or Laurence had walked away, the grim and miserable outcome would have been different.

In that moment, life made no sense. There was no plan or rhyme or reason, no goodness or mercy or great love.

Jack took his anguish to the page and to poetry.

———

When Megs looks up from the pages, there are tears in her eyes.

"Why are you crying?" George takes his hand from below the hospital sheet and touches her fingers. "He lived and went home and attended Oxford just as you do, and then he wrote all these books and—"

"But all the terrible things he had to go through. The misery in *our* world." Megs looks around the hospital room as if her eyes are cataloging all the terrible things she is thinking.

"Yes, I know." George watches her face as she tries to stop the tears. "Tell me what else."

She glances at the pages and a tear drops, spreading the ink of a word into a blue blob. George knows she's crying about him, and about loss.

She clears her throat before she tells him. "That mate of his that I told you about at the beginning? The one he met in training?"

"Paddy," he tells her.

"They promised that they would take care of each other's family if one or the other died. And Paddy . . ."

"Died," George finished for her.

"Yes, and Mr. Lewis has been taking care of Paddy's mother and sister all this time. Her name is Mrs. Moore, but he calls her Minto. Paddy's sister is Maureen, and now she's married and the mother is in a nursing home. He visits Minto every. Single. Day."

"Loyalty," George says. "That's in the book."

"Yes." She nods. "Loyalty."

A nurse enters the hospital room, bustling about George and Megs, tucking and checking and fixing. George ignores her, speaking to his sister. "Did Jack go right back to university?"

"Yes. And he eventually graduated with firsts in Greek and Latin literature, philosophy, and English. Not too shabby for a boy who almost wasn't admitted. And"—she smiles as if the war was finally fading in her mind—"that book of poetry he wrote during the war? He published it."

George sits up straighter. "That was his first book?"

"Yes, it was. He published it under the name of Clive Hamilton."

"Who is Hamilton?"

"It was his mother's maiden name."

"Oh, something wonderful out of something awful." George lies back and feels as full of story as if he'd been given a huge meal of something so satisfying that he could drift off to sleep without worry.

# SEVENTEEN

# ANSWERS WITHOUT ANSWERS

I'm back in Oxford for only one reason: to get more stories for George. Michaelmas term has ended and students
have gone home, but Mr. Lewis has invited me to his tutor
rooms at Magdalen College. As I walk up High Street, the
sky is blue and cloud-free.

I cannot wait until after holiday to hear more from
Mr. Lewis, because . . . what if . . .

I try not to allow myself to think about the what-if.
After one night in the hospital, George returned home, but
there was nothing new: no cure, no hope, real or even false.

I pass through the imposing wooden gates of Magdalen
with trepidation. Although I am invited, the sheer lack
of women students at Magdalen makes me feel like I am
trespassing, breaking some kind of unwritten rule about
entering by the gates without a secret password.

I take long strides and then begin to walk across the
sprawling frost-tinged lawn between the main building and

the New Building where Mr. Lewis's study is perched on the second floor. *New* means it was built in 1733, two hundred seventeen years ago. One side of the wide stone edifice is snuggled near to the River Cherwell and Addison's Walk, and the other to the front of the college at the street. In front of it lies a lawn so beautiful I want to roll around on it, but that wouldn't be proper, and I am long past rolling on icy grass. I spy two deer in the distant field.

"Megs!"

I glance around and can't spot anyone, then I hear it again.

A thought soars across my mind: how lovely it is when someone, out of nowhere, calls your name. You can be going about your business with your mind fluttering and thinking its thoughts, and the call of your name can make your heart rise.

I look up, and a hand waves out of a window. Shifting, I lift my hand and shield my eyes from the afternoon sun. Padraig! The wind animates his red curls.

"Ahoy, there!" he hollers.

I laugh and call back, "Ahoy! Are we on a ship?"

"Where ye headed?" he asks with a poor pirate accent.

"To the treasure," I say, pointing to the New Building, surprising myself with this giddy greeting. There I am, standing on the lawn of Magdalen College and playing verbal games with this red-haired boy who makes my stomach feel as if a swarm of bees have burst from their hive. Padraig makes me think of things I've only heard silly girls talk about.

"Ah, I'm betting you have another meeting with the maker of Aslan."

I smile at him, and he leans farther out—too far, for an image of him falling to the ground swoops through my mind.

"Stay there!" he says.

Then he's gone. But I stay, looking twice at my watch although only seconds pass. I don't want to be late for Mr. Lewis.

Padraig appears, bounding like a deer across the lawn in his jacket with the Magdalen crest open over a waistcoat and blue trousers. When he reaches me, he stops dead short, almost running me over. "Megs Devonshire, fancy meeting you here."

I smile. "You're going to freeze without your coat. What are you doing?"

"When a girl walks across the green, a gentleman doesn't take the time to button his coat or put on a scarf."

"Padraig." I say his name as he'd said mine and hope it has the same effect.

"Are you in a rush?" he asks.

"I am." I nod toward the second floor. "I must meet Mr. Lewis. It would be rude to be late."

"Yes, it would." He leans closer, and the cold begins to bite his nose red. Folding his arms around himself, he rubs his hands up and down. "Did he tell you anything else? Have you heard more stories?"

"I have," I say. "About the war."

"You must tell me about it."

My glee vanishes. I feel like I'm stealing the thunder and the lightning, all the goodness of the stories that are just for George and me. As if by sharing with Padraig I'm robbing my brother. My smile fails. I feel it.

"Are you okay, Megs?"

"I must go."

"Then off with you," he says but with a smile.

I try to grin back at him, but it feels shaky and false as I walk off, hurrying into the New Building and climbing the stone stairs and then reaching a door on the left. A sign hangs on it: Mr. C. S. Lewis—Tutor of English Literature.

The door is slightly ajar, and I peek inside and see him sitting at his desk with a pipe in his mouth and a nib pen in hand. He dips it into an inkwell and begins to write quickly. I hear him mumble the words he is writing out loud. He is whispering them into existence on the paper and through his pen. Something otherworldly is happening while he dips and writes and mumbles. I almost expect a faun to jump from beneath his desk or a witch to perch on the windowsill.

I don't want to interrupt, but then he looks up, as if my gaze has distracted him. His smile is wide, and he sets his pen down. The room smells of tobacco smoke and sunshine, if sunshine has an aroma.

"Welcome, Miss Devonshire."

I take a few steps and pause. "I don't want to interrupt."

"You were invited here. By me. Do come in." He stands

there in his carpet slippers wearing a welcoming grin. I think, for the first time, how he looks much like a jolly countryman instead of the learned man of letters and books he is.

"Thank you for having me," I say. "I know you usually don't have girl students in here."

"Oh! On the contrary. I do tutor some young women."

I lift my eyebrows at the lovely news, then gaze at the room. There are so many books they seem to have taken over, making it hard to focus on anything else. Heavy curtains cast shadows. Papers are scattered across his desk like fallen leaves. "Are you working on another Narnia book?"

"Oh yes." He stands. "But just then I was answering a letter."

"Oh?"

"I have a pen friend in America, a most fascinating woman named Joy Davidman." He pauses with a smile that could warm the White Witch. "Her deep questions and curiosity remind me of yours."

"Oh, I hope that is a compliment?"

"Indeed it is."

I feel happy to have been compared to his pen friend in America. I want to keep chatting with him before he tells me another story. "How is the newest Narnia coming?"

"It is much harder than the others. I'm trying to write the prequel. You see"—he grins—"I am telling the story of the professor before he appears in *The Lion, the Witch and the Wardrobe*, and you'll learn his real name."

"What is it?" I ask.

"Digory Kirk."

I nod and think about Professor Kirkpatrick but don't say a word about it, like a treasure I save for George. "So you're writing the first book second?"

"Oh, I am writing the first book fourth. I am going backward. It's not as easy as all that."

"When I read your story, you made it all look so easy. I couldn't just sit down with a pen and make a whole new world."

He laughs that beautiful laugh and says, "Well, I couldn't sit down and solve a physics equation." His balding pate glows with the sunlight falling into the room through the two windows facing west. "And meanwhile I'm working on an autobiography the publisher seems jolly keen to have from me."

"An autobiography!" I say. "I will read that straight away." I think for a moment whether to say the next thing on my tongue and then I do. "Seems like I'm getting an early performance."

"Indeed." He gives me what seems a secret smile. "They think I have salacious secrets I will finally tell. They are going to be truly disappointed."

He motions for me to sit in a large green armchair and I do. In my mind I have a list of direct questions prepared, ones I think will let me return to George with all the answers. But in Mr. Lewis's presence, these questions fall away.

We settle in, and I consider his huge wooden desk sitting

in the middle of the room, piled high with papers and what appear to be an inordinate number of letters. There is no typewriter. A standing grandfather clock looms over the study, its numbered face elegant and large. The rug is threaded with red and green. On the wooden coat rack, a robe of red and black hangs with a fisherman's cap on the top rung.

Mr. Lewis sits back in his chair and lights his pipe slowly, tapping down the tobacco as if he has all the time in the world. It's obvious his pipe has been fashioned by hand from the deep brown brierroot and soon glows under the smoke that rises toward his eyes. He blinks. I break the silence.

"I read *Phantastes*," I tell him.

"Oh, did you now? And what did you think, Miss Devonshire?"

"It was very enchanting, with all the fairies and the adventure. Honestly, I had a hard time stopping." I pause and realize in that small space of time that he also knows I've read his book too. "Just as I did reading yours," I add.

He bellows with laughter and leans forward, his cheeks ruddy and cheery, his rimless glasses falling lower on his nose. "You can love more than one book. It's not like a husband. You also don't have to feign loving both books."

"I'm not pretending, sir." I try to fix my hair, which is falling into my eyes, but then give up. It is unruly and will stay so. "I loved them both. I don't know why I believed . . ." I pause, because I don't know quite where I'm headed with the sentence, but he does.

"That fairy tales were only for children?"

"Yes."

He settles back into his chair. "Now where were we in our stories for your brother?" He pauses. "For George?"

"The last story I told him was about the war. It made us both so very sad." I think about telling Mr. Lewis that I wish we were, at long last, at the part of his story where he tells me exactly—word and literal word, like a math problem spread across the blackboard—where Narnia came from. This plus this equals that. This plus this equals the faun and the beavers and . . . the lion!

Instead, he nods and says, "Have I told you about the next war?"

"You went back?" I hope this isn't true.

"No, Miss Devonshire. Warnie did, but no, I did not. What happened during the next war is that children, many of them, came to live with me during the Blitz."

"Children?"

"From London," he says.

"Like in your book!" I feel the thrill of solving a problem. This is a direct line, an answer, an equation solved. The children in Mr. Lewis's book came from London to live with a professor. The children in World War II came from London to the Kilns. I settle back in my chair with a self-satisfied smile.

He sees it and laughs, as if he knew all along this next story might satisfy my logic.

———

Later that afternoon, I wait for the train at Oxford station, the floor slick with melted snow from the hustling feet of those rushing to the platform to catch their trains. I glance at the flicking tiles on the board announcing the time and platform of each train, at the cart of sandwiches and beers, at the stand with the bitter tea I love sipping on the way home. I think of Mr. Lewis stepping off the train at this station and walking out the opposite side of the building and into the wrong town. How disappointed he must have been! There is a slide of disappointment when a self-told story doesn't match what you encounter. But then there can also be a wonderful surprise when despair changes to rejoicing merely by turning around.

I hand my ticket to the conductor in the blue uniform. I walk onto the platform just as the black hulk of train approaches, sliding to a full stop and breathing out like a smoker with a deep cough.

I slide into my seat, and a woman with a large red hat and a wide smile sits across from me. She unwraps her sandwich, and just as she opens her mouth to speak to me, I lift the book I brought with me to block all conversation. Thinking of George, I have no desire to engage with her right now. I'm always within two breaths of crying. I hold myself together by being alone. Her long exhale tells me of her disappointment, but I want to read *Spirits in Bondage*, Mr. Lewis's book of poetry from the war, the book he published under the name Clive Hamilton when he was twenty years old.

He'd done so much at twenty: fought in a war and written a poetry book. It makes me wonder what I will have accomplished when I am twenty. What will become of me?

On this day, Mr. Lewis told me stories about the wartime London bombing, Operation Pied Piper, the friendships that changed his life, and a peculiar literary group called the Inklings, which was the anchor for so many of those friendships.

After I left him, I ran by the library and quickly wrote in my notebook what I could recall from his stories. Then I checked out two books to carry home: his book of poetry and a history book that includes information on Dunluce Castle. If I can't take George to Ireland, which of course I can't, I'll take Ireland to him.

Eager to read, I turn a page in Mr. Lewis's poetry book. I want to compare his younger self to the man who wrote *The Lion, the Witch and the Wardrobe.*

I begin to read the lines:

> Woe unto you, ye sons of pain that are this Day
> in earth
> Now cry for all your torment; now curse your
> hour of birth.

I am stunned at the poem's misery. Jolly Mr. Lewis hardly seems the kind of man to write of such despair. I have heard that war changes people, but I can't quite put together these pieces of his biography.

My mind wanders as the landscape passes by: villages glistening in snow and cows roaming wire-fenced fields, lifting wet noses at the sound of the train. When I finally arrive home, after taking the long way along the River Severn to watch it never give up its incessant journey, the sun is sinking. Mum waits in the kitchen with warm bread and a bowl of lamb stew. I shed my clothes and drop my satchel onto the table before hugging her so tightly that she lets go first.

I sink onto the chair and begin to gobble the dinner, realizing I haven't eaten since the porridge early that morning before I caught the train at dawn. After I finish, Mum and I sit in amiable silence as sleet ticks against the windows. Day slinks toward night.

"Why did you return to Oxford today, dear? Are you concerned about your marks?"

I look up and shake my head. "Not at all. Have you been worried about that all day, Mum? I thought I told you; I took Mr. Lewis up on his offer to come to his rooms and tell me a few last stories."

"You didn't let this silly storytelling ruin your status at Somerville, then, aye?"

"Mum." I pause because I want my words to be real and true. I want her to understand that although I had been the first to call Mr. Lewis's stories silly, I no longer can. Indeed, I am well aware they have changed me. I don't yet know how, but I want to convey this without worrying her.

She waits patiently, a wide-open space of love between us.

Finally I say, "It's not silly."

She nods, stands, then absently wipes the counter.

"I might have thought so too," I say. "But there is something in his stories, Mum. Answers without answers."

"You know that makes no sense, right, my dear Margaret Louise?"

"I know it *sounds* like it makes no sense." I put down my teacup and dig into my satchel to bring out my notebook. "Look. It's full of stories. Why would such an important man spend so much time with me if it weren't meaningful? He wouldn't do this if it meant nothing, if it were silly."

Mum takes the notebook from me and opens it smack in the middle, reads a few lines quietly and looks as if she wants to say something, but George's voice interrupts. He's calling for us, and after a few steps down the hallway we are both at his side. I sit next to him in the chair and Mum perches at the end of his bed. She still holds my notebook open and continues our discussion.

"You've written all of this." It is not a question.

"Only as much as I can remember. Mr. Lewis and I walk and we have tea and I can't take notes, so some of it might not be exact, but it's all true."

"Why would he waste his time telling you about things like"—she runs her finger down the page—"a horrible boy who teases him in public school?"

George pipes in now with a sincere laugh that is his alone. "Maybe because that's what Edmund is like when he teases Lucy about finding Narnia. Maybe the cruel boy who tortured Mr. Lewis for not being good at football shows up in Narnia as Edmund."

Mother and I lift our brows, and Mother walks to the head of the bed, leans down, and kisses his forehead. "My brilliant son."

I look at George and say, "I hadn't thought of it that way."

He sits up straight, then swings his legs over the edge of the bed. "Did he tell you more stories when you went to Oxford today?"

"He did, and I'm afraid these are the last. I can save one until Christmas."

"We don't know such things! He might tell you more." He suddenly sounds to my ears like Mr. Lewis himself. "Now tell me everything," he orders.

## EiGHTEEN

# THE FIRST START

Megs settles back in her chair and opens that black note-book that George has come to love so much. Its pages chronicle a man who turned all he was and all he is into a magical story about Peter, Susan, Edmund, and Lucy.

Mum leaves the room to clean up the dinner dishes and Megs begins to read. "Now we skip all the way to World War II. There were, astonishingly, only a little more than twenty years between the two wars. This means that men who fought in the First World War could fight again in the next, or their sons or their brothers or their nephews would be fighting in it."

She pauses; they give each other a knowing look. Yes, they are in the middle of their own kind of war.

She continues. "Mr. Lewis told me that Warnie said it was like he went to sleep after the first war and had a pleas-ant dream and then was called back up to return."

"Warnie had to go back?" George asks.

Megs nods. "But as you know, he returned unharmed. Now let me tell you what happened."

George listens, moving over on the bed so his sister can climb in beside him. She scoots closer to him, and they are shoulder to shoulder, his head nestled against her. "Once upon a wardrobe, not very long ago . . ."

"And not very far away," he says.

"During the war, there was a government program called Operation Pied Piper. In 1939, the Nazis were taking over countries across Europe, and even France had fallen. But Britain held out, keeping Germany from totally dominating Europe. After Jack graduated from university, after a stint as a subbing philosophy tutor, he was eventually hired at Magdalen, where he still teaches today. He and Warnie had been living in the Kilns for nearly ten years already at this part of their story."

She looks away from her notebook toward the memory of the story, as if finally getting the hang of telling a tale. She speaks in a soft voice.

George stood on a busy London street, where the threat of bombs was whispered day and night. Notices that read "Evacuation of Women and Children" fluttered from lamp posts and were slipped inside children's school knapsacks.

The war was coming, and any sense of safety in London was obliterated. Trenches were dug around the city, sandbags scattered around doors and windows, tape placed across glass to keep it from shattering. What was a mother to do? A father? How were they to keep their children safe?

In September of 1939, the signs about Operation Pied Piper were posted and sent home. Train schedules were established, and mothers and fathers began to pack up their children, who then gathered at their schools with their valises overflowing. To keep them safe from bombs, the children would be sent to live with relatives or even strangers in other cities.

Every parent was given a list of what their children must take with them on their journey: a gas mask, a change of underclothes, plimsolls, spare stockings and socks, combs, and more. They must label their luggage and take a warm coat, for who knew how long they would be gone?

Some children were sent off with nothing. Their families didn't have the money or the time to gather it all.

It wasn't just their luggage that was labeled. Every child wore a tag as if they, too, were baggage that could become lost in the shuffle of travel. These tags stated their names, schools, and other important evacuation information to help officials keep track of them. After taking their seats on departing trains, children waved out the windows to their parents and older siblings, clinging to teddy bears or their suitcases or their siblings' hands.

Some of these children were sent to the Kilns.

That autumn of 1939, at the Kilns, Jack Lewis sat in his upstairs study writing a letter to his friend Arthur in Ireland, his ink nib hoisted in the air and a drop of ink falling to his desk. He looked away from his letter and stared out the window to see the clutter of gold and red leaves.

He stood and walked over to gaze down at two young girls chasing Jack's big lopey dog, Bruce, through the hedges. He smiled.

He'd written to his brother, who had been stationed in Yorkshire, "Our home will be a harbor." And now it was.

At the time, in addition to the gardener and man of all work, Paxford, women now lived in the Lewis household: Minto and her thirty-three-year-old daughter, Paddy's sister, Maureen.

Only weeks before, on September 1, as the air had turned colder and winter hinted its arrival with morning frost on the grass, Jack had said good-bye to Warnie, who again donned his military uniform and set off to war through Catterick. The very next day three girls from London arrived: Annamaria, with long dark hair; Sheila, with a scared look of the lost; and Rose, with the defiant stance of the frightened trying to look brave. They'd arrived carrying their little bags, bundled in their coats and hats with their names hanging around their necks, their socks puddled about their shiny shoes, their tentative smiles dampened by the unknown.

Although Jack had felt completely inadequate around children and was quite nervous about it all, he wrote to Arthur, "Oh, the pencil boxes of childhood. How could I have known?"

The girls seemed happy, but Jack thought that nights were possibly quite frightening for them without their mothers and fathers and their familiar beds and homes.

He hoped that his house—with loads of rooms scattered about like secret places, with enough books to keep anyone busy for two lifetimes, with warm fireplaces, with Bruce, and with acres of land on the property to run about, which included two old kilns where bricks had once been made—would make them happy. Although there was only one bathroom, the children all bathed in the one lake, as it were.

Jack opened the window a crack to hear Sheila complain to Maureen, "Oh, there is nothing to do! Nothing at all!"

And Maureen, now about to be married, crouched down next to the young girl and said, "There are books enough to find a thousand worlds. You can play in the woodlands or write home or mend your socks. It is only for lack of imagination that you are bored."

Jack laughed loud enough to have them all glance up at him. He waved. Maureen was right. The echo of his own childhood rang in his ears—the wondering about what to do all day as the grown-ups went about their very important business, how to fill the time and the imagination as he and Warnie had in the little end room.

Jack closed the window and sat down. He thought of these children and of their lives upended. He thought of their parents and of their grief, and he thought of the war. Jack didn't know what to give them but his home and stories. So he began regaling the children with long-remembered childhood tales, and he'd told them about his favorite childhood books by E. Nesbit and about Squirrel

Nutkin and about fairies, about the Northern Norsemen. Jack tutored some, read to others, and showed them about his acreage.

A month in, Sheila had grown taller and a bit more confident. Her little gingham dress was too short already. She had pointed to the old family wardrobe and asked, "Is there anything behind this linen cupboard?" Jack had looked at her and at the wonder on her young face. Was there anything behind the wardrobe?

Later, as Maureen gathered the hollering girls outside for a hike to the lake and a bath, the rambunctious one, Rose, who always disappeared into the woods and lake, ran ahead of them all. Jack picked up his pen and wrote:

"There were four children, Ann, Martin, Rose, and Peter." The first sentence flowed from his pen. "But it is most about Peter, who was the youngest. They all had to go away from London suddenly because of air raids, and because Father, who was in the army, had gone off to the war and Mother was doing some kind of war work. They were sent to stay with a kind of relation of Mother's who was a very old professor who lived all by himself in the country."

He stopped and went no further.

Not yet.

Those days during the war, as various children came and went over three years, Jack tutored his students and met with the Inklings. He lectured and he walked and he wrote letters. There were air raids and bad news from the front; there were missives from Warnie telling of his safety and bringing news of the horrors. There were rations of eggs and butter and tea. Minto and Maureen helped with the children, and they in turn helped in the house. There were interesting dinners at the long table in the front dining room, where they talked about the books they read, or the games they played, or their parents in London or gone.

When the war was finally and blessedly over, the children returned to London, a city that had been gutted but not destroyed. On a cold night with a house empty of the footsteps and laughter of children, Jack looked to Warnie over a long pipe draw and said, "I don't think I ever appreciated children until the war brought them to us."

Even as he said this, the story Jack had started about four young children arriving at a professor's house in the countryside sat quietly in a drawer.

# NINETEEN

# THE TRUE MYTH

Megs lifts her head and closes the notebook while George feels doubt in his sister's tales for the first time. It's a bad feeling and he wants to dismiss it, but she must have made that story up, the part where Mr. Lewis used different names, the wrong names altogether. Maybe she's been making all of this up and she never even spoke to the author.

"Those are the wrong names," he tells her firmly. "Except for Peter, those aren't the children in Narnia."

"They are the right names for his first go-round." She tries to keep her smile from rising, but she can't and she laughs. She knows he would have noticed and doubted her; she toyed with him.

George shakes his head at her and then thinks about all of it: about first and second go-rounds. About how the genesis of a story isn't necessarily clear or straightforward. A story can change with time, just as people do. "So," he finally says, "Mr. Lewis worked on the story of the children, then put it away and changed it later."

"Yes, he picked it up nine years after he started. He says he went back to it in the summer of 1948, but that's a different story." Her voice is fading, like the color is leaving the sound.

She is tired, he can tell, but this is too important to let go.

"That's only two years ago," George says.

Megs nods. "Yes. I guess, just as most stories, it changed."

"Okay, so what's next?"

"George, there's only one more story. Don't you want me to save it?"

"No!"

"Well, he told me about a night he had at the edge of the river with two friends. A night that changed his life. We have to go back about ten years or so, but then we catch up to the day he sat down to *really* write *The Lion, the Witch and the Wardrobe*."

She rustles the pages of her notebook and flips to the end. The bound pages are almost full of her handwriting, not many blank pages left.

"This one is a story about how friendships change the course of our lives." She stops as if she's thinking of someone, then clears her throat and continues to read. "So Mr. Lewis first met his dearest friend, Ronald Tolkien, whom he calls Tollers, on May 11, twenty-five years ago and—"

George holds up his hand. "Tollers as in J. R. R. Tolkien?"

"Yes. I am sure . . . yes."

"Megs! That is the author who wrote *The Hobbit*."

"Oh, well, yes, that makes sense, doesn't it? He's the Merton Professor of English Language and Literature."

"Wow. Can you imagine what their conversations are like?"

"I can," Megs said. "I can."

George stops his sister with a little pull of her hair and a smile.

"So," she says with a smirk. "Once upon a wardrobe, not so long ago."

"And not so far way," he says as if their voices are combining.

————

The River Cherwell rushed by as evening turned to night and the water found its way to the Thames. As Jack and two other men walked along a path behind Magdalen College, Jack's walking stick swung with the rhythm he always used: *tap* swing, *tap tap* swing. Autumn had turned the leaves of the beech trees crimson and gold. Fallen ones crackled beneath their shoes; others stubbornly clung to almost bare branches.

Jack ambled with Tollers and a lecturer at Reading named Hugo Dyson. The men's heads were bent toward each other in conversation, stopping now and again when a point must be made.

The mile-long pathway called Addison's Walk was accessible only by an arched stone bridge over the Cherwell. They trod around a small island, the dirt path lined on either side by grass. The regal trees, their roots exposed and grounded both, looked as if they might begin to step across the river and into a nearby field of purple flowers.

Jack walked so quickly that, although they were in deep conversation, the other two had trouble keeping up. Then Jack stopped abruptly. He pointed at a bush, and the other two men looked. "Well, by Jove," Jack said, his booming voice echoing among the trees. "I was wondering where I left that!"

There, on a flat, low shrub of hornbeam next to a silver birch, rested a brown angler's hat made of coarse wove wool, its brim holding a puddle of water that reflected twilight's pink hues. He lifted the hat and shook it, bounced it twice against his trousers, then placed that hat, damp and limp, on his head and kept talking.

Tollers and Dyson looked at each other with a knowing smile, for they admired their friend's eccentricities. Tollers's voice rose above the branches as he continued the conversation with Jack. "You, my friend, believe in the importance of myth, as do Hugo and I."

Jack tapped his walking stick on the soft earth as a young couple floated by on an evening punt ride. "Believing in its importance and believing its facts are not the same. Myth conveys power. Myth gives import to the story. Myth guides us. Myths strike and strike deep. Myths have deep power over our human psyche. But that is not the same as being factually true. We all know that. We've all studied the Norse myths and the Celts and the Bible."

This particular discussion among these gentlemen had been going on for quite some time. The men were debating the truth of Christ's story, the actual story of Christianity. Jack was an atheist, as his teacher Mr. Kirkpatrick had been, and he argued with his two dear friends. Jack knew of their solid Catholic beliefs, but their friendship did not require his agreement with them.

When he first met Tollers, Jack was already immersed in the myths. Tollers had invited Jack to join the Coalbiters club, a private club that read Nordic texts in the original Old Icelandic language. Jack learned the Norse language just to join the group. Hugo was also a member of the Coalbiters. They, all three, were also part of the Inklings. So this discussion alongside the river, although started only an hour before, had been going on in different forms for years.

Tollers stopped short. "Jack, a myth can be true on more than one level."

"Yes," Jack said. "A myth tells a truth without the facts. You do not have to believe it is true to see the truth. In this, we agree, but myth is still myth. It is not something to believe *in!*"

They continued their walk as the trees turned blue in the shade of day's end, and the birdsong quieted and the creaking sounds of night began: branches rubbing in the wind, wings flapping the air. Jack sensed a deep longing, a personal echo he'd heard all his life that told him truth waited somewhere near. He lifted higher the collar of his coat to guard from the wind.

"Myths show us the way the world should be, or could be, instead of how it is," Tollers said, stopping to watch a squirrel scamper up the tree and disappear in the higher branches. "That is why we want more and more of them."

Jack already knew this. "Yes," he said, "that is their power."

"Think of all the myths and origin stories," said Hugo with his jowly smile, his rumpled tie loose. "Of all the gods who sacrifice their lives to save others." He stopped and straightened his hat, eyeing Jack with a look both casual and intense.

Jack stopped. "In almost every tradition there is the dying god who rises again," he said, turning to his friends. His eyes, always alert and warm, held their gaze. He was never tired of this conversation about myth and story, and yet this one seemed to be going in circles. "Yes. Balder. Adonis. Bacchus." He named just a few gods from his favorite pagan myths. "And of course, Jesus Christ."

"The difference," said Tollers, "is that the story of Jesus Christ is true. It really happened. Christianity is not *less* than a myth, but *more* than one. The true one."

"The only true myth," added Hugo.

"The myth of the dying God . . . ," Jack said, and the three friends continued their walk and talk.

Jack resisted.

He debated.

He listened.

They talked into the night, walking round about that river island until well into the early morning when Jack saw light—not of a rising sun, but of a spiritual conviction. He finally understood what his friends had wanted to show him, what he could see only in the middle of the night while the birch trees swayed in the wind alongside the river. All those years with the Knock, arguing logic, Jack had known that his intellect stood over his imagination, that the two hemispheres, as it were, of his mind were in sharp contrast. He realized that all he'd loved, he believed to be imaginary, and all he'd believed was real, he thought grim and meaningless.

Near dawn, Jack went home, and morning rose over the Kilns to see him a different man.

Something within him had shifted.

"Even if Christianity isn't my favorite myth," he told Warnie, "it's the only one that is true."

———

George sits quietly and stares at his sister, who is still gazing at the notebook. There's more, but she's stopped.

"What's wrong?" he asks.

She looks to him with brimming tears. George hates when Megs cries because there is rarely anything he can do to fix it. "I don't want this to end," she says.

"I don't either, but everything ends."

"Honestly, George." She shook her head and put down the notebook. "How do you know more than me when you are so much younger?"

"That's silly. You can add numbers in your head. You can—"

"But in the things that matter, you know more."

George thinks about this. Maybe it's true he knows more than her about some things, but he doesn't have the time to know about *everything*. He wants to know if it's true that there's something more when this something ends. Not whether there is a doorway in the back of his wardrobe; he knows that is just a way to tell a story about something more. But maybe in the back of his life there *is* a place he will go, a place they will *all* go.

He wipes a tear from his sister's face. "Tell me what's left in the notebook."

"Well," she says without even looking at it, "after that night with his friends, Mr. Lewis began to write books, almost a book a year—stories, allegories, and arguments for God's very existence: *The Problem of Pain* and *The Screwtape Letters*. He wrote *The Pilgrim's Regress* and *The Great Divorce*. He met with his writer friends, the Inklings, in a pub called The Eagle and Child—Bird and Baby is its nickname—every Tuesday between one and two in the afternoon."

"Have you been there?" George asks.

"I have. It's a lovely place, and they have gorgeous fish and chips."

"Have you ever seen the Inklings there? Reading to each other and such?"

His sister shakes her head. "No, when they read their manuscripts out loud it was in Mr. Lewis's Magdalen rooms on Thursday nights. They stopped meeting years ago, but they are all still friends. Mr. Lewis's dearest Inkling, Charles Williams, has died. But this group of men all shared their stories and work." She half smiles. "No women far as I can tell."

"Did Mr. Lewis take Narnia to them? Did he read it to them when he wrote it?" George is afraid she'll skip over the part that matters. The part where the author shares his story with his friends.

"Let me go on," Megs says and opens the notebook once again. "One afternoon at the Bird and Baby, pints on the dark wood table, low lighting casting shadows across their pages, Jack turned to Tollers and a conversation among the Inklings began about what they should write next."

She stops and takes his hand.

"Once upon a wardrobe, not very long ago . . ."

George smiles and closes his eyes. "And not very far away . . . in a pub in Oxford."

———

Jack, Tollers, Warnie, Hugo, and man named Dr. Havard, those Inklings who were there that afternoon at the Bird and Baby, were settled on chairs and on the long bench along the wall. Frothy pints, tobacco tins, and matchboxes littered the table under a circle of lamplight in a small alcove called the Rabbit Room. Wood-paneled walls almost glowed. The men's hats hung on a stand in the corner with their coats.

Tollers, his thinning gray hair swept back from his high forehead, his angular features beginning to soften with age, tapped his pipe on the table and ordered another pint. Spectacles low on his nose, he said, "I despair for the state of children's literature these days. They are reading pure rubbish."

Jack nodded, his laughter at something Warnie had said fading. "Yes," Jack said, "no more Edith Nesbit or Beatrix Potter. That's true."

"If we"—Tollers took a long swig of his pint, then slammed his hand on the table—"if we are to read something like that then . . ."

"We must write it," Jack declared, crossed his right leg over his left, and nodded as if he'd just won a debate point.

There under the low-slung ceiling and on hard benches, with their rustling papers and ink-stained fingers, all the Inklings agreed.

Jack Lewis and J. R. R. Tolkien decided they would write what they would have wanted to read when they were children. Tollers began working on a story called *The Lost Road*. His book *The Hobbit* was already a huge success. And Jack remembered the story with the four children who tumbled out of his pen in 1939.

One afternoon in the summer of 1948, after Jack had completed a lecture at the library and answered his correspondence, he sat down in his study at the Kilns and began the story.

"Once there were four children whose names were Peter, Susan, Edmund and Lucy . . ."

And this time, he didn't stop writing.

---

Megs ruffles the pages of her notebook, turning to the end. George interrupts the jolly good story to tell his sister, "Look at you!"

George sits straight and turns to her, placing his hand on her shoulders. "Did you just hear what you told? That was so beautiful. You described it perfectly. Megs, you're . . . a storyteller!"

She blushes, truly blushes, and kisses George's cheek. "This is fun."

"So what did his friends think of it? Surely he brought those pages back to the pub, right? To the Inklings."

"Yes. Some loved it, but sadly, Tollers didn't like it so much. He said that Jack mixed up too many mythologies."

George nods. "Maybe he did, but it worked to make something mighty, so what does that matter?"

Megs laughs at George, and a warm flush of love flows through his chest. She is everything good and true, he thinks.

George remembers something from the story and it rushes to the top like cream. "You said he also started his autobiography a few months before that. So he's been writing about his life at the same time as he's been writing about Narnia."

"Oh, yes. Yes," Megs says, kicking back a blanket. "Look at you, making connections that skipped right by me. Maybe that's why he's sharing it with us, his life, I mean, because he's writing about it and it eased its way into Narnia. That's as good a guess as any, but he's working so hard on writing more Narnia stories, so I don't know where his head is exactly. Maybe his thoughts are in both places—his life and Narnia . . . so . . ."

"Yes!" George exhales. "So maybe his imagination is in both places while he writes both books, real and made up, and they crisscross." He closes his eyes and sees the stories, words weaving over and around each other, fashioning a net of a story to catch him in. "Like a web, all those stories making another story, flowing in and out of one another."

"That's as good a guess as any," Megs says.

"It's more than a guess," George says. He wants his sister to truly understand what he means. "Like when you know the answer to a math equation but you don't know how you got there."

She nods and her lips draw in and there are red splotches mixed in with her freckles. He knows the look; she is going to cry and doesn't want to.

George also knows the stories are over, even as in some ways they are just beginning.

He can't find anything else to say, so he closes his eyes to imagine the man who wrote *The Lion, the Witch and the Wardrobe*. He sees C. S. Lewis walking at the edge of a river on a small island behind Magdalen College. A lion is hiding in the far woods, and the man's heart is filling with a truth that years and years later he pours onto paper—another myth, another story to reveal the truth.

TWENTY

# IT ALL BEGAN WITH A PICTURE

It is three days before Christmas, and even as I'd spent the previous night in my own bed at home, telling myself not to bother Mr. Lewis again, that Mum needs my help preparing for Christmas dinner while Dad works extra hours to get the Christmas orders in at market, and that George knows I've reached the end of Mr. Lewis's stories, I arrive uninvited at the Kilns with a written list in my pocket. I stand in front of the green door, waiting for someone to answer my knock. I still have questions.

I must ask now or never.

Mrs. Rounder, her hair still askew, opens the door and wipes her hands on her apron.

"Miss Devonshire! So happy you've returned. You know, we've been getting the most annoying visitors. People who think that if they come here they will find a knight in shining armor or the White Witch. They arrive just knocking at our door as if this wasn't a private home. But the brothers will be happy to see *you!*"

The aroma of sage and rosemary fills the hallway as I enter. Something's cooking.

"Mr. Lewis is in the common room. Go on in," she says.

I slip off my coat and hang it on the peg by the door before entering the common room. There, before the bright fire, sit Mr. Lewis and Warnie, right as can be. Each has a book in his hand and a cup of tea at his side. Looking up, both beam smiles at me.

"Hallo!" Mr. Lewis says. "Have a seat. What a surprise. We didn't expect you today."

"I know." I stumble as I walk in, suddenly self-conscious. It was rude to just show up. They might have had holiday guests. I dig into my satchel and pull out my notebook. "I don't want to bother, but I have a list of questions. They are for George, so forgive me for the bother."

"Oh, these questions are from George?" Mr. Lewis taps his pipe against the edge of his chair and ash falls to the carpet. "Are you sure they aren't for you?"

"No!" My defensiveness flares and then sinks under his warm gaze, beneath Warnie's laugh. "Well, maybe a little."

Mr. Lewis sets down a G. K. Chesterton book and grows serious. "What else would you like to know? Is there something you don't understand?"

"I *do* want to understand. And I still can't answer when George asks, 'Where did the lion come from? The faun?

The lamppost and the names of the children?' So now I ask you, Mr. Lewis, are they *real* in this world at all?"

"I don't fully know," he says. Mr. Lewis's voice is quiet but sincere. Maybe I have disappointed him by not seeing what needs seeing in the stories he's told me.

"But how can you not know? It is you who wrote it."

"Miss Devonshire, I had hoped to show you, and show George, how our lives unfold in so many different ways. How our individual stories become part of something much bigger. But I see now that you need more."

"I only need more because I want to tell George where it all came from."

"Here is the thing, Miss Devonshire: you must not believe all that authors tell you about how they write their books. When the story is finished, he has forgotten a good deal of what writing it was like."

"How on earth can you not know about a book that you wrote?"

"I shall end our litany of stories with the place I usually start when asked about Narnia. My story all began with a picture. One day when I was sixteen years old, I imagined a faun with an umbrella carrying packages in a snowy wood. Then, on another day when I was in my forties, I decided to write the story that went with the picture. But even then, I didn't write so much of it. Not until two years ago."

I nod, feeling something opening up, a cloud cover breaking under blue skies.

"Meanwhile," he said, "I'd been having dreams about

lions, and I'd read my friend Charles Williams's book—you heard me mention him, another one of the Inklings. He's gone now." Mr. Lewis closes his eyes and grief runs past; I feel it.

Warnie pipes up as if to fill in the spots where Mr. Lewis is faltering. "Charles's book was called *The Place of the Lion*."

Mr. Lewis nods. "But who is to say where the idea of Aslan arrived in my own story?"

My heart beats fast and I lean closer. "Aslan is George's favorite. He draws that lion everywhere—picture after picture of him." I pause before I tell Mr. Lewis that he is in the pictures too. I am not entirely sure how he will take this, so I keep it to myself. "Who is he? Who is Aslan?"

Mr. Lewis looks to Warnie, then to me. "Who is Aslan?" he asks. "He is the King of Beasts. Son-of-the-Emperor-Over-the-Sea. King above all High Kings. The Great Lion. High King of the Woods."

"Oh, Mr. Lewis, I know all of that. But who is he *really*?"

"That is who he is."

"Is he . . . God?" I ask outright the question I've been thinking. This is what I want to tell George: Aslan is God; all is well. There is a place where things are made right and good again. There is hope.

"That is the question I get all the time. What I did when crafting this tale, Miss Devonshire, was to suppose that there was another world, and God entered it in a different way than He did here on earth. And so there you have Aslan. It's a supposal, if you will."

"A supposal. What's that?"

"Something supposed, an idea of another world. And if there was this other world, how would God show Himself?"

I smile. "Or herself. And who is the Witch?" I ask, hurtling through my prepared list as quickly as possible, not wanting him to stop answering, believing I am at last finding my way to the missing puzzle piece.

"She may be any number of things."

Warnie laughs at this answer. Even though he remains otherwise silent, he seems to be enjoying this conversation, like a show.

I toss out an idea. "Is she Hans Christian Andersen's Snow Queen?"

Mr. Lewis lifts only his right brow. "Or, Miss Devonshire, is she Circe from Homer's *Odyssey*?" He leans forward. "Who knows? But don't we all know the White Witch? Must she be someone in particular? We can try and find the source, but we are all born knowing the Witch, aren't we?"

"Yes. We are." I think about the disease that has ravaged my brother's heart, making it weak. His illness is the White Witch. War is the White Witch. Cruelty is the White Witch. I take a breath. "There are so many things in your novel, Mr. Lewis. And then I've listened and I've written down the stories you tell me as best I can in my notebook, and I've read fairy tales and George MacDonald. I see, of course, that there is Greek, Roman, and Norse mythology in your Narnia story. There are British fairy tales, Irish folklore, and . . . even Father Christmas."

His laugh bellows across the room so loudly that outside I spy a flock of birds loosening from their branches and flying away with their black wings. "Yes, indeed," he says. "That is what my friend Tollers doesn't like."

I sink inside, drop my chin into my scarf. "So there isn't one answer for each question."

"There rarely is, Miss Devonshire."

"I wish there were." I look up. "And the character Lucy, she's named after someone because I see that name in the front of your book."

"Yes. My godchild is named Lucy. She is the daughter of my dear friend, Owen Barfield, an author and poet, a fellow Inkling. When I started the book, she was four years old. Now she is fourteen." He shakes his head.

He is quiet for so long that I think perhaps he's done talking, that I have finally, *finally* outdone my welcome. Then he speaks. "Megs," he says, calling me by my first name for the first time. "We rearrange elements that God has provided. Writing a book is much less like creating than it is like planting a garden—we are only entering as one cause into a causal stream that works, so to speak, its own way."

"In its own way?" I repeat.

"Do you know Psalm 19?" he asks.

I think for a breath and then another, moving myself backward through my memory to catechism days. "The one about the heavens or the sky showing God's handiwork?"

"Yes. The cosmos reveals God's handiwork."

"So you're saying maybe stories are the same? That they

reveal . . . God's handiwork?" I think for a better word. "Or truth? They reveal some kind of truth about the universe? That's what physics is all about."

"Yes, that is partly what I am saying. Megs, stars are made of dust and nitrogen; they are balls of gas and hydrogen. But that isn't what a star is; it's only what it is made of."

"I . . . hear you," I say and think about how this is the phrase young Jack Lewis wanted to hear from Mr. Kirkpatrick. *"I hear you."*

I don't want to say I understand, because I don't.

Not yet. Not fully.

"Did you want your book to have a spiritual message?" I ask. "To really say that . . ." I falter.

"I continue to hear this idea, that I have set out to write a Christian allegory, but it is all pure moonshine. I couldn't write in that way at all. Like I said, everything began with images: a faun carrying an umbrella, a queen on a sledge, a magnificent lion. At first there wasn't even anything Christian about them; that element pushed itself in of its own accord. And archetypes," he says. "You know about those?"

"I do," I say. "Carl Jung. I learned in secondary school how there are . . . what? Twelve types, I think. And they each show a kind of person or trait. Is it that each one represents a universal pattern of human nature? Or . . . I can't really have any kind of intelligent conversation about it. Which is the only kind I would like to have with you. I would be mortified to be considered daft."

"You, Megs, are far from daft. But yes, archetypes are

patterns. They are there in Narnia." He glances at the notebook on my lap, open to the end with only a few pages remaining. "I do believe your notebook might be full, and it's time for you, my dear, to live and tell your own stories."

Tears fill my chest like a balloon. I don't want this to end, whatever *this* is. I need to continue bringing stories to George. It seems they are keeping him alive.

"I don't know if I shall be back," I say, feeling overwhelmed. "It feels as if we are done."

"You may visit anytime, Megs."

"This has felt . . ." I stumble and forge through my thoughts for the right word. "This feels important."

"Megs, every human interaction is eternally important." He smiles, and I swear those eyes that usually twinkle are swimming with tears.

# TWENTY-ONE

# THE KISS

I step off the bus in downtown Oxford. It is eerily quiet. Most students have gone home for holiday. Without the crowds bustling by, the stone and brick buildings seem larger, more eternal, as if they have always been there and always will be, even without us. I kick my way through a snowdrift. I want to be home by dinnertime.

I bundle my scarf and coat as tightly as I can. I've forgotten my hat at Mr. Lewis's house and my hair is growing damp with the few snowflakes falling, leftovers from a swollen cloud that has already sent an inch to the ground. I shiver. I will go home and I will tell George the last of what I've learned today, but it doesn't seem enough.

It will never be enough.

I pass the Bird and Baby, the pub where Mr. Lewis met with the Inklings. Through the dusty window I see a small crowd inside. I remember meeting Padraig in a pub. I thought I'd never be able to *really* talk to him, but now we are friends. The warmth of the light draws me forward. One pint of cider might warm me up before I get on the train.

Also, I need to catch my breath. I want to write down everything Mr. Lewis told me—the lion and the faun and the umbrella—before I forget.

When I push the wooden door and step inside, warm air rushes toward me. I brush the snow from my hair and find my way to the bar. It is dim inside, the lights low. Its wood-beamed ceiling makes me almost feel like I'm within a ship. I set my satchel on the floor and my elbows on the bar. Behind it are shelves and shelves of liquor and glasses that glisten. The bartender, a short older man with white hair and a nose that appears to have been broken a few too many times, walks over and tosses a towel over his shoulder. "What can I get you?"

"A cider, please. Warm."

"Just the night for it," he says.

I sit and glance around the room and see others, students who haven't gone home yet or are local, talking to each other as if it's the easiest thing in the world, being witty and gabbing about as if they are in a movie.

I will never be able to be like that.

Then I see him: Padraig is across the room, in a thick Irish fisherman's sweater. It is the first time I've seen him without his school uniform. He's with a crowd, and the blonde girl—the one who giggles as if it's an art form—is hanging on his arm. Turning away, I quickly pull my notebook and pen out of my satchel and begin writing as furiously as I can, thinking about Mr. Lewis in his campus rooms, writing with an ink nib and mumbling his words out loud. My cider appears and I take a long swig, my pen moving fast.

Connections are coming to me: Mr. Lewis's voice, his laughter, and his hints. Lucy is his goddaughter. The lion might be from dreams or from Mr. Williams's stories. Or somewhere else. The idea had come with a picture of a faun when he was sixteen. He talked about the firmament of stars and planets.

These things begin to turn into a catalog of facts.

I am scribbling as though the world is held together by these very notes, as if the planets spin according to the correct order of all that could have contributed to the universe that is Narnia. As if I can unravel the beginnings of this world the way Einstein tries to unravel the beginning of our universe.

Padraig's voice startles me from the writing frenzy. "Stop!"

I come back to myself and the pub and the crowd.

Padraig swipes the notebook out from under me and begins reading it. I have made lines that connect one event or idea to another, attempting to make sense of it all: a web of scribbles and circles to show where one thing came from and how it might turn into another, proof that Mr. Lewis's story is logical and connected to the pieces of his life and his favorite myths. This diagram of interconnectedness would make sense to no one but me.

Padraig's gaze still on the paper, he speaks too loudly. "Lucy might be his godchild. Peter is Peter Rabbit? Edmund is Edmund Spenser?" Now he looks at me. Is it disappointment that paints his eyes? "The lions of Trafalgar Square and the Maid of the Alder?" He sighs. "Oh, Megs."

"Give me that back," I say as fear crawls up my neck. I am on the verge of understanding, of figuring it all out, and he will spoil my efforts.

Can I solve it?

I must!

I jump up and reach for my notebook, but Padraig is holding it over his head while still reading. Seeing how he's five inches taller than I am, there's not much I can do except hop off the barstool and jump up and down, looking the fool.

I stop my jumping. Take a breath. Stare at him and use my sternest voice. "Give me that. Now."

Padraig lowers his arm and sets the notebook on the bar next to my empty cider glass. Disapproval is set hard on his face and in his green eyes. "Why do you want to ruin it all with a chart and a list? Meaning and knowledge cannot be measured or calculated like this! Mr. Lewis didn't give you a list. He gave you these beautiful slices of his life."

"I know all that, but it helps me think." I want to back away from Padraig, but the bar is behind me, its edge digging into my spine through my thick green sweater.

Padraig's full lips flatten to a thin line and his brows bend in a V. The scolding expression on his face is more powerful than any words on paper.

My brain clicks back to defiance. Of course Mr. Lewis didn't give me the stories to make a list! But there I am, *wanting* to make a list. "I thought it might help George."

"Oh, did you?"

"Yes, I did."

"You might want to rethink that." He looks down at me, his hands on his hips.

Anger rises in a defensive heat that hurtles me off the stool. I shove my notebook into my satchel and grab my coat, squeeze past Padraig, past the students in their black turtlenecks and the girls in their red lipstick, past the wobbly Christmas tree and the wreath with the loosened red bow that hangs pitifully by a thread. I rush out the pub door into the snow and freezing air.

Anger warms me.

"Megs!" Padraig's voice chases me, dampened and softened by the snow.

I ignore him and walk faster. I'm too frustrated to be kind; I can't find the answers I want, and Padraig is teasing me. I do *not* want to be teased. At the same time, I know my anger is unrighteous, parceled out to a sweet boy who doesn't deserve it.

I hear him slogging behind me. He reaches my side, slipping and stumbling to keep up. He grasps my arm just as we both step onto hidden ice.

Together our feet fly from beneath us. We tumble to the ground in a heap, landing in a snowdrift that had been cleared from the sidewalk.

I'm still angry. I pound my fist on his arm, my legs tangle with his, and my neck burns cold.

He grabs both my hands. "Why are you so mad with me?"

"I'm not mad at *you*. I'm mad. Just flaming mad."

"Then why are you taking it out on me?"

I pull out of his grasp and slam my fist into the bank and attempt to sit, sliding and falling back into his chest. He laughs. I don't.

"I'm not taking it out on you. I'm just trying to get away from you." I wiggle until I sit up straight. Ice is melting through my wool tights, seeping cold onto my thighs.

Padraig finds his way to sitting and there we are, covered in snow. With a gloved hand, he brushes some from my cheek.

I shiver, not with the cold so much as his touch. But I will not show emotion. I have other more important matters to attend to.

"Why are you trying to get away from me?" He claps his gloves together, then takes my hands in his, easing me closer. "I'm trying to talk to you."

"You were making fun of me. Making light of what I'm trying to do."

"I wasn't. What you're trying to do is as noble a thing as any sister can do. I only meant for you to slow down and look at why you need a list. Or why you don't need a list."

"I was making connections—"

"You think turning imagination into logic will help

ONCE UPON A WARDROBE

George? Will that answer his most important questions? In my opinion, lists never answer the biggest questions."

"Padraig, I don't know. I can't give him what he wants for Christmas. I wanted something solid. I can't give him that either."

"And what's that?"

"To see Dunluce Castle." Hearing the words come from my mouth, I want to cry. The impossibility of it all. And then Padraig, here, now, confusing me even more. I have wasted too much time and need to get home, but I tell him, "He thinks the castle is Cair Paravel in the Narnia book."

"Let's go!" Padraig says, his voice strong and a laugh hidden within. "I have my father's car and I know how to get there. Let me take you both."

"What will your girlfriend say?"

"She's not my girlfriend."

"She's just a girl you let hang all about you?"

"Are you jealous?" He winks at me, joking when I am serious. I am furious and elated. There are too many feelings at once.

"No, I'm just wondering why you would spend your holiday with us when you can be muggling with her."

"*Muggling* isn't a word."

I push at him, trying to stand but instead managing to plop back in the snow again. "I know it isn't a word," I say, trying not to look ridiculous as I attempt again and slip again, failing to get off the ground. "But you know what I mean."

"Megs, sometimes a man changes his mind when he

sees the truth of things. I ask you to have a little confidence in my sincerity."

"I don't know what you mean."

He smiles. "Do I need to tell you in a math equation?"

"Tell me what?"

"Let me take you and George on a grand adventure to Ireland."

"I can't."

"But you can." His face is the picture of confidence. It scares me a bit.

"And why do you even care?" I ask. I'm angry; I'm frustrated. I want to throw my arms around him and let him hold me until I stop shaking, and at the same time I want to push him away. All the feelings are banging up against each other, fighting for first position. "What does it matter to you at all?"

"Megs, are you dotty?"

"Most likely."

"I care because I care about *you*."

Time freezes. The winter evening's steady course toward night pauses. Something is about to happen, and I'm fairly sure what it is.

Padraig leans forward and his lips are on my lips, kissing me. I've imagined kissing in an abstract way, something that would one day happen. But not in a snowbank outside a pub.

My first kiss.

I've been waiting for it and expecting it, even as it totally surprises me. I close my eyes.

Padraig pulls me closer, and there's nothing in the world but the feel of his lips on mine. I have a giddy sense of rightness and goodness that has nothing to do with logic or lists or facts.

"Whoop, whoop!" a voice calls out, and a chorus of others laugh in return as a group of students stumble past.

The kiss and the moment are over.

"That was Megs Devonshire," says a girl.

"And Padraig Cavender," says another.

"Miss Prissy Lane won't be too pleased," says the first girl. The laughing resumes until it turns into a group singing a rough ballad about a farmer and a milkmaid. The gaggle of students round the corner to High Street.

Embarrassment floods me. Me, Margaret Louise Devonshire, canoodling in the middle of a snowbank. I jump up, slip, banging my elbow against the curb so rightly that electric shocks run up my arm and I cry out.

Padraig stands slowly and carefully, reaching his hand down to pull me up. I face him and shake out my arm. "I must go, Padraig. Please don't follow me."

And off I go. He doesn't follow, just as I'd asked.

## TWENTY-TWO

# A GRAND ADVENTURE

The morning arrives with a slow lazy snow, its flakes falling fat and quiet, gathering on windowsills and fences. Tomorrow is Christmas Eve. Out the cottage's kitchen window, the sky peeks blue behind low clouds, and hints of the snow peter out to a weak sun. Around me are the remains of breakfast that I am to be cleaning up. Mum and Dad have gone market shopping in town while George sits quietly at the kitchen table, drawing in his thick sketchbook, which to me has become a symbol of all that is good: George's vital passion to create something marvelous in the middle of uncertainty.

I watch out the window, my mind wandering from exams (Did I do all right with such a scattered mind?) to the presents I want to get for Mum and Dad (a new cast-iron pan) to Padraig and the kiss. Always back to the kiss. Thoughts of Padraig are persistent and never fail to bring a thrill, even as I try to tamp it down.

A blue car stops in front of the house.

The door of the sedan opens, and my thoughts snap to the present. Did Mum order something delivered—a Christmas present perhaps? A young man bundled in a black wool coat and hat climbs out of the car, wraps his red scarf tighter about his neck, and looks up to the house as if checking the address before walking toward the low gate that opens into the garden path to the front door.

Padraig.

Had my thoughts become so muddled that I made him up? Had I become so preoccupied that I could think of someone and then imagine he is ambling up my familiar stone walkway to the front door?

I rush from the kitchen, my breath puddling in my throat. I don't have a name for my feeling; it's a peculiar mix of excitement and worry.

He can't be here. Not at my house. Not with George sick and me looking all mussy from sleep and not yet fully dressed and my parents gone shopping and . . .

He knocks.

George looks up. "Who is it?"

"I'll get it," I say. I walk past the hall mirror and glance at myself: a disaster, just as I thought. Messy dark curls are mushed up on one side from sleeping. I run my fingers through my hair, then hurry to open the door.

Padraig grins at me from beneath the flock of his cap. "Well, hello, Megs!"

"What in the world?"

"I have a surprise for you."

I glance back to the kitchen. George still sits at the table and his back is to us. He's drawing as if that's all there is to do in the world. I grab my coat from the hook by the door and slip on my green wellies before walking onto the front stoop.

"A surprise for me?"

"Well, it's for you . . . and George." From his pocket he slips out a map folded in neat creases. He opens only the first flap. "See this?" He points.

I lean to look where his finger rests. In tiny words I read *Dunluce Castle*. I lift my gaze back to Padraig's. "What's this about?"

"We're taking George there. Today."

I cough a laugh, a kind of relief that this is a joke. "He already has a map. He's drawn all over it."

Now it's Padraig's turn to laugh, and it's a full one. "No, silly. I'm taking you both there. In the car. On a ferry."

I shake my head, look behind Padraig. When a car passes, I think it might be Mum and Dad and they'll wonder why I'm standing outside in the snow with a boy they don't know. But it's not them. "That's impossible. George can't take that kind of journey and—"

"I have it all figured out." Padraig jabs his finger at the spot on the map. "Well, perhaps not *all* figured out, because that's part of the fun of an odyssey, not having it all squared away. Don't you agree? But I have enough of it figured out to get us there and back home safely." He pauses. When I have nothing to say, he plows ahead. "The castle is near my hometown of Crawfordsburn."

"No," I say even as I want to say yes. I must be sensible. If Margaret Devonshire is anything, she is sensible. I shake my head, then make a resolute face.

"I sort of expected you'd say that," Padraig says with no hint of giving up. "That is, of course, a perfectly logical reaction."

I want to be insulted, to be indignant and have a quick-witted response, but I fear he's right. These last few days I've been questioning the fundamental value of *only* logic. Of logic's ability to withstand what lies ahead in my life, in all our lives.

"Hear me out, Margaret Devonshire."

I laugh when he uses my full name, then place my hand over my lips.

"It is an eight-hour trip. A day to be sure. A journey, but worth it, and such beauty along the way." He opens the map wider and it flaps over his hand. "We drive from here to Holyhead, then take the car ferry to Dublin. After the boat ride, it's a three-hour drive to the castle."

"To the castle . . . ," I say, like I'm starting to believe.

"Yes, but if we're to keep to my schedule, we'll have to go now." He looks at his watch. "It will be dark early, and we'll need to get up to the northern tip of Ireland. No worries about food. I have a full picnic basket and a thermos of warm cocoa. I have a blanket in the back seat where George can lie down and—"

"So that means we'll need to spend the night. Do you intend for us to sleep on the side of some Irish road?" I am clicking through every reason that this adventure is a terrible idea even as a growing and frightening giddiness indicates resistance is futile.

"My aunt Mary lives in Crawfordsburn. Well, honestly, many of my aunts and uncles and cousins and second cousins live there, but Aunt Mary is my favorite. She'll take us in without alerting the family forces, I know it."

"My parents will never allow it. Not at all. Not for a minute."

"Are they home? I can talk to them." He grins. "I'm good with parents."

"I'm sure you are. I'm sure you're charming enough to talk anyone into almost anything, but they aren't home, and besides that, they aren't easily charmed."

"I don't want to charm anyone, Megs. I want to take you and your brother on an adventure for Christmas. I want George to see the place he longs to see. I want to spend today with you."

I could not have been more stunned if he'd picked me up and swung me around and kissed me again—but this time on my front stoop. A flash of sadness told me that the snowbank kiss was a one-time thing. A mistake at best.

"That is so nice, Padraig, but we just can't. I just . . . can't."

"You wanted adventure . . ."

"I never said that."

"Okay, then it's George." He smiles because he knows that will hook my heart like a fishing line.

"I can't take him away from home on Christmas Eve . . . Eve."

"We'll be back home in time for Christmas Eve, for whatever your family has planned. To my mind, there's no time like the present."

"What if we get stuck? What if—"

"What if we don't go and your brother never has his adventure? Actually, your parents not being home might be just the thing. We'll leave a note. We'll be safe. I promise."

*We'll be safe. I promise.*

I believe him. I believe the deep echo in his voice. The sky clear and bright, I think of George in front of the fireplace asking for only this for Christmas. I think of next Christmas when George likely won't be here, and me wishing I'd taken the chance, broken through the stone wall of logic and fear. There is a courageous girl I want to be—not this girl I am at the moment.

I look into Padraig's green eyes and I believe him.

*We will be safe.*

"Wait here," I say.

I rush inside, running toward an adventure. Before I fully know what I've done, I write Mum and Dad a note.

Please forgive me in advance. I am taking George on a short overnight trip. I promise he will be safe and warm.

My heart is hammering with delight. Something is coming alive in me, racing toward the unknown. It's an untested feeling I indulge, a surge toward adventure.

This is dangerous and wrong.

It is safe and right.

Everything is all mixed tighter.

I am taking him to Ireland to see the castle. We are with Padraig Cavender from university. His father is a mathematics professor at Reading, and Padraig has an aunt at Crawfordsburn. We will stay at her house. All will be well. I am sorry to take him without permission, but this is all he has asked of me for Christmas.

> I love you.
>
> Yours, Megs

Within minutes, a perfectly thrilled George with a self-satisfied smile is bundled into the back of the Wyvern on a bench seat of leather with blankets and pillows piled all around him.

I've brushed my hair and donned my favorite thick gray lamb's-wool sweater, grabbed a hunk of cheese and a loaf of bread. I bring George's sketchbook and his pouch overflowing with colored pencils. Padraig has a big wicker basket on the floor of the back seat. The car radio is playing "A Nightingale Sang in Berkeley Square," and George's cheeks are aflame with adventure.

Padraig starts the car and then turns around to George.

"It is lovely to meet you, George. If you look on the floor back there, you'll find I've brought something for you."

I sit in the front of the car, knowing I have about one minute to change my mind, but then George lets out a holler of glee that I haven't heard in ages and I know I won't. I turn in my seat to see that George has pulled from the floor a huge world atlas. He opens it as Padraig presses the gas.

We are off on the London Road of Worcester, heading toward Holyhead, then through Birmingham. It's all too wonderful to believe.

"George," says Padraig, "I think you are very, very brave."

George nods solemnly and says in a very big voice, "Yes, but Peter didn't feel brave when he stabbed the wolf chasing Lucy; he felt sick with fear, but he did it anyway."

Padraig and I look to each other and smile; he reaches over with his free hand and pats my leg just as Bing Crosby's voice sings from the car radio, filling the cab with the music and words of "Jolly Old St. Nicholas."

Padraig joins Bing, singing in a tenor voice that gives me a thrill of happiness. "Lean your ear this way."

George joins in. "Don't you tell a single soul what I'm going to say."

Without breaking the stride of the song, I sing off-key, "Christmas Eve is coming soon; Now you dear old man . . ."

The three of us join in laughter.

Padraig sings the entire song, tapping the steering wheel, knowing every word. His voice is beautiful with the lilt of his Irish accent, but also with something I hadn't known: his singing voice is as melodious as Bing's. My voice, meanwhile, is as out of tune as an abandoned piano, but I care little for how I sound. I am singing with Padraig and George, and we are with St. Nick.

Watching the English countryside fly by the windows of Padraig's car, I am as nervous as I am excited. Every mud-splattered sheep, every black cow, every thatched-roof house and smoking chimney are brilliantly vivid in the snowy countryside.

George naps and I put my feet on the dashboard, something Dad never lets me do. We laugh, and the feeling is like growing wings. Within a few hours, we arrive at the ferry port, where we see the monstrous metal ship that will carry us across the Irish Sea with Padraig's father's Wyvern inside.

Once the car is in the ferry and we're riding the waves, Padraig and I get out of the vehicle and walk to the metal railing. We feel the wild wind that makes it too difficult to talk. George naps in the back seat. It's so cold I can't feel my fingers. Mum will be frantic with worry, and I can only hope my note will soothe her somewhat.

We land in Dublin. Back in the car, Padraig tells George stories. One here, another there, sometimes nothing more than a poem or song. We drive along winding Irish roads where hedges sometimes brush the side of the car. Villages with small churches and corner pubs rush past.

Both George and I had faded off to sleep when Padraig stops the car. We awake with a jolt, my neck cranked to the right. I am mortified: Padraig has probably watched me sleep with my mouth open like a turtle's. Just before winter's early nightfall, we arrive at Dunluce Castle's ruins on the basalt outcropping of the seacoast.

George opens his car door and jumps out before I can say a word. Padraig and I get out and join him. He's standing with his face lifted to the castle. He is bundled in coat and sweaters, his scarf about his neck and high above his lips, his black wool hat low on his forehead. All I can see of him are his eyes, and they are as wide as they have ever been, taking in the view of the castle in the evening's fading light.

"We made it just in time," I say. "George, we made it."

Padraig nods. "Yes. We don't have long."

The three of us gaze up at a luminescent Dunluce Castle as the sun eases low behind it.

———

It is just as George had imagined, and this is all he wanted for Christmas. To know and see a place in the real world that can be transformed into something wondrous and unknown in another world.

Yards out past the cliffs, the sea thrashes the jagged and steep rocks with all its might, then retreats, only to try again. These broken walls and half crumbled towers had been seen by a young boy named Jack, who turned it into a magical place where goodness and love conquered winter, and a lion rose from the dead, and four children unexpectedly sat on royal thrones.

If George squints just right against the setting sun, he can see the castle intact and whole.

Padraig crouches next to him. "Jump on my shoulders, and we'll get closer," he says, his Irish accent flowing like a song.

George does it and instantly is above the ground, taller as if he has grown, as if he has become a man who can walk seven feet high and see the world from there. As the castle looms closer, George thinks of the Irish fairy folk Padraig told them about on the drive. Padraig said they live inside this world, in a fantastic place where seven years equals one. George thinks of Lucy in Narnia, gone for hours and hours, though her sister and brothers think she's been gone only for minutes. George thinks of his life and how short and how long it will be. He thinks of Jack Lewis at nine years old, gazing at this castle, tucking it away in his memories, turning it into Cair Paravel.

George knows this quest will be the adventure of his life. He snuggles closer to Padraig's warm woolen scarf as Padraig talks in a lyrical storytelling voice.

"The Scottish clan of McQuillan built the castle on the cliff edge—"

George interrupts. "When Megs starts a story for me she says, 'Once upon a wardrobe not very long ago and not very far away' and then she tells the rest. It's the beginning."

Padraig laughs and his shoulders shake. "Well, look at

that. Your sister is a storyteller." He glances back at her and jiggles George's legs. "Okay, here we go. Once upon a wardrobe, not very long ago and not very far away, the Scottish clan of McQuillan built the castle on a cliff edge, believing it would keep them from being conquered, but it didn't." He points. "The McDonough clan had spies that helped them scale the cliff walls there with ropes and baskets to conquer the McQuillans."

George listens. He doesn't have to dive so deep into his imagination as when Megs tells him all the facts, because Padraig is really good at telling a story.

"And there"—Padraig points up to the far edge of the castle—"Is where the kitchen crumbled and tumbled right into the sea."

"You're making that up," George says.

"Sure, I make up loads of stories, but that's true as true can be."

George laughs. "Were people in the kitchen when it happened?"

"Oh, yes. It's said that a young boy ran to get something for the cook, and when he returned they were all gone—kitchen included, as if it had disappeared into thin air."

"Oh, tell me another one." George realizes that real stories can be just as fantastic as made-up ones.

"Underneath the castle," Padraig says as they bow into the wind and make their way closer, "is a cave. They call it the Mermaid's Cave."

Padraig keeps talking, and his words whip about them

as he weaves stories of mermaids and pirates. Padraig walks across a long stone bridge that arches over a craggy furrow of land. George feels safe on Padraig's shoulders, watching as an eagle might. The stone bridge leads inside the castle, which of course is nothing but squares of earth and rock, of broken walls, the rooms and furnishings centuries gone. Where they have gone—the people and the kitchen and the furniture and the decorations—is a mystery, but what remains are stories. And George wants to hear every one of them.

After they cross the bridge, Padraig sets George down on the earth. Megs is behind them, and they are the only people there. "It is Cair Paravel," George says.

"You know," Padraig says as if he's just thought of it, staring far off over the darkening sea, "in Gaelic, *kaer* means 'castle.'"

Megs takes in a quick breath and George feels the night coming fast. No one speaks. They stand at the edge of the cliff, roped off and safe high above the rocks where waves crash, turning into white and silver foam.

———

I look at George, and he is more spirited than he has ever been. I see it in his eyes and in his straight shoulders. He's facing the medieval world that helped build the world of Narnia. Our trio stands there for a long while above the wild sea, silent and watching. George wanders a few feet away to the far end of the ruins, hobbling in the layers and layers of coat and sweaters I have made him wear.

"This is . . ." I pause for a lack of words.

Padraig fills in the blank spaces. "It's an adventure of our own making."

"Yes, it is," I say.

Dunluce Castle is not just a pile of old stones on emerald hills. It's an ancient whisper of Ireland and her stories. It's the seed of a story where a great lion appears, and it is the symbol of my brother's bravery.

It is much, much more than a pile of old stones.

George stands at the edge of a shattered wall where he runs his hand along the rocks.

"You know why he wanted to see this, don't you?" I ask Padraig, my voice tremulous. I am so grateful to him, and I don't know how to tell him. It's too big of a feeling for me to speak.

"Yes, I know why," Padraig says. "George knows you can take the bad parts in a life, all the hard and dismal parts, and turn them into something of beauty. You can take what hurts and aches and perform magic with it so it becomes something else, something that never would have been, except you make it so with your spells and stories and with your life."

Tears overflow my eyes. I can't stop them. I don't even want to. "Mr. Lewis said not to try and assign bits of a life to a story—"

"I know," Padraig says.

"But all the bits and pieces and scraps of a person's internal life are the ingredients of a life story. Here I can see that clearly," I say.

"And there's something more," Padraig says, so quietly that it almost sounds as if the whistling wind in the stones repeats his words. "Something undefinable. That's where Mr. Lewis's stories break all the bonds, Megs."

I'm transported by Padraig's wisdom. With Dunluce Castle rising above us, I start to understand. "Mr. Lewis's kinds of stories—the fairy tales, the myths, the universes all wrapping themselves around other worlds—are inside ours." I look to Padraig. "These stories make us remember something we forgot. They make a young boy want to hop out of a bed and see the ruins of a castle. These kinds of stories wake us up."

"Yes!" Padraig takes my face and the rough wool of his mittens scratch. I smile and feel my cheeks lift, cradled in his hands.

"The way stories change us can't be explained," Padraig says. "It can only be felt. Like love."

Time stands still, I swear it does. It takes a huge breath and holds it, waiting for what? I'm not sure.

Then George is next to us and he pulls at Padraig's hand. "Hurry! See the sun melting into the water."

And time lets out its breath.

The three of us look toward the remnants of a sunset, the wind trying to steal our hats and whipping hair into our eyes and mouths. As night falls, we are quiet, the only tourists audacious enough to brave a windy winter evening in a ruined castle.

# TWENTY-THREE

# CHARA

I wake in the creaky cottage of Padraig's aunt Mary in Crawfordsburn. Her house is a tiny thing, made of white-washed plaster with a thatched roof. I hear a fire crackling in the main room as morning rises outside, painting the world alive. Padraig slept on the couch out there, while his aunt has slept nearby in a tiny alcove on a cot. They've given George and me the bed.

George is asleep, curled next to me like a puppy. His soft sounds of sleep are comforting. He breathes in and out so easily, as if this journey has made him healthier. Dare I hope?

I lie as still as I can, recalling yesterday as one remembers the lines to a poem recited over and over.

We arrived at Crawfordsburn after dark. I called Mum and Dad on the pay phone in the village to let them know all was well. After assurances that we'd kept George warm and fed, Mum hadn't sounded mad—although she was reserved. I wondered what I would come home to today: anger or fear, disappointment, or worse.

Amazingly enough, right now none of that matters so much.

Yesterday matters.

George's adventure matters.

*Our* adventure matters.

My heart feels as if it dropped a rock in the sea below the broken castle. Or perhaps my heart has opened up in a swirl of laughter and wind, sweeping aside logic that had kept me so locked up. Logic—it can't help me in the soul things that matter.

I sneak my tingling arm out from under George and shake it awake. Morning creeps through a window covered in white lace, and I see George's notebook. His many-colored pencils are poking from a leather drawstring bag. I lift the notebook to see what he drew in the late-night hours before we fell asleep. He hid the pages from me, and I drifted off to the sound of the pencil scratching across the pages.

In his notebook is a rendering of Dunluce Castle.

George's drawings are becoming better and better. His talent can be observed roaring to life in the progression of these sketchbook pages. Dunluce Castle is jagged on a green hillside overlooking a riotous sea. But here is not the castle we saw. Here it is restored and whole, triangle flags flying from the highest towers, walls intact, and windows reflecting the sunlight and overlooking the sea. He found its hidden wholeness.

When I turn the next page, I see a lion standing at the edge of the cliff, his head thrown back and his mane tangled in the wind. His mouth is open in what must be a mighty roar, bellowing across the sea.

I begin to cry. All that has been locked inside bursts forth. I shake with the tears, and it wakes George, even as I try to swallow my sobs.

He stirs and then sits, touches my wet cheeks.

"Don't cry, Megs," he says. "All will be well."

———

When we emerge for breakfast, Padraig's aunt is as congenial as one might dream up an aunt to be. She is as round as she is tall, and her hair is bundled up like a ball of wool on top of her head just as it was last night when I met her. Her dress, resembling a tablecloth we have at our cottage with blue and yellow flowers scattered across the fabric, is swaying about her as she bustles to make porridge and tea.

"Oh, Padraig, my boy," she trills. "You must stay and say hello to Uncle Danny and Auntie Sorcha. Liz and small Padraig and Thomas and James will be so disappointed."

Padraig rips off a piece of the soda bread she is wrapping up for our journey. He gobbles it with a smile. "Aunt Mary, I must get these two Devonshire treasures home. I took them away and their parents are quite worried. They don't yet know how trustworthy and kind I am." He winks at his aunt and she bursts into laughter—not because it's not true, I can tell, but because he's so frank and unassuming.

They love each other; I can see that.

I realize that Padraig is a boy—no, a man—who says the truth. He is the man he appears to be. His charm isn't a cover, as it seems most boys' charms are, but instead is an outgrowth of his true-blue character and wit.

Soon enough, though, loaded down with bread and apple jam in a basket she gives us, Aunt Mary kisses me straight away on the cheek, holding my face in her hands as if she has known me all her life and loves me the same. She then sits in a chair to face George and places her hands on his shoulders, looks him in the eye so long that he eventually throws his arms around her and she around him. I look to Padraig, who watches them, and we both blink back the tears.

After a few hours' drive, during which George reads the names of countries and towns he flips to in the atlas, we are back on the ferry to England. The sun brightens the sky with a new day. For the rest of the drive home to Worcester, George sits in the back seat with the atlas as his friend, a smile on his face.

We are quieter on the drive home, the radio playing while the countryside flashes by. We are each in our own worlds, thinking of yesterday and what it might mean. My absolutely stunning realization that stories are a kind of answer, the same as any physics equation, will take me some time to fully absorb. It was as if I had seen the periphery of a large foreign landscape, and soon all of it would come into view.

When we finally drive through Worcester, it is late afternoon. The town is preparing for Christmas Eve services and gatherings. Padraig stops the car at the main square, and we all glance around.

The village twinkles under lights that have been strung from lampposts to storefronts and back again, a zigzag of lights swaying in a biting winter wind. Tonight everyone will be out. The local parish will perform a live nativity scene after finishing communion and a candlelight service. The townspeople will greet each other cheerfully with "Happy Christmas" and "Noel." Hugs and cheek kisses and all-around gaiety will surround the small makeshift stable in the middle of the square.

"Your town is so jolly," Padraig says.

George leans forward from the back seat. He's just woken up and sees where we are. "We are almost home."

"Yes," I tell him. "And tonight is Christmas Eve."

"You know, Padraig"—George touches Padraig's arm— "in Narnia, it is always winter but never Christmas."

"I know," he says.

"But tomorrow," George says, "we will have Christmas."

Padraig puts the car in drive, and in a few moments we reach home. After he stops again I meet his beautiful eyes. "This was an amazing gift you gave us. I could never have done this without you."

"Oh yes, you could have. You underestimate yourself."

He grins out the windshield, but I know the smile is for me. "But of course without me you wouldn't have had nearly as much fun."

I laugh and glance at my home. It is four in the afternoon. The sun is weak in the sky above a thin layer of icy clouds that can't decide whether to snow or not.

"Padraig," I say, "don't come in, okay? Let me bear the brunt of however cross they might be. You can meet them another day when their faces might not be so red and angry."

I climb out of the car and lean down in the open passenger door. "Thank you so much, Padraig." The words get caught for a moment, and I have to clear my throat. "These two days were the most astonishing I've ever had. I really believe that to be true."

He nods quickly, and I realize that if he speaks he, too, might cry. I close the door, then open the back door. George crawls out and into my arms, resting his head on my shoulder. I set his feet on the ground, and Padraig jumps out of the car. "Wait!"

Padraig comes to stand with us. He leans down and stares at George so hard I'm uncomfortable, but George isn't. George gazes right back into Padraig's eyes as straightforward as an arrow. "George," says Padraig. "I want to tell you I am so happy to have met you. You are the kind of wise, curious, and clever man I would like to become when I grow up."

George laughs. "But you're already grown-up."

"I *am* trying." Padraig takes George's face in his hands and kisses his forehead.

Then Padraig stands to face me. He smiles, brightly and clearly, sending wings of a thousand birds to fill the middle of me.

"Happy Christmas," I say.

"*Nollaig Shona Dhuit.*" He returns the sentiment in Gaelic. I want to kiss him. It is a sudden and irrepressible desire, but I am sensible.

I merely smile. "We need to get inside," I say. "Are you traveling back to Ireland today for Christmas or staying in Oxford?"

"Father and I are staying in Oxford until tomorrow afternoon, then we're off to visit family. Though I will see you soon." He leans again to George. "And you too, *chara*, you too."

"What is *chara*?" George asks with a tilt of his head as he grasps the atlas to his chest.

"It means 'friend' in Irish. It is pronounced *cara* but spelled *c-h-a-r-a*." He grins. "Friend."

"I like it," George says and laughs. "*Chara, chara, chara.*" He walks toward the front door and I follow.

*Chara.*

Friend.

I will not get seduced into a fantasy about who and what Padraig and I are. *Chara* is lovely and sweet, and I'm lucky to have even that with him.

Padraig drives away, and I know our adventure is over. Now I turn to my family.

It is enough. It must be enough.

George and I reach the door, and he sets his hand on the knob and then looks up at me. We both wonder silently what awaits us inside.

George opens the door.

Mum and Dad are sitting at the kitchen table. Between them is a plate of uneaten scones and a pot of tea. Mum has been crying; that is clear. Dad is holding her hand, and they both look to us as we walk in. Mum jumps up from the table and takes us both in her arms, hugs us close. "You're home!"

"Mum!" George's voice is muffled in coats and scarves and Mum's embrace. "You're hurting me," he says, though laughing.

Mum lets go and looks at us both. George yanks off his scarf in the warm house, and then his mittens and coat, all the while talking as fast as a runaway train. "Mum, it was the jolliest adventure in all the world. The wild sea and the fairy folk of Ireland and a castle that had a kitchen that fell into the waves. There were seabirds and I have an atlas. Padraig's aunt has a little house that looks like it's in a fairy tale and—"

"Whoa!" Dad interrupts and stands. He steps toward us, and I feel the problems brewing. This is the part where we'll be in trouble. I'll be sent to my room or lectured.

But Dad stuns us all. "Did you see a talking beaver or

a faun or"—he bends closer to his son and whispers—"a white witch?"

If Dad grew wings and flapped about the room like a madman I would not have been more amazed. That's when I see the book next to the flowered teapot and the folded green napkins: *The Lion, the Witch and the Wardrobe.*

George's book.

Our book.

And my notebook.

I had left it behind in the rush, and Mum and Dad had read my tight handwriting, the jumbled stories of Mr. Lewis's life that tangled with the land of Narnia.

"You have written a most beautiful story." Mum puts her hands on my shoulders and speaks, tears in her eyes. "The love you have for your brother will carry all of us through. What you have done for George is more than anyone could ask."

Dad sits and motions for George, who crawls into his lap. "You are so brave," he tells his son.

"You've been reading the story!" George says.

Mum and Dad look to each other and nod. Dad says, "Tell me everything about the castle. Everything."

"It is wild and free and sits on the top of a green hill at the edge of a cliff, and . . ."

As George tells his story, Mum's tears drip onto my notebook of Mr. Lewis's life.

# TWENTY-FOUR

# THE PROWLING LION

I wake on Christmas Day feeling like I've barely slept. In the middle of the night, a terrifying fear swamped me. What if George didn't make it to Christmas morning? What if, for George, it stayed winter and never Christmas? I found my way to George's bedside, to the upright chair where I've been half-asleep ever since.

In dawn's light, with the streaky pinks and reds striping the horizon and lighting George's room, I know my fears are ridiculous. And also that George, even if he didn't wake on Christmas morning, wouldn't find himself in the icy wasteland of the White Witch.

I stretch and crank my neck, which is stuck to the right with a pain that shoots down my shoulder. George breathes in and out softly. The covers are up to his chin, and one arm has flopped out to reveal his flannel Christmas pajamas with lambs in Santa hats. I hear a rustling sound and look to see Dad standing in the doorway.

He's already dressed and shaved clean, his face gleaming in the morning sun. He puts a finger over his lips for silence and nods for me to follow him to the kitchen.

We stand there, waiting on the kettle, fatigue like a heaviness in my head and shoulders. "Happy Christmas, Dad," I say quietly. He slips his arm around me and pulls me close.

"Happy Christmas, my little one."

He hasn't called me that in so long that I feel myself a child who needs comforting. He lets me go, and I turn to see the fir tree with the silver tinsel and the presents piled underneath. They are wrapped in red and green. Some white with tinsel bows. Only a few, but enough to make me smile. Across the mantle of the fireplace are four stockings, once knitted by Grandma Devonshire. Somehow my parents, just as they do every year, have managed to hide the presents, then sneak them under the tree without me hearing a thing.

Dad's voice comes wrapped in a cough. "When I read your notebook last night . . . What do any of these tales have to do with what George wants to know?"

I take a breath and step back while the kettle heats up and Mum and George sleep on.

"To people like Mr. Lewis, life isn't a math equation. Everything he says seems to have layers and layers of meaning. George wanted me to ask just one question: Where did Narnia come from? All I was trying to do was answer him. But meanwhile, it changed me, Dad." I pause.

"Megs, you're doing everything you can, I know that . . ."

"George is going to die," I say, shocking myself by saying it aloud. "I can't do anything to save him. But I can tell him the stories that Mr. Lewis told me. If Mr. Lewis's answer to a question is another story, who am I to argue?"

As if someone has startled him, Dad drops his tea, hot brown water flowing over the table, the teacup rattling to the wooden floors. He sets his face into his hands and begins to sob. His shoulders shake. His pants are soaked with tea unnoticed. His voice breaks the air. "I don't want to lose him. I can't fix it. I can't work hard enough or pay enough . . ."

I place my arms around my dad and pull him close. "I know. I know," I say as a knock startles us both and we look to the front door, confused.

"Santa?" Dad askes with a funny grin. He wipes the tears from his face, blows his nose with a loud snort into his handkerchief.

"Maybe?" I say and walk to the door in my nightgown, a flannel gown with flowers around the sleeve cuffs.

I regret this ensemble as I open the door to see Padraig standing there in a long black coat, his curls freckled with snow beneath a bright cherry-colored Santa hat. His cheeks are red and I am filled with delight. Pure delight, though simultaneously I wish I were dressed in my Christmas best with a hint of red lipstick.

"Padraig!" I grab my coat from the hook and slip it on before I step outside and close the door. "Why are you here?"

"Do you mean Happy Christmas?" he asks with a sly grin. Then I see in his hand a piece of paper rolled like a scroll with a red ribbon wrapped around it.

"Do you mean *Nollaig Shona Dhuit*?" I ask.

He laughs. "Yes, I do." He pauses, looks behind him and then back to me. "Beautiful Megs, I don't want to bother you or your family, but I wanted to bring this to you before I go back to Ireland today with my father." He nods toward the car idling in front of the house. "He's waiting."

I glance toward the blue Wyvern and I feel the heat of a blush rising. "Oh splendid. An Oxford professor seeing me in my jammies. Jolly brilliant."

Padraig almost laughs. "He let me come out of the way to give this to you." He hands me the paper. "I told him all about you. About George. He's happy to be here."

From behind the Wyvern's windshield, Professor Cavender, wearing a blue hat and red scarf, waves at me. I wave back timidly and look to Padraig.

"What is it?" I ask.

"It's a story . . . or a poem . . . I'm not sure what it is. I wrote it last night. For you and for George."

"Why did you come here? Why not mail it?" I wonder why I am ruining this moment with all the questions even as I ask them.

"I'm here . . . for *you*. Are you a dolt, Megs?"

"I don't think so." I almost smile at the same words he'd used in the snowbank when he'd kissed me.

He lowers his voice and steps so close to me I can feel

the heat from beneath his coat. "I'm here because I'm rightly in love with you. That is why. And I want to be here for you. You don't have to love me back. It doesn't have to work that way, but it would sure be nice if you did."

There I stand in my pajamas and love enters my world like lightning from a blue sky, surprising, unexpected, and completely meant to knock me over. I can't say the words in return, not yet, although I know I will. Someday, and soon.

Instead, I take the paper and open it. I read as Padraig watches me.

Once upon a wardrobe, not very long ago and not very far away, a little boy entered the world in a small stone cottage in the English countryside. Some babies are born closer to the end of their story than others, and this little boy was one of those.

For a short while the boy named George remembered where he came from, and then the memory faded, almost disappeared into the bright light of this loud world with all its talking adults and worries and sickness and words. But when the boy read a certain kind of story, or heard a very particular type of tale, he had the nudge of a memory, a thrilling kind of prescient joy, an echo or reminder of something more, of somewhere very important, of somewhere where it all began.

That feeling returned with every book he picked up and with every story he begged his sister, Megs, to tell him.

And Narnia was his favorite of all. The young boy wanted to know how the author found this story of a lion and a witch and a wardrobe, a tale that carried him to new adventures.

He asked Megs to find out for him; he asked her to discover how Narnia had roared into this world.

I look up to Padraig and I don't even try to hide my tears. He takes off his leather gloves and holds my face in his hands. "You will write the rest of this story. And hopefully I'll be in it."

And with that, he kisses me. Right on my front stoop on Christmas Day, smack in front of his father and the sky and the unseen stars above us. And I kiss him in return with a promise that can't be yet voiced, but one as sure as a blood oath.

Dad opens the door.

"Dad," I say and take Padraig's hand in mine, unashamed of the kiss he interrupted. "This is my friend Padraig Cavender."

"The boy who carried you to Dunluce?" Dad asks, straightening his cardigan and squinting into the morning sun.

"Yes, sir," Padraig says without flinching.

We both wait and then Dad smiles. "Thank you; you are a good man."

"It was one of the best days of my life, sir," Padraig says. "And now I must be off. My father is waiting, and there is a ferry to catch."

"Happy Christmas," my dad says.

"And to you." Padraig tips his hat and then he leaves.

I watch him as he saunters to the car, opens the passenger door, and looks back to me. I wave with the rolled-up paper and hope he can feel everything I feel, because it is the only Christmas gift I have for him.

Dad does me a great favor and doesn't say a word about the kiss that still has me feeling untethered and grounded both. We wander back to George's room. On the way, I hide the paper in a drawer in the kitchen hutch.

"Happy Christmas," Dad and I call out as we reach George's sunlit room, where Mum is waiting.

"Happy Christmas," he says, and he's smiling, so pure, so bright. Then he holds up my notebook, which I'd left at his bedside table, and I see the list I'd made in the pub. "What's this?" he asks.

"Oh." I reach his side and kiss his cheek. "I was . . . I was trying to make a list to show where I thought each thing in the story came from . . . and . . ."

"Like a math diagram?"

I feel stupid. I should never have tried it.

"How did that work out?" he asks with a teasing voice.

"It didn't, really," I say. Our gazes meet and we laugh.

Dad perches on the end of the bed, picking up George's sketchbook.

"These drawings are jolly marvelous." Dad flips through the pages, and Mum and I walk behind him, peering over his shoulder to watch the sketches go by. Each page is a scene from Mr. Lewis's life, and each page has a colored lion in the background: fierce, tender, curious, or protective. George has captured all of them in the expressions and stance of his lion.

"George," Dad says, "it looks like you think the lion followed the author around for all of his life."

George nods. "I think the lion follows all of us around. We just have to look for him."

I scoot George over, wrapping my arm around his shoulder as I sit on the bed. "Well, how do we see him?" I ask.

George looks at me, then at Mum and Dad. He opens his hand and then rests his palm over his heart, leaving it there on his chest as his only answer.

After that, we're all silent for a time.

"Dad," George finally speaks, "I heard you in the kitchen. Please don't be so hard on Megs. She did as I asked. There is no *real* answer. I never thought there was."

"I maintain that there is an answer," I say. "Or many answers."

"And what are they?" Mum asks, either skeptical or curious, I can't tell.

George looks to me and nods. He now trusts me to answer, and I want to keep every ounce of that trust.

"Maybe . . . maybe Narnia also began when Mr. Lewis sat quietly and paid attention to his heart's voice. Maybe we are each and every one of us born with our own stories, and we must decide how to tell those stories with our own life, or in a book." I stop and clear my mind, my heart, and my eyes. "Or . . . could it be that all our stories come from one larger story? Maybe Narnia also began before Mr. Lewis was even born in Belfast, Ireland. Maybe . . . Mr. Lewis's tale already existed in the bright light where every story, legend, and myth is born."

"Yes, Megs," George says so quietly that Mum leans closer. George's eyes alight not on any of us but on the wardrobe across the room. "Yes. The bright lamppost light where all stories begin and end."

# THE END AS THE BEGINNING

Once upon a wardrobe, not very long ago and not very far away, a little boy entered the world in a small stone cottage in the English countryside. Some babies are born closer to the end of their story than others, and this little boy was one of those.

For a short while the boy named George remembered where he came from, and then the memory faded, almost disappeared into the bright light of this loud world with all its talking adults and worries and words. But when the boy read a certain kind of story, or heard a very particular type of tale, he had the nudge of a memory, a thrilling kind of prescient joy, an echo or reminder of something more, of somewhere very important, of somewhere where it all began.

That feeling returned with every book he picked up and with every story he begged his sister, Megs, to tell him.

And Narnia was his favorite of all, and he wanted to know about the author and how he found this story.

You see, there was once, and is even now, a city on the banks of the River Cherwell, a city as abundant with timeless tales as any city in the world. The slow river begins its journey in Hellidon and meets its destiny in the Thames at Oxford, a city of stone towers and pinnacles where this story, and many, many others begin. Some stories imagined in this ancient place rise above the others; they ascend from the towers, from the quiet libraries and single rooms, from the museums and the cobblestone streets. Some of those stories become legends.

Myths.

Tales that are as much a part of us as our bones.

"Wait!" Young George's voice stops me. He jumps from where he's been sitting on the floor of the library and rushes to my chair, climbs into my lap.

"Start over. Say it again."

I laugh and tousle his red curls. "We're only on page three."

"But if you start again, it will last longer."

I understand this logic. It's why I wrote the book in the first place, to make it all last longer.

I kiss my grandson's round cheek. Growing up in the countryside, he's as wild as the land and his parents' farm of sheep and goats and cows. His wild red curls are an imitation of his grandfather Padraig's in his younger days. The Devonshire cottage in Worcester is his home, only a few houses down from the cottage where Padraig and I live, married for thirty years.

This George is the child of my daughter, Beatrice. He's squirming to no ends in my lap. I wrap my arms tight around him to still him, and he exhales, snuggles closer.

Our cottage, Padraig's and mine, where we are right now, is the one we built right after we married to be near Mum and Dad while we taught at Oxford. It has become our permanent home in retirement, although I can't rightly call it retirement when Padraig and I are both still writing books and articles, and lecturing when called. But to be here in the countryside with Beatrice and my grandson is about as right as the world can be, even when it's not.

The library here is just like the kind my brother dreamed for himself, the kind George talked about and wished for. I designed it with his imagination in mind. The high shelves of dark wood, with leather-bound books of classics, include an entire collection of the Narnia chronicles, signed by Jack. There came six more after *The Lion, the Witch and the Wardrobe*. There's a ladder that rolls along the hardwood floors so I can reach the top shelves and grab a George MacDonald, G. K. Chesterton, or one of Mum's many Dorothy L. Sayers novels that she left me. On the middle shelves, alphabetical and orderly, are my physics and mathematics books, from Einstein to the new theories of a man named Hawking. And across the room is a fireplace big enough to walk into, snapping and crackling with a fire to warm our early spring afternoon.

"Tell me the part about the trip to Dunluce," George says. "And the castle." He exhales the next words with a smile. "In Ireland."

Ireland, the place his grandfather comes from, the land of wild dreams and adventures. We've taken him to visit many times, always on Christmas Eve Eve.

"Oh, we'll get there," I say.

"Go there now!" He is almost bursting.

"But all that comes before the castle matters just as much."

George settles in and flips to the next page for me. "This is my favorite picture," he says.

He points at a mighty drawing of Aslan standing behind a young Jack Lewis as Jack draws his own pictures in a little end room in Belfast. The image is colored in with the pencils I once brought to my brother from Blackwell's bookshop. "My favorite too, love," I say. "Mine too."

Outside, wind rattles the new leaves of the beech tree against the glass. It is March. Spring is moving, hidden beneath the hard and cold ground, rising up to new life.

I read to my grandson. I read of meeting Mr. Lewis after Warnie found me hiding in the woodlands behind their house. I read to him of Mr. Lewis's life stories that twist and spin into and out of Narnia. I read of George's adventures in his imagination, and I read of our journey to Dunluce Castle. At each page, I pause for my grandson to stare at the sketches of Aslan near young Jack Lewis: in an attic where Jack is writing of Boxen; in the classroom of a horrid boarding school; in the trenches of France; in an office at Oxford. The well-wrought sketches change from page to page, the lion's expression as wise or as caring or as fierce as the scene demands.

I am near the end when we're interrupted by a deep voice.

"Hello, my loves." Padraig enters carrying a stack of wood. My heart reaches for him; it has never stopped moving toward him since the evening at the castle, or maybe even before, on a bridge over the River Cherwell when he ran after me to walk me halfway to the Kilns.

Padraig's hair is silver, pure silver, as if a child with a paint box took his bright red curls and painted them. His face is lined with wrinkles to mark his smiles. Twenty best-sellers my husband has written now, fairy tales and legends of the Irish countryside, even while tutoring at Merton for all these years. But the book young George and I are reading?

*Once Upon a Wardrobe.*

I wrote it.

My brother illustrated it. Of course, he hadn't known he was illustrating a book; he merely drew while I told him stories.

The book came later.

Much later.

Padraig drops the logs into the fire and comes to kiss us both. "What part are we on?"

"The end," George says, "until we read it again."

I look up to Padraig, and he smiles down at me with that crooked and dear grin that melts everything in me. I think of the first time I knew what that smile meant—on my front porch on Christmas morning—but it was at my brother's final good-bye that I knew for sure.

It was the end of 1950 when we bid farewell to my brother. The whole village was there. Almost everyone to the end of every lane had come for my family. They whispered and they cried and they kept their eyes downcast.

I sat on the front row with Mum and Dad, and I wasn't crying because I'd cried as much as one body knows how to weep. I'd believed—fool that I was—that because I knew this end was coming, I was prepared, that I would not grieve as I had. As if one can pre-grieve and get it out of the way. It's not true. Grief is the price I paid for loving fiercely, and that was okay, because there was no other choice but to love fiercely and fully.

In the church, I hadn't looked behind me, because I knew I'd have to stand and speak, and I didn't want to see all the familiar and mournful faces. Mum and Dad had asked me to talk about George. It wasn't customary, getting up and speaking in such a way at an Anglican service where the priest usually just reads the *Book of Common Prayer* pages for the Burial of the Dead, but I'd said yes. George would have wanted me to say something. I knew he would. That didn't make it easier, just necessary, and there was a difference.

When I stood and walked to the center of the church

and faced the pews, I saw Mr. Lewis and Warnie in the third row. Next to Mr. Lewis sat Padraig Cavender himself. I was already shaking, and to see their sorrowful faces made my hands flutter like wings, almost sending my handwritten pages to the stone floor. The choir sang a gorgeous hymn in Latin, a hymn whose words I knew in English, but for some reason the Latin itself was squeezing my heart in grief.

"*Come, Thou fount of every blessing . . .*"

The choir finished. Padraig gave me a sad smile and nodded as if to say, or as if I imagined him to say, "You can do this."

I was scared. All the thoughts flew through my mind at once like a flock of wild birds. I thought about George and his last breath with his gaze on the wardrobe. I thought of Mr. Lewis and Warnie and the Kilns' warmth and books. I thought of Padraig's kiss. I thought of the snow outside and how George would never again see spring, or not the kind of spring we would see when the baby lambs were birthed and the crocuses burst from the ground. George's would be a new spring I couldn't yet see.

I thought how we are never, any of us, in one place at a time, but in our minds and in our imaginations we are many places all at once. We were here and there at the same time; it was my body in a black dress at the front of the church, but my heart was with George.

I stood at the lectern and took a breath; everyone waited.

I meant to read what I'd written the night before in one

long exhale of words. I opened my mouth and let the words flow with the beauty of all George was and is.

When I finished, I was undone by it all. I had nothing left. I walked back to the pew in a haze. I sat between Mum and Dad and their arms were around me lickety-split, pulling me as close as they could. We stayed that way for what remained of a service I don't remember, the sounds and prayers sliding off of me.

An hour later, as we stood in the warm narthex crowded with people, Padraig walked toward me with his long strides and his green eyes and his kind, sad smile.

"Megs," he said. I loved hearing my name on his lips in the midst of despair. "It was beautiful. You are beautiful."

"Some of those words are yours," I said. "The words you gave me Christmas Day."

"They are ours." He moved closer just as my uncle Brian approached and swooped me into his arms and held me so tight I had to give him a light punch on the arm. "I will miss him every day, Megs. Every. Single. Day."

"Me too," I said. "Every minute."

"He was something special, that lad. Not meant for a place like this." Uncle Brian kissed my forehead. "And what you read, that was beautiful. Who wrote it?"

I lifted my eyebrows and sensed the swollenness of my eyelids. "Padraig and I did."

"Huh." Uncle Brian stepped back. "Well, look at you. A writer to boot." He kissed me again, then he was off to another cousin.

Padraig had taken a step or two back. I reached for him. He came closer and knit his fingers through mine and held tight. It was the best I could do at that moment, the only way I knew to say, "I love you."

But he knew. I could see that he knew.

Mr. Lewis and Warnie approached. It was an odd feeling to see them together outside their home or acreage or college, as if a storybook had come to life. I didn't think about it as I let go of Padraig's hand and threw my arms around them, both of them, one arm each, and embraced them.

They hugged me in return, and I marveled at this. In a matter of weeks I had come to know these two men better than some of my own family. They had changed my life, my heart, without telling me what to do or think or believe, and I didn't understand how.

And they had eased George into a new world.

"Thank you for everything. Both of you. Thank you. You gave my brother beautiful last days."

"No, Megs," Mr. Lewis said. "You gave your brother beautiful last days. Your heart shines as bright and clear as the stars."

Padraig piped up. "He's right, indeed. Your heart does do that."

The doors of the church opened as people began to make their way outside, and our group of four did the same until we stood on the grass that was turning to slush under everyone's shoes.

Warnie coughed past his sorrow-drenched voice. "We wanted to meet him. I am so sorry that didn't happen."

"He met you in your stories," I said. I looked away from these men I had come to love. I looked to the sky, to the stars hidden in sunlight that would reveal themselves in the night. I looked to wherever my brother might be. "And you've allowed me to see that we are enchanted not by being able to explain it all, but by its very mystery. That is—finally, that is—enough."

Padraig squeezed my hand so tightly and Mr. Lewis said, "I hear you. I hear you."

Now, yanked from the memory, another hand pulls at me—my grandson's. And I am back in my library with my husband and young George.

Padraig sees my faraway look and he asks me, "Love, are you okay?"

I tilt my face up for another kiss as George squirms in my lap. "I am more than okay." I glance down at the last pages of the book and I read the ending, the words I'd read at a service all those years ago when we said good-bye to my brother.

The brave boy's story was short but full of just as much courage as any knight in shining armor fighting a dragon, just as full of bravery as any explorer journeying to the ends of the world to save a maiden, just as adventurous as any odyssey to the center of the earth.

The young boy understood now, after all the tales

and adventures, after all the drawings and stories, and he told the grown-ups, who aren't as smart as children, "There is a light, a bright lamppost light where all stories begin and end."

Then his bedroom filled with the feeling of snow and light and warmth and darkness and joy and grief—everything of the broken and whole world, incongruent and holy, overflowing with mystery.

This feeling in his room was far better than the stories he loved, and yet the same. The hints had always been right in front of his eyes and inside his heart. The stories that thrilled him were echoes of the world that waited for him.

And he heard, as loud as a new world thundering out of the cosmos, the mighty roar of a lion.

# A NOTE FROM

# DOUGLAS GRESHAM

Patti Callahan Henry is already becoming known for her works, which indeed are well-admired books—full of good stories and a steadily deepening understanding of people.

But for me, all her previous books were overcome by the first book she wrote about my mother, Joy Davidman, and her marriage to C. S. Lewis, my stepfather. And this is not simply because she is a good writer (which she definitely is) but also because of the delicacy and care with which she wrote *Becoming Mrs. Lewis*.

For me, naturally enough, that is a very good book but also somewhat emotional for me to read. I was there, in that desperate and despairing world to which she was so carefully taking her readers. And yes, it did stretch my heart to some extent. But in her previous writings and in *Becoming Mrs. Lewis*, she was swimming in a calm, delicate sea.

In her new book, however, things have changed

radically; she writes taking us adeptly through the storms of life that will face many of us and will move us deeply.

In *Once Upon a Wardrobe*, Patti smashes through the steep waves and torrents of life in ways that will leave us all astonished, searching and looking hard ahead. This is not merely a book worth reading, it is a book that will drive us through the difficulties of love and of sorrow, to struggle, gasping onward and upward, our emotions surging with us until we are brought, once again, to love.

In this amazing book Patti's portrayal of my stepfather, C. S. Lewis, or "Jack" as he preferred to be known, comes once more to life, and he shows a very full understanding of what is needed to make us understand a little less carelessly, what the world expects of us—no, indeed, demands of us—until finally we get there! I advise you to read this book, then wait for a while and then read it again. For while it may not be Narnia, there is magic in it, and that deeply moved me.

Douglas Gresham
Stepson of C. S. Lewis

# A NOTE FROM THE AUTHOR

This novel, *Once Upon a Wardrobe*, is a story that grew out of many other stories, and I'm starting to see that maybe that's always the way it is. When I was writing the novel *Becoming Mrs. Lewis*, I realized that the year that C. S. Lewis and Joy Davidman met through letters was the same year that *The Lion, the Witch and the Wardrobe* was released: in 1950. Eventually, five Narnia books later, Lewis dedicated *The Horse and His Boy* to Joy's sons, Douglas and Davy Gresham.

I often wondered about the time in C. S. Lewis's life when he decided to start *The Lion, the Witch and the Wardrobe*. What was the origin story? What made him start and then stop and then start again? Had he meant to create this land, or did it grow into Narnia as he wrote? I began to ponder how much his life ended up in his stories. How much of our life ends up in our stories? How much is conscious and how much is unconscious?

I leave that final answer to the experts in psychology, philosophy, and religion, but as usual I turned to story for our answer.

Most likely you feel the same as I do if you hold this book in your hand—Narnia was and is a powerful part of our collective lives and imaginations. I've never felt the need to dissect it like a specimen on a laboratory slide, or to take it apart to find its inner workings, but I did find myself wanting to convey the power of it in our lives. I felt a story stirring that might reveal exactly what C. S. Lewis meant when he said, "Sometimes fairy stories may say best what needs to be said."

I fell through the wardrobe door of Narnia as a young child, wishing for my own Wardrobe. I would wager some of you did the same. I read the books to my children, and we've all cried through the movie.

As I considered *The Lion, the Witch and the Wardrobe*, a young boy named George Devonshire and his sister, Megs, visited my imagination. Living in Worcester, England, in 1950, seven-year-old George is dying and his seventeen-year-old beloved sister can't save him; she loves him fiercely and will do anything for him (just as C. S. Lewis and his brother Warnie loved each other). This young boy asks his sister to find the answer to his most pressing question: "Where did Narnia come from?" You see, Narnia comforts him. Narnia thrills him. He wants Narnia to be *real*. And although he asks his sister a question that can't be truly answered, his sister goes looking for that very answer.

Megs, a mathematics student at Sommerville College in Oxford—who wants logical answers, ones that might be ticked off like the equations she solves—sets off to track down Mr. C. S. Lewis and timidly ask him about Narnia's origins. He answers her, but not as we expect. He doesn't give her the pat answer or logical ties; instead he tells her stories from his life for her to take home to George. Stories both dark and light, stories of triumph and heartbreak: *true* stories.

Although an author's life and reading might inform a story in some ways, there are also large swaths of story-source that are altogether imaginative, mysterious, and transcendent. *This* is what I wanted to express.

As the Irish poet and philosopher John O'Donohue once wrote, "A book is a path of words which takes the heart in new directions." And that is what I long to show you: how Narnia does that for us all.

I think of this novel as a story about a story—nesting stories, if you will. I have no desire to ascribe logic, facts, and theory to the world of Narnia. That has been done, and done well, by so many others. There are scholars and academics who've spent their lives studying Lewis and the creation of the seven-book series. I've read most of these books and I'm beyond grateful for their insight and wisdom.

Yes, in this novel I was, and am, *only* fascinated by *The Lion, the Witch and the Wardrobe* and how its world transforms the lives of Megs and George (and a few others along the way during their adventures). I'm fascinated by the ways in which Narnia transforms *us*, how the power of its tale can't be fully explained no matter how much we want to quantify and list its logical associations.

My editor at Harper Muse, Amanda Bostic, once said to me, "I've always believed that if we can find our way to Narnia, we can find our way home." May it do the same for you.

# ACKNOWLEDGMENTS

This novel, just as many others and possibly more than any other, does not belong to just me. It would not and could not have been written without so many other authors, scholars, and artists before me. Most notably, of course, C. S. Lewis who wrote *The Lion, the Witch and the Wardrobe*, therein capturing our collective imaginations for generations.

My gratitude extends far and wide, backward through the years and into now. Let me start with Lewis, of course. When he sat down to write this novel in 1939, he began the tale and then set it aside for many years. Thank you, C. S. Lewis, for picking it back up, for pouring your imagination and heart into this story and into the land of Narnia.

There are many books I read and studied for this novel, and I want to thank the scholars who penned them: Christin Ditchfield Lazo, Rowan Williams, Joseph Pierce, David C. Downing, and Paul F. Ford. To Diana Glyer, whose work on the Inklings allowed me to write that part of the novel with care. The work of Dr. Crystal Hurd on Lewis's parents, childhood, and early life set me wondering what his family life had been like and how it might have influenced a book he began more than thirty years later. To Dr. Don W. King—your work on Lewis and his life influenced the way I see him as both human and vulnerable. I am grateful to you!

I want to thank the kind souls who gave this an early read and said, "Whoa there, you went off course here and here and here." Or as Andrew Lazo might say, "There's a howler." This book would not be what it is without Dr. David Downing, Dr. Crystal Downing, Andrew Lazo, and Christin Dietrich Lazo. I am humbled by your generosity and kindness.

The profound work of Max McLean of Fellowship for Performing Arts helped me see C. S. Lewis through clearer eyes, and from those eyes I started to see the pieces of Lewis's life that have influenced Narnia.

To Amanda Bostic—you have journeyed with me from the start and you have been the greatest advocate, friend, and coconspirator. Your strength and your wisdom have carried us through so many stories both on and off the page, and I am profoundly grateful.

To Marly Rusoff, who took this story to Amanda and was its champion.

To my Friends & Fiction cohort who listen and cheer and keep me straight and sane, who understand that story is one of the most important things in our life—Mary Kay Andrews (Kathy Trocheck), Kristin Harmel, Kristy Woodson Harvey, and Mary Alice Monroe. You are my trusted allies.

To Paula McLain, Beth Howard, Ariel Lawhon, J. T. Ellison, and Signe Pike, who listened to the whispered idea at its genesis and didn't say, "That's nuts," but instead said, "Go finish that book."

To Dana Isaacson, who read the pages and helped me understand where this story might be going and why. A book whisperer they call him, and it's very true. And a good friend—that's true also.

To Meg Walker of Tandem Literary, my friend, marketing guru and wizard, you are the calm in the storm, and what would I do without you? I do *not* want to know. And to Judy Collins, webmaster and newsletter genius—I can never say thank you enough. You don't miss a beat.

To my literary agent, Meg Ruley—our partnership has been one of the greatest joys of this year, and I am sure it will be for many more years to come. Thank you for believing in me and in my work, for loving England as much as I do, and for understanding the power in this story. To the entire team at Jane Rotrosen Agency: to Chris Prestia, Sabrina Prestia, Hannah Rody-Wright, and to Jessica Errera, Andrea Cirillo, Jane Berkey, and the entire crew who have welcomed me into a family—and a damn fine one at that.

For the team at Harper Muse—you are the dream team of the wardrobe. I am so thankful for you and for your patience, curiosity, creativity, and commitment to the written word. To Nekasha Pratt, Margaret Kercher, Laura Wheeler, Matt Bray, Marcee Wardell, and Kerri Potts. To

Latasha Estelle and the sales team—without you we are just a finished book; with you we are a book on the shelf!

To the readers and librarians and booksellers—you inspire me and spur me on; you make me want to become a better writer and a better person, and I hope you love this book.

For Douglas Gresham—Joy Davidman's son, C. S. Lewis's stepson, and my friend—I will never find enough words to thank you for your wisdom, thoughtfulness, and kind words. In writing about your mother, I found a friend in you. I think she'd be happy about that! And to the C. S. Lewis Company, including Melvin Adams and Rachel Churchill, as always you are the keepers of a legacy, and I am always honored and humbled to work with you.

To the C. S. Lewis community far and wide, I am full of deep gratitude—including the astounding work of the C. S. Lewis Foundation, who have welcomed me and helped me along in my understanding of Lewis's work and life. To Steven Elmore who keeps the fire burning, and to Stanley Mattson who founded the extraordinary foundation.

Always last and never least, for my family—Pat, Thomas, and Rusk, for Meagan, Evan, and to Bridgette Kea Rock, to whom this book is dedicated. For my parents, Bonnie and George, who introduced me to Lewis and let me dwell in novels such as Narnia for as long as I wanted or needed. For Barbi Burris and Jeannie Cunnion and to their extraordinary families. To Serena Vann, and Stella and Sadie who always listen to me talk about stories. To all the Henrys—I love you all fully and irrevocably.

# DISCUSSION QUESTIONS

1. Was *The Lion, the Witch and the Wardrobe* part of your childhood? Your children's childhood? When did you first discover the story?
2. Did you ever wonder, "Where did Narnia come from?"
3. At the start of the novel, Megs Devonshire doesn't care much for made-up stories. She's concerned with math, facts, and figures. Why do you think her heart changed? Have you felt the same? What stories have changed you?
4. Megs Devonshire attempts to make a logical list of Narnia facts, and her friend, Padraig, stops her. Why do you think he does this? What does this mean to you? Would you have stopped her?
5. George Devonshire is looking for more than facts when he asks about the origin of Narnia. What do you think he is really asking? What does he really want to know?
6. If you could ask C. S. Lewis anything about Narnia, what would it be? Did his stories answer any of those questions for you?

7. In Patti's author's note she states, "What I've set out to do is show that an author's life (and reading) might inform a story in some ways, and yet there are also large swaths of story-source that are altogether imaginative, mysterious, and transcendent." Do you believe that to be true about stories? About Narnia?

8. What means the most to you about *The Lion, the Witch and the Wardrobe*?

9. Patti deliberately kept this novel in 1950, which is the year that *The Lion, the Witch and the Wardrobe* was released, keeping the story to *just* the first novel in the Narnia series. If you have read all of the books, do you have a favorite?

10. As you read about the seven events in Lewis's life, which one do you think contributed the most to Narnia? Where do you see these events in his life in the pages of *The Lion, the Witch and the Wardrobe*?

11. Megs, Padraig, and George went on an adventure. What struck you the most in those scenes? Why was it important that they went on this adventure?

12. How did you feel about the ending of the story? Would you change it if you could? Was it what you expected?

13. Megs moves between two family homes in the course of the novel—the Devonshire's cottage that is her family place, and the Lewis brothers' home.

Both give her a feeling of ease, contentment, safety, and security as she enters from the winter cold outside. What is it that makes these places feel so soft and rounded? What is it that defines home—rather than just a house—for you?

14. Patti opens the novel with a quote from C. S. Lewis: "Sometimes fairy stories may say best what's to be said." Have you found that to be true? Why do you think it is or isn't?

15. When Jack is living with the Kirkpatricks, the thing he most longs to hear from his tutor are the words, "I hear you." Why does knowing that someone hears you matter? How does it change you?

16. Was there a scene in this story that was particularly meaningful to you? Which one was it?

17. George tells Megs, "I think the lion follows all of us around. We just have to look for him." Do you agree with George? If so, have you ever seen the lion?

18. C. S. Lewis endured many hardships in his life, as did George and Megs. How did each of them respond? What do you think might have been different in each of their lives if they had different experiences, or if they had responded differently?

19. Padraig tells Megs, "I can't really understand my life without stories." Do you agree? What stories have best helped you make sense of your own life?

In a most improbable
friendship, she found love.
In a world where women were
silenced, *she found her voice.*

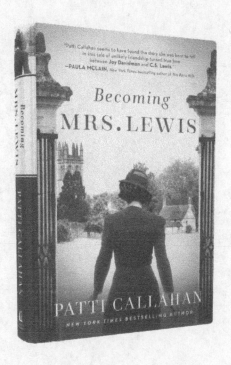

"Patti Callahan seems to have found the story she was
born to tell in this tale of unlikely friendship turned true
love between **Joy Davidman** and **C. S. Lewis.**"

—Paula McLain, *New York Times* bestselling
author of *The Paris Wife* and *Love and Ruin*

AVAILABLE IN PRINT, E-BOOK, AND AUDIO

# PROLOGUE

1926

BRONX, NEW YORK

From the very beginning it was the Great Lion who brought us together. I see that now. The fierce and tender beast drew us to each other, slowly, inexorably, across time, beyond an ocean, and against the obdurate bulwarks of our lives. He wouldn't make it easy for us—that's not his way.

It was the summer of 1926. My little brother, Howie, was seven years old and I was eleven. I knelt next to his bed and gently shook his shoulder.

"Let's go," I whispered. "They're asleep now."

That day I'd come home with my report card, and among the long column of As there was the indelible stamp of a single B denting the cotton paper.

"Father." I'd tapped his shoulder, and he'd glanced away from the papers he was grading, his red pencil marking students' work. "Here's my report card."

His eyes scanned the card, the glasses perched on the

end of his nose an echo of the photos of his Ukranian ancestors. He'd arrived in America as a child, and at Ellis Island
his name was changed from Yosef to Joseph. He stood now
to face me and lifted his hand. I could have backed away;
I knew what came next in a family where assimilation and
achievement were the priorities.

His open palm flew across the space between us—a
space brimful with my shimmering expectation of accept-
ance and praise—and slapped my left cheek with the clap
of skin on skin, a sound I knew well. My face jolted to the
right. The sting lasted as it always did, long enough to stand
for the verbal lashing that came after. "There is no place for
slipshod work in this family."

No, there was no place for it *at all*. By the time I was
eleven I was a sophomore in high school. I must try harder,
be better, abide all disgrace until I found a way to succeed
and prove my worth.

But at night Howie and I had our secrets. In the darkness of his bedroom he rose, his little sneakers tangling in
the sheet. He smiled at me. "I've already got my shoes on.
I'm ready."

I suppressed a laugh and took his hand. We stood stone-
still and listened for any breaths but our own. Nothing.

"Let's go," I said, and he laid his small hand in mine: a
trust.

We crept from the brownstone and onto the empty
Bronx streets, the wet garbage odor of the city as pungent
as the inside of the subway. The sidewalks dark rivers, the

streetlights small moons, and the looming buildings protection from the outside world. The city was silent and deceptively safe in the midnight hours. Howie and I were on a quest to visit other animals caged and forced to act civil in a world they didn't understand: the residents of the Bronx Zoo.

Within minutes we arrived at the Fordham Road gate and paused, as we always did, to stare silently at the Rockefeller Fountain—three tiers of carved marble children sitting in seashells, mermaids supporting them on raised arms or sturdy heads, the great snake trailing up the center pillar, his mouth open to devour. The water slipped down with a rainfall-din that subdued our footfalls and whispers. We reached the small hole in the far side of the fence and slipped through.

We cherished our secret journeys to the midnight zoo—the parrot house with the multicolored creatures inside; the hippo, Peter the Great; a flying fox; the reptile house slithering with creatures both unnatural and frightening. Sneaking out was both our reward for enduring family life and our invisible rebellion. The Bronx River flowed right through the zoo's land; the snake of dark water seemed another living animal, brought from the outside to divide the acreage in half and then escape, as the water knew its way out.

And then there was the lions' den, a dark caged and forested area. I was drawn there as if those beasts belonged to me, or I to them.

"Sultan." My voice was resonant in the night. "Boudin Maid."

The pair of Barbary lions ambled forward, placing their great paws on the earth, muscles dangerous and rippling beneath their fur as they approached the bars. A great grace surrounded them, as if they had come to understand their fate and accept it with roaring dignity. Their manes were deep and tangled as a forest. I fell into the endless universe of their large amber eyes as they allowed, even invited, me to reach through the iron and wind my fingers into their fur. They'd been tamed beyond their wild nature, and I felt a kinship with them that caused a trembling in my chest.

They indulged me with a return gaze, their warm weight pressed into my palm, and I knew that capture had damaged their souls.

"I'm sorry," I whispered every time. "We were meant to be free."

# ABOUT THE AUTHOR

Photo by Bud Johnson Photography

Patti Callahan is the *New York Times, USA TODAY,* and *Globe and Mail* bestselling novelist of fifteen novels, including *Becoming Mrs. Lewis, Surviving Savannah,* and *Once Upon a Wardrobe*. A recipient of the Harper Lee Distinguished Writer of the Year, the Christy Book of the Year, and the Alabama Library Association Book of the Year, Patti is the cofounder and cohost of the popular web series and podcast Friends & Fiction.

———

Visit her online at patticallahanhenry.com
Instagram: @pattichenry
Facebook: @AuthorPattiCallahanHenry
Twitter: @pcalhenry

# the
# PERFECT
## *love song*

NEW YORK TIMES BESTSELLING AUTHOR

## PATTI CALLAHAN
## HENRY

### *the*
# PERFECT
## *love song*

A CHRISTMAS STORY

*"Patti Callahan Henry is quickly becoming one of my favorites."*
—DEBBIE MACOMBER, *New York Times* bestselling author

From New York Times bestselling author Patti Callahan
comes a perfect Christmas tale of love lost and found.

*Available in print, e-book, and audio*

THOMAS NELSON®
*Since 1798*